T0196528

The
MISGUIDED
EMPATH

The MISGUIDED EMPATH

SEAN NEWBERG

THE MISGUIDED EMPATH

iUniverse books may be ordered through booksellers or by contacting:

iUniverse
1663 Liberty Drive
Bloomington, IN 47403
www.iuniverse.com
1-800-Authors (1-800-288-4677)

ISBN: 978-1-5320-5516-4 (sc)
ISBN: 978-1-5320-5517-1 (e)

Library of Congress Control Number: 2018909832

Print information available on the last page.

iUniverse rev. date: 08/16/2018

DEDICATED TO

My UNCLE STAN WHO encouraged me to write. Thank you Stan! Also to my mother, Linda Ryan. My Aunt Cindy Welsandt and my beautiful grandmother Juanita Lathrop. This book couldn't have been written without them

MOSQUITO LAIR AND CRAZY TRAVELS

DREW SHAW LIVED A carefree life from day one. He believed in living as if tomorrow did not exist. He believed in adventure. He believed in living more so than merely existing. Moreover, by living he believed happiness was in doing as he pleased. He somehow believed that laws about public intoxication and buying illegal drugs every now and then shouldn't apply to him. To him, those laws were for the idiots who couldn't handle themselves. He'd narrowly escaped death on numerous occasions during his career as an absolute nothing. The streets had done nothing more than harbor him while preparing him for a journey he never saw coming. A journey he truly never expected and for years never accepted.

Growing up in the very hot southern land of poverty and violence, Drew had no clue what the north had in store. Before he would know, he would first have to make it out of the south. Backpacking it up the interstate would be his means. Easy enough, he thought.

Eight hours into his trek, Shaw grew tired. He entertained lying down until morning at the next viaduct or overpass on this peaceful August night. He wouldn't need a blanket and his backpack would make a great pillow. Yes, sir, a nice pillow. What he hadn't counted on was a nearly transparent army that seemed to have long awaited his arrival.

Pillow down. Head down. Exhausted and ready. At last, the sleep he longed for would soon be upon him. Almost instantly, he heard the distant buzz of what at first he thought was sleep. Within moments, the slight buzzing sound of a streetlight became one with the sound of mud grip tires fleeing the woods.

Mosquitos. Mosquitos in his ears and mosquitos in his mouth. He was under attack plain and simple. He didn't know where to go next but he could not stay here. The flying aggravation was unbearable. They hung in his ears like light fixtures buzzing and screaming. Making his way out of Mosquito Lair, he fled from the aggressive Arkansas mosquitos.

For the next three hours or more, he found a mesh of buzzing biters anywhere he tried to lay down. Biting through his clothes, they nearly drove him crazy. He would find relief in a nearby field as the sun rose and the cool morning dew began to set in. The bugs sought refuge from the morning sun and seemed to drift back into the woods. He slept…

Drew was not raised in the wild but raised himself as wild. A shady childhood made for an early runaway. He'd been abused, molested, and traumatized at a very young age. So much so that before age eight he slept with his eyes open and often walked in his sleep. He was in and out of juvenile court before graduating to jail and prison, as the usual sad story goes. Drew wasn't the average seed one would expect to be sown from such an upbringing. He was a seemingly good man at heart, full of hospitality and consideration. Rarely seen without a smile he was a very polite, two-hundred-pound gentleman with honest blue eyes and jet black, corkscrew hair. Quick to hold the door for the elderly or anyone for that matter, he was often mistaken for a pushover by hoods in the alley. With his incredibly strong, six-foot-one-inch tall frame, predators weren't quick to try him out unless they knew they could outwit him. He was usually left alone and alone is how he liked it.

Waking up just before nightfall, he was excited about exploring the world ahead. Now 30-years-old, he was actually happy just to leave his old world behind like an old sheet of paper tossed in the basket in exchange for a nice crisp, clean sheet – a new slate if you will. Eager and excited, he stretched out and accompanied it with a deep yawn just before lighting a cigarette. After smoking a joint, his night would begin. Where it would lead him was unknown. He always expected the worst while hoping for the best. Drew maintained a confidence in himself and the world he lived in. He knew that just when you thought you'd seen it all you hadn't and that every day brought him a new smile. A new adventure.

In his current state as an adult, he'd begun to realize that he was perceiving life in a very awkward way. He'd begun to suffer not only an odd world of extreme coincidence in much of his everyday life but to also understand that in some way he was different from most. In a world he could no longer help but try to understand, he remained positive. Before he knew it, a driver in a yellow box truck picked him up and he was in Washington State. Shaw had traveled as far north as he could from his hometown of Memphis, Tennessee. Relief entered him like a breath of fresh air. He knew this was his destination. He didn't know why but he knew he was tired and it was time to settle down. What he didn't know was that he would sooner than later realize that his problems were of his own imperfect choices. He would ultimately discover that no matter where he went, his problems would always be close by. There was no escape. No matter where he'd gone, life would follow. His first day in the north was beautiful#. He loved the fresh cool rain in the air and the smell of wet evergreens. He took notice because after all he was in "The Evergreen State." The ladies seemed to show interest in him that he wasn't familiar with. People commented on his southern accent. People were overall nice. They spoke phrases new to him like "right on" and "I'm stoked". In agreement, they often said "right?" It was all new and he was very excited. Almost immediately, he was offered a job with a local telephone base collections agency. On one hand, they made him feel special. On the other hand, he was skeptical. Why were these people being so nice to him? Whatever the case, he accepted what they had to offer. He wanted a respectable life and thought this could be his ticket.

Months into his new job, he felt a security in his once embarrassing financial life. He could finally show an interest in the women who'd first shown him interest. He also felt more confident around other people now but he would always have a shy cord about him, especially with the ladies. It was only natural for him to be the clumsy goof on the first impression. He'd have to work on that.

Time came and went. For nearly a year, he'd developed everyday relationships with people he felt were ... well... actors. Not that they were actual Hollywood style actors but people who tried too hard possibly. He couldn't quite make it out but over the years he'd developed an acute sense of feeling for what people were thinking. He couldn't read the actual words that they were thinking; he merely knew when people were trying not to be themselves. He could sense their emotions if you will. He felt their animosity towards one another. When someone physically close to him was sad he felt it in his bones. The same with anger and hatred. He reserved no hate of his own and couldn't stand to feel it from anyone else. He also had a knack for thinking about minor things before they happened. Such as thinking about apples just before the news aired a segment on poisonous apples.

It was a Tuesday afternoon and he'd decided to retire to his apartment for the day. When he'd first got a job, he roomed up with a roommate who not only thought he was God's gift to collections but also a bean head who smoked opiates on aluminum foil. It had been what felt like an unusually long day at work and Drew was glad to be home. He'd been high on amphetamines throughout the day, as it seemed to be company culture. In using he hadn't been so out of touch with reality that he ever hallucinated. It did, however, give him a boost of false self-confidence and it opened up an inquisitive side in him. It also helped him to talk on telephones and thus made his boss a lot of money. As he entered his apartment he heard an odd sound like a cord being dragged across his kitchen floor. He was sure he'd beaten his roommate home already. He looked around but found nothing so he dismissed the sound.

Women had often given him the opportunity to have sex but he knew about the attachment aspect all too well. He was passionate and from what he gathered was good at what he did. One-night stands often turned into relationships that felt like boat anchors two months down the road. He'd been through it 89 times. He counted them one day while experiencing solitary confinement for the first time in prison. He wasn't in pursuit of another ball and chain relationship.

Drew was in pursuit of nothing more than happiness. He knew that each day carried with it a new experience. New ladies to flirt with. New goals to reach at work. New coincidences. His daily coincidental experiences usually consisted of something as small as perhaps watching a TV program and then later hearing people openly discuss the same topic without having watched the program. Or as much as saying a prayer and later hearing a television pastor preach a sermon about the very topic he'd prayed about. Coincidence was somehow built within his shadow. It seemed to be part of him. The more Drew analyzed his life the more he wanted to know about himself and his purpose. In recent years, he realized his life had been spared on numerous occasions for it had been far too often to be mere coincidence.

He had once been at a girlfriend's house where he made plans with her brother to go out frog giggin' later at night when the time was right. Frog giggin' used some fairly simple tools: a flashlight to blind and vaguely hypnotize the cute green guys and a miniature three-pronged pitchfork that you stabbed into them with. He thought frog legs were tasty. Frog giggin' was gonna be fun later. At least one would think so…

CHAPTER

FROG GIGGING AND NEAR DEATH

LATER IN THE EVENING in the backwoods of Helena, Arkansas, his girlfriend's brother, and a friend tried waking Drew up to go frog giggin'. Alcohol had once again gotten in the way of good clean fun. Despite their good-hearted attempts, he was overly exhausted from the drink. Out of commission. He shunned them with a "go away" and he slept.

As he slept they made their way down an old dark highway called Lexa Highway. There were no streetlights on this rather straight stretch of quiet country and there were no headlights on Fred's truck. As Fred roared down Lexa Highway having just left the bar, he didn't have a care in the world. The moonlight was his only source of light. At 80 miles an hour in the dark, his eight-cylinder truck unwound quietly enough to purr smoothly through the two unsuspecting victims almost like a lawnmower mowing grass. By the time Fred realized what he'd done, he had already dragged one frog hunter under the truck for nearly 180 yards. The other was killed on impact as he was knocked nearly 80 yards through the air. Drew escaped death because he was drunk.

Another time, a bad drug deal caused an enraged man to try and run him over. However, it began at close enough range that he was able to stay close enough to the side of the culprit's vehicle so as not to be hit or run over. One wrong move and he would have been under the vehicle. His near misses with death went on for years before he realized it may well be chasing him. He knew of death very well although he was very much alive.

Drew believed firmly in his Maker. However, he didn't believe in forcing his beliefs on anyone so one would never know of his religious beliefs judging merely by his actions. Stand for nothing; fall for anything. He was a tough guy who took pride in knowing his Maker who had spared his life so many times. He felt somehow protected by his beliefs. Fear had long since left his life though wonders and mystery never would. He couldn't help but love life no matter what it had to offer.

Being a believer didn't bar him from temptation, wrongdoing, and flat-out sin. He lusted over beautiful women sometimes in a way that he knew he shouldn't. He sometimes wondered about dominate sex in fashion or making a woman grimace with his manhood. Although he would never intentionally hurt anyone, he wondered what the rough sex that women seemed to enjoy was really like. He questioned whether they truly enjoyed it or not. Was it all a facade? Was it a way of control?

He grew up at a time where that not so unfamiliar smell of old dirty magazines lingered from under the bathroom cabinets of common households. Where uncles and dads alike explored sex without cheating on their old ladies. A time when kids could make a trip to the sex fantasy shop magazine porn world by merely going to the bathroom and locking the door. He sometimes wondered if he could watch a specific porn video that might somehow release the memories of when he was molested as a child. He'd been told he was molested at an early age. He'd also been told that if one could trigger the actual memory of being attacked, one could somehow deal with it and become a better person. He'd tried about all the pornography he could stand for one lifetime. None of it ever opened any doors or satisfied him. And while he once believed he had a pornography problem, he now knew he did not. As he matured into his 40s, he outgrew the smut that had haunted him since childhood. These days he deemed it gross but refused to judge other people for not being as strong as he was.

While the feeling of someone watching angered him and rendered him uncomfortable, he managed to keep his cool and with that his sanity. It seemed as though every time he used uppers, a distinct feeling of paranoia without fear came over him like an irritating cloud full of raw stench. He couldn't place it. It was as if he'd already known he was being watched but uppers intensified the sense 10-fold. He couldn't even imagine the thought of another person or people watching him like uninvited bugs. Their beady little gross eyes pierced into his privacy, stabbing their way into something he trusted like he did a chair to hold his backside off the ground. He trusted in the privacy of his own space. In essence, he trusted too much in people to afford him his privacy.

He noticed a pattern of coincidental noises that seemed to begin when he was alone. Every time he was alone, there were slight noises at his wall or people called him on the phone at a time that he was about to shower or was extremely busy. It seemed always something as if they were playing a game to take away his peace. It had never occurred in Memphis where he would have had reason to be paranoid, only here in Washington.

Up late one night, Drew cleaned his room and wiped all of his furniture, which consisted of a dresser, a TV, and his headboard. It wasn't much and didn't really match but was all black by design. It collected dust all too obviously. As he lay down having turned off the lights to relax into sleep, he heard what sounded like wind being blown through a pipe of some kind. Simultaneously he began to itch ever so slightly but enough to sense. He scratched his chest. He'd heard the sound before while he itched. This could no longer be classified as coincidental. He'd put two and two together.

CHAPTER

CHUMP WITH POWDER

COULD SOMEONE ACTUALLY BE blowing some sort of powder into his room to make him itch? Who would be so juvenile? And why would anyone want to play games with him? He'd played no games with anyone else. He decided to check it out this time. He braced himself before leaping to the floor and running through his bathroom and into the living room. He'd caught him.

His roommate Alvin was scurrying back to his room when Drew cut him off.

"Can I have a smoke?" Alvin asked him with a look of guilt or surprise, like a deer caught in headlights.

Drew gave him a cig and said nothing else about the night in question. He went back to his room while turning his light on. He could see the white film on his black furniture. The blowing through a straw sound never returned. He never itched again in his own apartment either.

Drew would later determine that his wormy rodent of a roommate Alvin was nothing more than an evil jerk who boasted of such atrocities as spitting in a policeman's food and stealing speaker systems from churches. He was a real loser. Alvin was a self-centered idiot who gave himself more credit than he deserved. Blowing itch powder into Drew's room was dismissed as a tactic to get Drew to move out as Alvin may have had another roommate in mind. Either way, it did not matter. He would stay put until they were evicted because Alvin couldn't pay his half of the rent. Once evicted, Drew moved in with his work colleague Alice.

Alice was a person who knew she could have pretty much any man she wanted. At least, that's what she would have you believe. She'd worked with Drew at the strange collection's agency he'd once worked for. She often gave Drew the opportunity for romance but Drew never took it. She enjoyed his company because she assumed she felt safe around him. She felt comfort in knowing he was a true gentleman of the south. Or she was somehow a fake.

On the other hand, Drew didn't entirely trust her. He felt something was fabricated about her as he felt with many people in this strange town of foggy mornings and black evenings. He read emotions well and he could sense some folks were hiding theirs and disguising hidden intentions, or at least trying to. Alice always seemed to have a hidden agenda; one that Drew would never care to see.

Soon, he'd lost another job because of his move. He had no car. He disliked buses and couldn't afford cabs. He was back to broke. Alice decided she wanted to become an escort and asked him to be her ride along. She dared not say the word pimp. She was too classy for that. In no time at all, he had gone from collection's agent to pimp. Just that quickly. His life consisted of running around with a woman whom he never trusted while protecting her from rabid tricks. The thing about it was he had a gut feeling that told him she was only acting like an escort and bringing him along for alternative reasons that for the life of him he couldn't figure out. Something felt all wrong about her. Unreal. Was she a man underneath? Was she a cop setting him up for a pimping charge? He did not know. He just knew it was better to get away from her. He took some money one day while she was out and left. He moved away, taking nothing but what he was wearing. It seemed his life would remain unpredictable.

He traveled by the city buses he so much disliked because getting to the next city would not be an easy task to walk. Seattle would be his next stop. Seattle was dirty, loud, obnoxious, and crazy. At five in the morning, he witnessed a man in the middle of downtown throwing garbage bins while screaming at them. Another sat on the corner murmuring that someone had put medication in his food. He wouldn't stay long before heading further south into Tacoma.

Tacoma would be a little hotter for him and with fewer people. Downtown boasted hills like that of San Francisco. More black people lived in Tacoma, which was cool for him. He'd never been prejudice towards any race and Everett seemed to be 90 percent white. Memphis, in the areas he'd called stomping grounds, was predominately black. He liked everyone accept jerks. He couldn't stand inconsiderate jerks. Other than that he was fine with anyone and everyone. He saw neither black nor white when it came to others. He saw people as one and people often took him for being slow because of it.

He arrived in Tacoma on a Saturday morning. It seemed as though there were more buildings than people and many of them vacant. He thought it was the perfect place to film a zombie movie. The downtown area seemed like a ghost town at first. There were many vacant buildings and oddly enough he didn't see any hobos like himself. Although he didn't refer to himself as a hobo he knew in his heart he was no better. No money and no job equaled hobo. Although not quick to judge others, he was quick to make fun of them in his own head. It kept him entertained and as sane as he was capable of being. He saw a city trolley that ran north and south and couldn't understand why the trolley didn't go east and west where the extremely steep city hills threatened a strenuous workout for both pedestrians and motor vehicles. "Oh well," he thought. He was sure no one else questioned or cared about it.

Drew thought differently than most people. Although he wasn't a "conspiracy theorist", he knew that conspiracies did in fact exist and were most dangerous when carried out by organizations, including the government. He'd been in and out of jail and prison enough to know that people were sneaky. And when people wanted things, they conspired to get them. He'd seen it time and time again.

He questioned things such as why red lights at all four corners of a four-way kept a hundred cars at bay for minutes at a time despite the fact that no one was coming. He thought perhaps Uncle Sam plotted it that way as to capitalize on the misfortunes of drivers who idled out millions of dollars in gas every year. Or perhaps car repair offered an abundance of tax dollars.

Tacoma was okay but offered little more than a nice homeless mission. For a homeless man it consisted of hills and heat; two things he thought he could do without. Even homeless he could feel that he was being watched. He felt as though an unseen spotlight shone on him even in the dark of night. His fear of it had long since numbed and he felt nothing more than a sense of mystery.

His Tacoma days consisted of nothing more than another experience. He gained nothing while there and it seemed he could never find even an hour's privacy. Even deep in the woods, it was impossible. He knew that somehow and for some reason, his life was being manipulated. His thoughts grew into "who" and "why". He knew it was of man.

A week into his homeless Tacoma exploration, he was relentlessly struck by the urge to relieve himself. He wrote off the public restrooms and was left with what he assumed was his only option to go deep into a wooded area. Like a rabbit, he would take refuge amongst the trees and dispose of his frustrations. Yet, as he went to relieve himself, he heard the stomping of another bum's feet venturing into the woods. "You have got to be kidding me right now," he thought. "Absolutely unbelievable." There were more coming in from other areas but they didn't seem to know one another. Just random hobos in a random area of woods. Some sitting and some walking with no particular direction in mind. They would normally be eating at the mission right now. What was going on and who was responsible?

Pissed, he left the woods in haste. "Of all the places for people to go," he said aloud as he left the woods. He made his way to another stretch of woods only to find the same thing happening over and over. It seemed no matter where he went people appeared out of nowhere and without intent. He couldn't make sense of it. But that feeling of mystery would soon turn to anger. He'd grown tired over the years of feeling like he was being watched by a fleet of eyes. Now he wanted it to stop. He refused to play this little game any longer. Whoever was directing people to play these games was a real loser – a bug to be squished on a later date.

Drew, the wanderer and the loner who felt closest mentally and physically only to his Maker, was beginning not to like people. He could either feel their hateful emotions or they seemed to invite themselves into his life when he simply wasn't okay with it. This life belonged to him and "dad-blast it" he had a right to privacy.

For years, he still felt the black cloud known only as paranoia without the fear factor gloom within his privacy. Why did he always feel as though he was being watched? Was it that jail had messed with his mind during months of solitary confinement? Was it all the drugs he'd experimented with? Was it the altitude change because he'd moved from the south to the north? He never felt this way down south, so why now? Why were there still strange noises? Why did it seem as though people wouldn't let him be? He'd never felt anything special about himself but began considering the possibility that somewhere somehow he had unknowingly done something that interested someone in such a way that attracted them to him. It left him feeling like an animal in the zoo. A specimen.

Before long he began seeing look-alikes of people he'd known in Memphis. He saw look-alikes reflecting his brothers, his grandfather, his aunt, his uncle and more. Was he losing it? He even thought he saw celebrities. A man in a city worker truck picked him up and gave him a ride once that looked like a famous bald-headed pro wrestler. He made the comment to the gentleman regarding his similarities only to have the man come back with, "Well, I am him. I just drive this city truck for extra bill money when I'm not wrestling." Drew blew it off as a joke but would never forget how striking the resemblance was.

That very same day he'd walked by a man who he could have sworn was a famous actor. It wasn't an actor that he ever really admired in his younger years with the exception of one movie. Drew apologized to the man for passing him on the sidewalk while smoking a cigarette. The man only said, "It's no problem. I've smelled worse." Again striking similarities but nah. "Couldn't have been," Drew thought.

One night after working all day on a temp job picking up wet toilet paper, he took his money for a ride into a casino. He figured he could hang out and drink all night while playing penny slots. Sure. That's it. Live like there is no tomorrow. What did he have to lose? He was already homeless. He remembered the times he was thankful to have ground to sleep on and it soothed him. If tomorrow never came then at least today was a blast. He didn't wanna get cheated. He valued life but accepted that death might well be out to get him. How many more times would he escape it? He had to accept it. Accepting it was hard to swallow and he often chased it with alcohol.

As he got older and braver, his need for the bottle began to diminish. Having taken his first drink at nine, he would "get over it" much faster than the average alcoholic. He had 20 plus years of experience at kicking his own ass with the bottle and had grown tired of it. Plain and simple. It wouldn't punish him today. Besides, he knew life had too much in store for him and he didn't wanna miss it. He was thankful for life: to breathe in the air and to catch the bastards he felt glaring but couldn't see. He needed their identities like oxygen. He wanted someone held accountable for stealing his precious privacy and seemingly manipulating his life.

As he played the slot machines, he started winning big time. Or at least to him, it was big time.

CHAPTER

NEAR DEATH PIT BULL ATTACK

Unfortunately, he couldn't leave as a winner. Eventually, as the usual story goes, he would leave the casino broke and tired. Again he afforded himself a suffering.

On his way to yet another unknown destination, the homeless Drew once again longed for sleep. He often traveled the unfamiliar road for excitement. Exhausted and drained of motivation, he stopped to rest at a bus stop and nodded off to sleep. He saw a shortcut path through a yard that would save him a few minutes of sidewalk travel back in Orange Mound, Memphis, Tennessee. He was dreaming. The path cut through from the southern sidewalk to the eastern sidewalk. The path was beaten enough that it seemed plausible. As he entered the immediate path leading from sidewalk to sidewalk, he heard the distinct sound of a large chain unraveling. He looked to his left only to see an adorable, two-hundred-pound, tiger-striped

Pitbull hauling nine kinds of ass towards him with its cute little tongue flopping out of the left side of his smiling face. He absolutely loved animals with a passion. He just knew within his heart that this big ol' puppy was running up to give him some lovin'. At least that's what he thought for the first three seconds of what seemed like an animated horror film in slow motion.

The house that the Pitbull was chained to was at least 50 yards from the sidewalk. Unfortunately, he would discover that the little old black lady who owned the house had long since protested pedestrians (crack dealers and gang bangers) cutting through her yard and hence the giant Pitbull with the 50-foot chain leading straight into his path. Just before the incident, he had awakened from a walking, drunken blackout. He was just about to understand where his drunken endeavor of homemade hell was about to lead him. It wasn't going to be pretty.

He barely got the words out of his mouth, "Hey puppy," before he realized the puppy turned demon was leaping for his neck. Had he not been so naive as to at first reach out to pet the Pitbull, his hand might not have been in the right position as to shove his right wrist into its razor-sharp mouth. The Pitbull locked at once onto Drew's wrist. Its intentions had been Drew's juicy neck. Instead of the throat it thirsted for, it sunk one K9 deep into Drew's wrist bone. The worst pain he thought he'd ever felt wouldn't come until later. For now, he felt nothing but adrenaline and betrayal, which as a combination also equaled anger and strength. He reached under the dog's belly with his left arm and with all of his might he picked the dog up high into the air and slammed it on its back to the ground. As it wobbled quickly on its back to get on to its feet it released his arm from a deadlock. He jumped back nearly a foot as the striped monster leaped again for his neck. The predator was stopped midair like one might see in a cartoon, clamping its teeth down on nothing but air. The chain had reached its limit just before the sidewalk. Drew jumped back just in time to limit his injury to one wrist shooting blood like a squirt gun. From across the street, a younger black lady ran up to ask Drew if he needed help and if she should call an ambulance. Drew's first response, despite the fact that he was bleeding to death from his wrist, was a simple "no" and a slight smile to assure her he was fine.

She looked at his wrist and could easily see that the furious land shark had made an attempt to take his hand off. At the same time, Drew looked too and swiftly changed his mind. "Yes, please. Call an ambulance," he said now as reality sunk in right along with new pain.

When the ambulance arrived so did the police. Laying in the back of the ambulance, he grasped his own arm with all his might in an attempt to subdue the pain he felt deep within his wrist. And as always it never failed that the police also wanted to know if he was okay – because they cared so much. An officer searched him while he was in the ambulance and found cassette tape player head cleaner on him. Drew told the officer what it was but the officer insisted on testing it to make sure it wasn't some sort of illegal liquid drug. Incidentally, the officer concluded that the substance tested positive for methamphetamine. Drew had never used meth at the time and laughed. But the officer didn't laugh. Drew went to jail on top of being attacked by the dog under false charges. When his court date finally arrived and he'd had all of the violent cage company he could stand, his attorney acknowledged that after deeper testing of the substance it was found to be legal. He wasn't getting off of their bureaucratic hook that easily though. His attorney advised him that if he didn't sign a guilty plea for sniffing glue in public then he would remain in jail for at least another year awaiting trial. It was more than obvious that the police weren't going to admit to being wrong. Left with no choice but to either sign for a crime he didn't commit or fist fight for his life every day, he opted for the least violent choice. He pleaded guilty just to be set free from a jail he had no business being in. When he woke from his dream of past memory he felt it time to head south into the next biggest city, which was Vancouver Washington.

With no casinos around and his lust for alcohol and drugs diminishing, he was able to work labor jobs here and there enough to save some money. Within a few months, he'd rented a small apartment with enough left over for a computer. He bought a Windows 10 laptop. He decided to explore more employment options than some jerk shouting how slow he was and to hurry up over his shoulder all the while he busted his ass. Working for "the man" wasn't for him. Disrespectful people were a pet peeve of his. Inconsiderate people had no respect coming from Drew Shaw. Hateful people he sensed quickly. He stayed away.

CHAPTER

COMPUTER HACK AND LIGHTNING ATTACK

WITHIN A DAY, FIVE thousand people tried to hack his computer or so his computer said. He wasn't good with computers but he knew this didn't sound right. He stopped for a moment to consider why he would be so important for them to do that or what would make someone think he might be important. Why on earth were people trying so hard to get into his life? Why were they prying? The only crazy motive he could come up with was an insane, ex-wannabe girlfriend whom he'd refused to sleep with had maybe put an x on his back. These were the most obsessive people he ever knew. Women he stood up for sex seemed to almost hold a special hatred for him. As they say, "Hell hath no fury like a woman scorned."

He did everything possible to ignore the thousands of attempted hackings. Then it came to him to return the computer and exchange it for another identical one. He did. He swapped it out for another brand new computer. On his way home, he noticed a lighter burn on a telephone pole about chest high. It reminded him of a time in Memphis when he was nearly struck by lightning five times within 20 seconds. He'd been walking down the road in the pouring rain just off of Beal Street in the pitch-black dark; Memphis was recovering from an earlier 90 mile an hour straight wind. Power was out for miles. Drew had been walking the streets aimlessly in the storm and could barely see a foot in front of him before the thunder rang in his ears like a gunshot next to his head. It was so loud that he nearly lost his balance. Following the gargantuan crack, a strike of lightning smashed the sidewalk next to his feet.

Then, up high, another strike that almost seemed blue hit the light pole. He started to remember what fear was as he felt his Maker lashing out at him. All his misdeeds flashed in his brain. "Please God!" he shouted directly. "Give me another chance!" Again lightning bolt smashed the top of a dogwood tree to his right. And then another light pole. It caught fire. Another crash of lightning appeared in the street next to him. Finally, the storm moved on and he felt relieved. He also somehow felt more alive. He felt direct communication with something far greater than he himself. He also felt a stern message. He would decipher it later because he was the king of procrastination.

Once he was home he would try again with a new computer. The very same thing happened yet again. "Where will this end?" he thought." He didn't believe in calling the police because the police had enough to deal with and it didn't seem serious enough to sound paranoid. After all, what could they "whoever they were" do at most? Watch him to death? He didn't think so. He knew that eventually what was done in the dark would be brought to the light. That's just nature. Just the way life worked in his world. What may have once been fear was replaced with curiosity.

He decided to trade that computer in as well but this time he would get a different device. This time he bought a Google Chromebook. Whether hacked or not he didn't care, he was keeping this one. In a sense, he was putting his foot down. Not giving up.

His feelings of being watched would ultimately cause him to avoid a social life. He had no friends and, at this point, he wasn't sure if he ever would. He wasn't entirely lonely. He definitely never longed for the irritating people he had to meet in order to make real friends.

CHAPTER

QUESTIONING THE
SPRINKLER HEAD

On a gloomy Tuesday, he lay in his bed wondering and thinking. His thoughts streamed through his mind as he focused solely on a sprinkler head above him on the ceiling. It was then that he noticed a violet, almost lens-like tip on the sprinkler head. He took a closer look before sourly entertaining the idea that he was being watched in his own apartment. He really didn't know much about sprinkler heads or systems enough to determine whether or not his mind was fabricating an unwanted scenario but he needed to know. He grabbed a chair from the dining room and used it as a step stool. He got up as close as he could before seeing small numbers along the metal head. After determining that he would need a magnifying glass he stepped down and dismissed the sprinkler heads as being surveillance equipment. What a hoot, he thought. He had a magnifying glass but undoubtedly he was entertaining an idea too far-fetched to pursue.

Moving on, he decided life was far too precious to spend worrying about anything, much less people staring at you. And besides that, hacking a computer and watching someone in their humble abode was quite a different can of worms. He was almost certainly not important enough to be watched in his room. He had no roommate this time and things were different. Weren't they?

He was nearly certain that despite his misunderstanding there must be a reasonable explanation. Brushing it off was far less complicated than worrying about something he himself couldn't change. He wasn't in any mood to research sprinkler heads. As nightfall crept in, he fell into a deep sleep and drifted into a dream. Before he knew it he was bouncing from the ground high into the air and high above the treetops from the sidewalk. Each time he landed a block further away. It was a re-occurring dream that he enjoyed every single time. Drew walked on his toes so that every time he took a step he seemed to bounce off of his toes and straight into the air.

Without intentionally jumping, he seemed to drift into the air as if he were on the moon and without gravity as he knew it. He didn't understand what it meant but he liked it. It was much more pleasant than his childhood nightmare of a man with a very hairy chest and a moose head chasing his mother. Of course, the moose-headed man without a shirt was wearing blue jeans, which also stuck out to him. He'd never imagined a moose wearing jeans but there it was.

The following morning he had coffee and watched the morning news. Something he saw reminded him of tourettes so he said aloud, "Tourettes." He remembered the movie "Speed" in which there is a scene with Jason Statham asking a man why he had hit him. The man replied that he had advanced tourettes. It had tickled Drew. He didn't believe in making fun of people and hurting their feelings but he had found it most entertaining. He even made fun of himself to himself.

He had no work lined up for the day so he set out to visit his local library. He was totally caught off guard when "coincidence" attempted once again to haunt his day. Sitting down at a computer, he logged on to the internet. He was looking for a better way and where else to find a better way than the worldwide web. In an instant, he heard someone directly behind him shout a loud seemingly meaningless yelp. It was a library. Anyone might expect quiet in a library yet today had started out a bit differently. In response to the huge and quick seemingly meaningless shout, a woman across from him said she couldn't understand why people could be so loud and rude. Eagerly the woman next to him stated simply, "She has tourettes." He left. He didn't particularly want to endure a bunch of coincidence today. He would turn around and go home to his own computer.

Soon he worked enough odd jobs to afford himself a car or at least a down payment on a junker. He bought a PT Cruiser. He didn't know much about cars but he knew it wasn't a muscle car even though it read "Turbo" on the back. It sounded rough but he figured it could last a year or two. He wanted a car that wouldn't act as a police magnet yet was cheap enough and running well enough to get from point A to point B for at least a year. The day he bought the car he sat in it for a while admiring the interior and the satellite radio. His hand stroked the scar just under his cheekbone. He drifted into a daydream and remembered how he got the scar on his left cheekbone.

It was the Fourth of July. His friend, Todd, was busy fighting a crack dealer and shouting to Drew to get the other guy. The other guy was half Drew's size. Drew and his friend were both white and fighting two black crack dealers in a predominately black community. They had been drinking in the hot sun of downtown Memphis, Tennessee when Todd decided he wanted to fight someone. The crack dealer on the corner was the target. The fight was over with fairly quickly. Drew hadn't even gotten his hands dirty. It was later in the evening that Drew would pay for his friend's lust for violence.

MORE VIOLENT MISHAPS

LATER THAT EVENING WHILE walking down the road, a man ran up behind him and smashed Drew's face with a brick in hand. In turn, Drew was knocked out for an instant. He came to just as he fell to the sidewalk and landed directly on the side of his face that had just been smashed by a brick. Blood poured down his face to his t-shirt as he got back up to his feet. The man who smashed him must've been startled by Drew's remarkably quick recovery. He turned to see nothing but the bottom of the assailant's feet as the black fireball faded into the distance like a star track runner.

Pulling out of his daydream, he thought once again that the brick attack could only have been a repercussion from the fight he'd been involved in earlier with Todd. But now he was in Washington, the good ole north. He'd come to realize that that southern heat played a manipulative chord on the human brain. A chord that affected people in a way that seemed to blindly agitate them. While they thought it was just life, he now knew the heat contributed to anger and violence. The American way of drinking a cold beer on a hot day was a way of life he thought that just didn't mix with true hot, humid days at least in the southern portions of the US near the mighty Mississippi. He liked the liberal state of Washington. He knew that no home was ever guaranteed at least as long as man rented it from man and were he left homeless again, at least the sun and river wouldn't attack him anymore. He wouldn't have to force cold liquor down his throat to feel better as cold water would do him just fine. The Evergreen State was remarkable whereas the Volunteer State simply wasn't meant for extended stays outside unless you were a mosquito.

It was a cool, sunny Thursday when he went for a drive that a policeman got behind him. His driver's license was insured and he was sober. While he knew he had nothing to worry about he was always leery of cops. From his juvenile life as a runaway all the way through his adulthood in Memphis, he'd seen and fallen victim to violent police officers. No doubt the sun and humidity had something to do with their volatile ways he thought. A few moments later, the officer did a complete U-turn and drove away. He thought it strange. The officer must have had an important call come in. Drew continued his drive long enough to consider gas cost money and he really couldn't afford joy riding for too long. He pulled back into his rented home after exploring the neighborhood.

Drew had a different outlook on life than most people due to his extreme experiences. In general, he didn't like people who abused power and authority. He was often fired up when he saw police murdering people on video during the news. He knew that the police had often murdered unarmed people but were only recently being exposed due to the rise in technology. More and more videos began to surface of police shooting and killing unarmed men now that cell phones could be used as video cameras. It seemed that every other day a policeman either did something as horrible as shoot a man in the back eight times or beat a man with a billy club for half an hour, and always without any repercussion. He didn't dislike anyone just because they wore a badge, just those who took advantage of it as to purposely cause harm behind that badge. He had never been one to judge people as a group because he knew it to be discriminatory. He knew every single person on Earth had something very special about them and that they weren't ever to be judged as a group but police departments might just be an exception.

BEATEN BY A CORRUPT SYSTEM

Recently he'd been somewhat confused about the good policemen standing up for the foul. If any of the rest were above this gruesome and violent mentality, why were they protecting the officers who undisputedly murdered unarmed men? Their motive could be nothing more than to hide something much greater within the departments themselves.

He entered his apartment where he kicked back on his bed and turned the television on. The news wasn't on yet so he flipped through the channels with the remote. He stopped on Cops Reloaded. Cops Reloaded was a reality show that involved a law enforcement officer driving while talking with a cameraman well into a high-speed chase or bust. The criminal usually turned out to be one of the dumbest idiots you could imagine and the cop talked them into confessing themselves straight into a jail cell once they believed he was sincere about helping them. Drew felt the show was also a slick way to lead the average Joe into believing that he had to put up with being harassed by police officers.

Minutes into his viewing he lost interest and again his mind wondered. Focusing on the sprinkler head's violet-colored tip, he thought back again to a time when he was in jail in Memphis. One day a black DRT officer four feet away from him had held a very small black man a foot into the air by his head and neck while jerking him around like a ragdoll. It was too much for Drew to watch without intervening in some way. He was the only white person in a cage charged with theft among 39 murderers and now 10 aggressive detention response team officers who would show him who was boss.

"Hey, that's not necessary." The words came to him almost accidentally as he stood in front of his cell with his hands on his head during the three a.m. shakedown. The officer who was abusing the small man dropped him and now focused his attention on Drew. White as a snowflake and standing out like a sore thumb in a pod of black men, Drew had to open his mouth for something he believed in and again it would cost him dearly.

Soon after dropping the small man, the officer cuffed Drew, took him to the only room in the entire jail without surveillance equipment, and proceeded to beat him with the help of seven more officers. Drew fought with everything he had, mainly using his feet as his hands were bound. When the match was done, Drew suffered a condition known as Bell's Palsy. His face was paralyzed as if he'd suffered a stroke, namely on the left side. In short, he'd taken steroids and his face restored within a month. He never received thanks from the man he'd defended because he was soon moved to a cell block for higher security risks and high profile inmates. He later tried to sue but it just so happened that the federal judge knew the sheriff and the jail professed to have already destroyed the videotape that recorded everything from the time he was bound to the moment he was taken into the cameraless room. He was railroaded with no choice but to move on and forget about it. Justice seemed to him to work only one way. The law only worked for the rich. He had known that since the day he'd watched Rodney King being beaten and tasered unmercifully by Los Angeles police who were found not guilty of any wrongdoing. Either you were a cop or a rich man. It appeared there was no in between. He fought them with a lawsuit for nearly two years before his grandmother rescued them by taking custody. She got him out of jail after two years of fighting them through the courts and took him into her house in the woods of Drummonds, Tennessee. There he could not meet deadlines rendering him helpless and unable to receive justice. He'd nearly gotten justice but it slipped away. His aunt and grandmother insisted he leave the lawsuit be lest the government kill him.

Glancing back to the television, he watched as a man pleaded with an officer to let him go after being caught with 10 dollars' worth of marijuana. His anger was aroused and he couldn't believe people were being stuffed in cages with murderers and rapists for possessing marijuana. To him, it didn't make sense that justice was filled with hypocrisy. There were other times he watched as people told such outrageous lies to the officers that he was disgusted enough to change the channel. He didn't like hypocrisy and he didn't like watching other people make the same mistakes he had that had cost him so many years of his life. He'd never hurt anyone. He had been put in cages for stealing as an adult and running away from home habitually as a child. It was never for being directly mean in any case.

Drew simply didn't want to see people being mean to each other. It wouldn't matter one way or another if he saw 10 civilians beating a police officer or 10 officers beating a civilian.

He always went with the underdog. No guts no glory. And besides, he had been the underdog most of his life except for when it came to being physically attacked. He somehow always blacked out and whipped pure ass when he was hit. Once in the seventh grade, he had been attacked for being clumsy in the gym locker room after taking seven valiums. His buddy Ronald had given him the valium before school that morning after stealing them from Mommy's medicine cabinet. Drew bumped into one of the crazier guys in his school who was hanging out with another of the biggest guys in his school. They attempted a two on one that seemed to have backfired. The next day he had a lot of new friends, one of whom praised him for whipping the two seniors' tails. After all, he was only 13 and they were both 16. When he found out what he'd done, he ran to apologize to the two. They gave a sort of grunt before running away. Drew felt genuinely bad for beating them up. He shouldn't have.

He fell into a deep sleep while the television continued to waste electricity. As he slipped into Neverland, his mind couldn't help but melt into yet another time past. He found himself back in the Mississippi River just off the bank when he was 19 years old. He was being pulled out by the current towards what seemed to be a whirlpool. He couldn't swim so well much less tread water. He thought staying close to the bank meant all the difference in the world but so did knowing how to swim.

He'd begun to panic. Flailing wildly, all he could get out was, "Oh, God, no." His friends who'd brought him here were looking at him from what seemed at that moment a thousand miles away. He couldn't believe they weren't running to help him. They merely stared with their hands shielding the sun from their eyes.

During his panic, he tried swimming in towards the bank. It felt useless. At the very moment when he realized it was over, his foot touched the bank. Then the other foot. As if the ground had magically appeared under his feet, he was secure. Nearly out of breath, he walked straight back onto land as if it had never happened. He still felt the near-death chemicals that his brain released and the fear of it lingered. It was an earlier episode of near-death he'd long since forgotten.

The next morning, he woke to hear a street sweeper driving into his apartment complex parking lot. It was still dark outside and he was in an usually quiet neighborhood. It ticked him off a little bit considering that the sweeper sounded like an old three wheeler doing donuts. It was quite loud and it hadn't happened before.

After brushing his teeth and washing his face he headed into his small kitchen where he made coffee. He turned on the morning news as he took his first gulp of hot coffee. He needed it and a cigarette to boot. His grandmother had always told him to quit smoking but he believed firmly that in moderation nearly anything could be appreciated. He appreciated cigs and pot. He had long since stopped abusing either of the two and now only enjoyed them in what he considered complete moderation. Marijuana was legal in the great state of Washington. He'd been slammed to his face from behind once as a youth by officers after being arrested for marijuana in the great state of Tennessee. They had to slam him because apparently, the marijuana might have killed him at any minute. It was a schedule one drug... He liked Washington but still loved Tennessee because at heart he knew he'd always be a southern boy.

The news stories consisted of electoral debates between Donald Trump and Hilary Clinton, flooding in Louisiana, and police shooting unarmed men and women in that order. It was sad, he thought. The majority of those caught being murdered on camera were the minority: black men and black teenage boys. He'd even watched as a California State Trooper beat the brakes off an old black bag lady on the side of the highway. He couldn't believe that people could simply drive by what was happening without intervening. Had he been there live, he thought he might have run up and kicked the officer's head across the sky like a football racing to a field goal. He wasn't violent but seeing people hurt had a way of changing him into a fight-fire-with-fire type of guy. Stand for nothing... fall for anything.

He was half done with his coffee when the news of protesters on the east coast, in southern areas, and California hit the screen. His surrounding area in Washington was calm. They were using a new slogan called "Black Lives Matter". It was a movement he thought could have done better without the word "black". He knew where they were coming from but he felt that they were cutting themselves short through their own segregation. Drew knew full well that poor white people were treated just the same. He felt it might have been wiser to coin the term "All Lives Matter" or "Citizens' Lives Matter". They could include a much greater crowd had the movement not sounded limited to black people. It was more about financial status than race. He knew but what could he do? The movement had already started and besides, he didn't want to take away from the fact that yes, black lives do matter. At the same time, he understood that by saying "All Lives Matter" we would be taking away from the subject, which absolutely was that black lives mattered. Racism was the issue.

Protesters had basically burned down their own cities as criminal opportunists looted nearby businesses small and corporate alike. The police arrested nearly 30 people during the protests gone riot. Drew knew for certain that the only way to win a protest against police was for all to band together and not allow ANY arrests whatsoever. Not allowing them to make arrests would make them "obsolete", for lack of a better word. They could actually get something done that way. It was his secret and he would keep it lest he be charged with something. He could see that freedom of speech was diminishing. People were becoming more and more outspoken about being, themselves, offended. Facebook was a chance for everyone to type the words that expressed how they felt and be heard. They hadn't counted on the ever-so-large population of cry-babies who would complain to the government about how "butt hurt" they were because someone else had posted a news clip they didn't like. He racked his brain trying to figure out how someone could cry about what someone else did with their fingers on their own computer. "Put your feelings in your back pocket and sit on them," he always said to himself. His own mother had asked him if he was going to become an extremist simply because he was saddened by murder and posted clips of brutality from the media on his Facebook page. Other family members talked down to him for posting news clips of what police had done. And his mother told them to just block out people they didn't want to hear from; he assumed that meant him. By now, he was considering closing his Facebook account for good. He felt like the bad guy even though he wasn't. He was only concerned.

He'd posted his views on Facebook where diehard Nazi cop fans ruled that they could do as they pleased as police officers. And that if people didn't resist they wouldn't need to be killed. He couldn't believe they were serious. He couldn't for the life of him believe that anyone could harbor enough hate to feel this way about another human life. He watched the video of a man running from police because he had a warrant for child support. About five steps into his run, the police officer pulled out his sidearm and fired directly into the back of the debtor. He shot him eight times in his back. The officer was charged and later released on house arrest.

Within a year or so, cops had managed to choke a man to death, Taser another to death, and sever the spine of another. Most of the murdered were shot to death while unarmed and/ or running from the ego of a trigger-happy-power-trip wearing a badge. In Drew's eyes, the videos alone were undisputable evidence of murder and hatred. He didn't feel trial was necessarily warranted. These guys were evil and the videos were showing America exactly how evil some of them could be. The spawn of cellphones with cameras now exposed what had been occurring over the last 300 years. The majority's eyes were being pried open and they were none too happy about it. Some people were actually refusing to accept it.

When his coffee was finished, Drew got cleaned up to go job hunting. He couldn't see working for some jerk that talked bad to him while he swung a pickaxe all day long. The laborer in him was tired. No one was ever appreciative of his work. He felt like a mule that had been smacked with a stick all day for most of its life. The collection's work had been a nice change of pace. He thought he would try that again. If not, then maybe telemarketing. Any job inside and out of the sun would do him justice. He longed for a job that did not consist of someone standing over him. He just wanted someone to tell him what they wanted him to do and then leave him to work uninterrupted. He often perceived most bosses as overly bossy. The truth was that they were. He could feel within himself that they felt a superiority and Drew didn't like it.

CHAPTER

MORE ATTACKS ON PRIVACY
AND CRAZY PEOPLE

HE LANDED A JOB that day with a fundraising company. All that would be required of him would be to get people on the telephone and pass the call to a closer. He liked the idea. He had a long three-day wait before his start date. When he got home he turned on his television and kicked back on his bed. He considered what to do for the rest of the day. As he stared into the sprinkler head above him on the ceiling, he thought to himself how boring it would be to sit and watch television for the rest of the day. Why not go tie one on? He could have some cheap whiskey and see where it lead. To him, tying one on once every month or two wasn't quite the abuser he'd once considered himself. For years it had been daily. He knew also that he shouldn't but like it always had, alcohol screamed louder than reason. Logic vanished and all that remained in control was instinct.

He already had the balls of a bull and alcohol turned him into superman except that he couldn't fly and was well aware of it, which added just a touch of restraint to his behavior. By five o'clock in the evening, Drew was well lit. He enjoyed listening to music on his iPod Shuffle and drinking alone. He sat and watched as suspicious people frolicked about the park dealing meth and heroin. There was the occasional couple or group passing through for a glimpse of adventure. He eventually returned to his apartment.

When he walked in he noticed a smell that was alien: the smell of another person. His sense of smell was strongest when he was intoxicated. He smelled someone. And although he couldn't describe the smell he knew it to be from a person. He knew no one was there now and he couldn't see his landlord breaking the law by trespassing without his permission. Whoever had been in his home seemed to have touched nothing. It didn't make any sense to him. He could do nothing more than dismiss it.

Glaring into his think spot again, a mere sprinkler head, he listened to an old heavy metal song about politics. He didn't understand the full meaning of the song but he loved the sound of it. He listened to a very wide variety of music including but not limited to hardcore rap and country music, not excluding everything in between. He was truly appreciative of all kinds of music. He'd even enjoyed classical on occasion. Music seemed to boost his adrenaline so incredibly much that he often felt the absolute need to drop and give himself 20 pushups. He maintained his size this way, not to mention the fact he drank milk like it was water.

He himself couldn't see he was built like a brick shit house. An innocence about him kept him blinded from seeing who and what he was. While he considered himself average, others saw something entirely different: a big nice guy, a man who didn't realize his size and age, and a gentle giant with a baby face who got along with most everyone. Drew was a likable guy. While he enjoyed a good debate he never wanted to anger others with his views on life. He felt it necessary not to offend people. The past had revealed to him how irate weaker-minded people could be when it came to introducing another point of view. He'd seen a man in Memphis once beaten down for arguing with another man about how he believed that the Bible was written in order to control the black man. Once the man was beaten to the floor, Drew watched as several others viciously stomped the man's head into the floor until a large pool of blood formed a red halo around him. He'd tried to save the guy before his black buddy stopped him. It could have been a grave mistake had his friend not pulled him back. Getting in the middle of a gang fight in Memphis would assuredly get you hurt.

Violent episodes he'd witnessed in years gone by seemed to haunt Drew's memory. As early back to when he was five years old, Drew could remember seeing some men in a truck drag a dog up and down the road on its back while it howled horribly. That same feeling lit him up every time he saw merciless violence. A burning rage inside made him want to flip the tables so that the violent culprits could feel the very pain they themselves had inflicted upon another. He wanted justice for the underdog. Drew was indifferent to hatred. He felt that if people could just imagine themselves in the victim's shoes, then everyone could live together more gracefully. They could also maybe learn to love one another. Unfortunately, he knew that this would never happen. People found it easier to hate than to love. It was easier to take than to earn. And easier to forget than to remember.

As he listened to his iPod, that dark cloud that seemed to rain on his mind through his scalp, felt again like a form of paranoia. It wasn't the change of music triggering it but something unfamiliar to him. Something outside of the music. Something hidden. Something very disturbing struck his senses, allowing him to focus on the feeling a deer might have just before it is shot during hunting season. He wasn't in fear but in question. He'd long since accepted that one day he must die along with everyone else. Millions before him had already done so. Death to him was an inevitable stage to something much greater than he could ever imagine. He was never so arrogant as to believe he was on Earth by luck or circumstance.

He had that feeling of quiet where a pin drop could be heard, yet he was blaring music into his ears unmercifully. His focus immediately turned to first his closet and then to the sprinkler head again. He felt compelled to look closer into his suspicions regarding the sprinkler head this time. He could only imagine just what this would look like to someone else who might be watching him from elsewhere within the apartment. If the violet-colored heads proved not to be a threat, then perhaps he was being viewed from somewhere else within the apartment. Camera lenses these days were made as small as pin holes.

Holding a small magnifying glass to the back of the inside of a sprinkler head 10 feet off of the ground would prove tedious. He grabbed a stool and wrote each number down with a grimace. Sweat dripping in his eyes from his forehead made seeing the numbers that much more difficult. He was nearly drunk and now agitated.

Once he'd taken the numbers down, he jumped from the stool and flopped his lazy drunk ass back down on his bed tossing the digit littered paper onto his nightstand. As usual with Drew, he'd lost interest and grown tired from the drink.

Before nodding off he would remember why he "quit drinking". He nodded into a nightmare.

In his nightmare, a man with a wide pig nose or snout was flying down at him from the sky. He seemed to want to attack but was not quite doing so as if he was awaiting a command or permission from a higher power. It was a dream that struck no certain chord yet cut into the memory like a hot blade driving through a stick of butter. It was there and there was no taking it out. And so as he slept and drifted from dream to dream, his body recovered from the drink. When he awoke the following morning he felt refreshed and ready to dive into another entire day of nothing. He still had two days before he would begin his new job. Today, he knew he had to enjoy because once work began it always seemed to capture his freedom. Off days were never enough time and with anxiety came the need for escape. Often times he'd left a job to go get drunk. The people he showed respect to as co-workers and or supervisors often seemed to take his hospitality and consideration for a weakness. More times than not a boss had hurt his feelings by talking to him in a disrespectful and demanding way. Instead of talking back, he merely quit and got lit. That was how he handled his problems with those people around him. Arguing could lead to violence and much more. Walking away was always better than hurting someone and later grieving their pain. He truly didn't enjoy hurting anyone. And, of course, he himself wasn't fond of pain though his tolerance was high.

He looked back on the night before and remembered how nutty he must have been to write down the serial numbers of a sprinkler head. He glanced over at the numbers he'd thrown onto the nightstand and thought to himself how embarrassing it would be to see himself drunk and paranoid. For an instant, he felt that there was more wrong with him than he could see. "Could I really be paranoid without the fear?" he thought as he looked himself in the eyes through the bathroom mirror. "Why do I feel this way? When will it stop and how?" While the questions bombarded his mind like ants on sugar he couldn't help but taste bitterness in each question.

For now, Drew would drop the questions and attempt to move on with his day. He would pass it off as another odd episode in his life. After all, "odd" was common with him. He knew his life was weird but couldn't accept that he himself might be a weirdo. Although it had crossed his mind, he knew everyone was weird in their own way. That's what made him different from Joe Shmoe down the road.

He took a cup of coffee outside with him to get some fresh morning air and to have a cigarette. The two seemed to have made the perfect couple in the stimulant world. Coffee and cigarettes were both legal and both invited him to wake up happily. He took a sip of coffee before he noticed a gigantic slab of notebook paper flopping around on the street near where he'd parked his car. He walked up and sat his cup on the hood of his cruiser then lit his cigarette. He reached down and grabbed the piece of paper only to find that it was a pamphlet for people who may be suffering from paranoia and where they could find help. It might have come to him as a surprise were he, in fact, not used to crazy everyday coincidence invading his life. He shoved the paper into his back pocket to toss it in the trash. He would be littering if he threw it back on the ground. He believed in keeping the Earth clean. He grabbed his sweet and creamy coffee and headed back into his apartment.

He fried up some bacon and eggs and had breakfast while he watched the morning news. The news that morning was no different except this time five policemen had been killed in Dallas, Texas. It seemed people were growing angrier every day about the police shooting people and now the people were killing police because of it. Eventually, the dead suspects would be written off by the government-controlled media as crazy lone wolves with PTSD and such. The government wouldn't allow the media to promote the idea that the "lone wolves" were part of an internal movement. It was the government's way of preventing any kind of forced change to their own comfortable policies and procedures. Keeping the people at bay consisted of keeping them divided into groups that despised each other: black and white, Muslim and Baptist, police and civilians, rich and poor. Both the privileged and the oppressed were divided in a way as to suit national security. No one group was big enough to put their American government back in check of the people. And no two opposing groups were willing to join forces. The American people seemed to be hopelessly at the mercy of the very government their forefathers founded for them to enforce their freedoms. Freedom seemed to be trumped by safety.

Drew wondered as he watched more news if anyone else could see what he felt was important about what was happening in our country. Most of what he saw on social media were people sticking up for those police who'd shot and killed or beat unarmed men and women. They boasted statements such as "Stop resisting and y'all won't git killed" and "Obey the law and that won't happen." He would never understand this mentality. Perhaps it wasn't in him to understand.

He began flipping through news channels looking for yet another perspective on the world. "A new outlook on life would be great right about now," he thought. He never liked what he saw on the news nor did he think he ever would. Why then did he feel so compelled to watch it day after day? He had many questions about himself to an extent that it made him feel guilty. The guilt came from thinking too much of himself. Analyzing himself felt somehow wrong yet he didn't know why. What was his major malfunction? He didn't know. But he did know that if he could identify his problem then he could fix it. Extreme self-consciousness and weird paranoia without fear could make for a stronger Drew. The crazier things he experienced, the closer he came to being humble.

Drew gulped down the last of his "pick me up" coffee and realized he'd stopped surfing on a channel that was playing a commercial for "people who have been diagnosed with schizophrenia or their concerned loved ones". At this point, he felt it was in order to hit the power off button. Coincidence in repetition was a bit too much.

He ventured out in his PT cruiser and cruised to the park to take a few puffs of a purple strain of pot. He knew a couple of puffs couldn't last more than a full hour in his system. He would park for an hour and a half after smoking so that he abided by the law. Heaven forbid a security conscious extremist smelt pot coming from his car. He didn't need them entertaining themselves at his expense by calling the police to create a scene.

HUMILIATION AND MORE CRAZY

During his peaceful smoke session, he watched squirrels chase one another up and down the evergreen trees. Butterflies tossed themselves around in the air and beautiful trees danced with the wind. There weren't many people and it was very pleasant. The birds sang and the bees did their thing. Were a person to get too close he might have had to worry about their being offended by his smoke whether from the small amount of pot or the cigarette he would smoke afterward. Inevitably, people seemed to bring problems to his life more often than not. He was more comfortable being left alone. Once, when he was a teenager, he attempted to break out of being horribly shy by speaking up while some girls were looking at him and giggling. He put everything he had into saying, "Hi. What are y'all laughing about?" He just knew they would flirt back when one of the three girls said, "You're ugly!" As they laughed, he pretended to brush it off while secretly feeling the most devastating humiliation known to mankind. He'd just realized he would never ask a girl out because it hurt too bad to find out how unattractive he was.

His hairline was never even close to normal, especially during his younger years of growing. And his eyes were extremely deep set. He knew he wasn't very attractive and he would have had no idea exactly how attractive he would become when he became an adult. His face and head would begin to form and fill out in a way that almost matched his environment. By age 25, he'd become a good looking young man. By 30, he would appear intense. And on to sexy by 40. Carved facial features would highlight his baby face to make him a very attractive man. In childhood, he looked like a sleestack with little pointy teeth and a very large forehead.

Being a moderate pothead, he put down his accessory after his second full pull and went for a quick walk through the park. He noticed a man in the woods who appeared to be trying to blend into the scenery as he walked his dog. The man wore camouflage pants and a brown shirt. His dog was brown. He'd seen the man come in but had paid very little attention until he felt the man's glare violating his senses. Drew didn't look directly at the man because he too wanted to observe the man he first felt and then saw glaring at him by way of peripheral. His set back eyes gave him an advantage that many didn't have such as extreme peripheral vision. He could nearly see behind himself.

He couldn't help but notice the man move forward in what appeared to be an attempt to further hide behind a small tree. Drew knew this man, for whatever reason, was watching him but also knew he couldn't prove it. He'd often concluded that approaching anyone who hasn't laid hands on you was a no-no. And besides, it could always be a flaw scratching his perception. He was careful to always remember that he wasn't perfect. Drew never for once felt like he was in any immediate danger. He only felt curious as to why anyone would focus their attention on a nobody. A nice guy loner. A stranger. He walked for a bit before dismissing the stranger's odd demeanor. By the time he got back to his car, he'd forgotten about what he concluded to be a nosy old man. He sat for a few more minutes and listened to the radio and then he left.

On his way out he saw a man who appeared to be his deceased grandfather's twin. His grandfather never had a twin but the old man appeared to have all the same character features as his grandfather. For a moment he felt a chill tickle the center of his spine. He forced his eyes on the road and continued on. He noticed people seemed to sometimes stare at his vehicle as he drove past them. Some actually pointed at it. He thought it funny and entertained the idea that anyone would be interested in him or even knew who he was but on the other hand... what in the hell were they pointing at?

It made him chuckle with a whim of insanity. He simply didn't get it. To him, the questions he had about being watched were overwhelming. So much so, in fact, that he found a way to throw them all into a file that lay within the outer realms of his mind. They weren't organized in the least; a kid's closet stuffed full of toys if you will.

Drew continuously had battles raging in his mind. With the knowledge that death had once followed him through life, he battled with questions like "why?" Why did those ladies in Everett set up yard sales so quickly just before he walked his homeless self by their homes? They must have known he was in desperate need of a t-shirt as they had one his size and still in a package. When he opened it, the shirt displayed a cartoon-like picture of a zombie's face and it read, "Zombie no want brains. Zombie want equal rights. "It nipped at his ankles like a small, cute, irritating little dog. He loved dogs—not this kind—but still, he accepted it. Death was inevitable. And then so was life. And so were games.

Drew pulled into his driveway and turned off his car. He went inside and, as usual, he sat down in front of his TV. He liked nature shows. They relaxed him. They could also excite him. Watching monkeys communicating was relaxing. Watching elephants was relaxing. Watching wild buffalo in Africa gang up on a half-dozen lions that were simultaneously playing tug of war with an alligator and its prey totally blew him away. His adrenaline went straight through the roof when he discovered how even buffalo would stand in loyalty against attacks on its own. He expected to see the herd of buffalo stampede away in fear. On the contrary, these bulky balls of horn turned completely around once the lioness brought down one of their bouncy youth. The lioness took down the calf and an alligator leaped forward from the water and seemed to glide across the mud in a mode brought on more so probably from desperation than skill. The tug of war began. Within a few seconds, buffalo were goring the vicious cats from the opposite side with their massive horns. Eventually, the baby buffalo got away and again joined the herd. This had to be the best nature show he'd ever seen. He saw real raw justice as the buffalo flipped lions with their coarse headpieces, hurting them yet sparing their freedom and life. The sheer desperation and determination of the alligator was admirable. When it lost its prey it gracefully sunk back into the water as if to say, "Maybe next time." It reminded him of how much more callous the human justice system was in comparison to wild animals.

Again, he nodded into a dream. This time the dream was from a time when he was very young and afraid of a crop duster that looked like it was gonna crash into his house. He was maybe five years old at the time but remembered the day well. The plane continuously swooped down by his home, which sat in a field in Kentucky. Somehow, even at five years of age, he gathered strength that night not to be scared anymore. The plane had gone and although he was still winding down from that fear he was healing from it emotionally. As bedtime came, he lay in bed under the covers, tired from being horrified the whole day long. In his dream, he began to nod off just when he heard a faint noise from across the room.

His room was huge, or at least it felt that way to a five-year-old. His bed seemed to be in the middle of the huge room. The window was huge and so was the moon. The carpet and the walls were both a gross puke beige color. The noise that he heard sounded like what a foot would sound like if it were slowly taking steps across the carpeted room towards his bed. He became so frightened that he covered his face with the blanket. His breathing began to quicken as the noise came closer to his bed. His heartbeat was stronger than life and smashing against his little chest like a bass drum. He hoped whatever monster was coming wouldn't hear his heart beating.

With his body shaking violently out of control and the eternal sound of a slow footstep as near as it could get, the frightened child jumped from the bed onto the floor in a karate-like stance. He knew nothing about life but what he'd seen on television and the horror of being forced to face his fears right now...

He woke up sweating. It must've been two o'clock in the morning. He went to the fridge to get a drink of milk. As he passed by the dining room window he heard what sounded like a hundred children screaming in terror from a good distance. He did a double take and turned to look out the window but saw nothing. Advancing to the refrigerator he opened the door to grab the milk. Midway into pouring milk, he heard something above him smack the Plexiglas skylight six feet above his head. Assuming it was part of a tree or possibly a pine cone he ignored it while he poured his milk. Then as he put the milk away he heard another small crack. And then another. And another. He looked up to see three crows pecking away at his skylight. "What on God's green earth are crows pecking at me for at two o'clock in the morning?" They seemed to be trying to communicate more than being aggressive. Another mystery of life. "Oh, boy." For now, it was back to bed. He would have time to analyze it tomorrow when he'd had his coffee.

The following morning he awoke and took care of the three "s" words that everyone should take care of regularly. Then he had his coffee. He listened to the weather lady rant about how beautiful the tormenting heat was going to be by noon. In all honesty, he joked to himself that she should smack herself and snap out of it. She was spastic and too fake happy. Maybe too commercial. Daydreaming about another time brought with it a déjà vu. A peculiar smell that reminded him of the southern U.S.

JASON AND MORE CRAZY

DRIFTING INTO THE ALMOST mental smell, it reminded him of riding bikes with his friend Jason when he was 13-years-old. Jason had been his brother in a sense. When Drew ran away from home he always hung out at Jason's house. Drew practically lived there. Jason was an interesting character. When Drew and Jason met it was their first year in the seventh grade. They didn't entirely fit in because they were neither one hip to the current style of dressing. The two wore what the other kids called three stripe buddies: the cheap stuff with three stripes going down the sides of the shoe.

Looking back, he remembered the day he first met Jason. Jason had shown him the cool stash of frogs he'd nailed into the ground while they were still alive. He also showed him the once-live snake he'd caught on fire with gasoline. They were all things Drew was totally against. Later, Jason matured in a way that at least he stopped hurting animals. Jason would also help the police to change their laws on high-speed chases. Jason was a country boy and an R-rated version of the "Dukes of Hazzard". He became an ass-kickin' vigilante that loved motorcycles and his people but hated drugs.

While Drew never participated in hurting any animals with Jason, he still remained a close childhood friend throughout the years. Jason wasn't really into hurting animals, it had just been something that a lonely little boy had experimented with. Later in life, he had too many friends to count. He admired a bravery about Jason until the day he passed away. A bravery that drove him to stand up for what he believed in. Twenty-two years into their friendship they had a violent misunderstanding and parted ways. Four years later, Jason was shot to death by a man with a badge who didn't understand anything but fear of another man and getting a paycheck. Jason was a hero.

Déjà vu and coincidence seemed to crowd Drew's life. No matter how he tried to deal with it, the irony would always be there. When he snapped back to reality, the television bombarded him with first a commercial about nails on sale at a hardware store, followed by another commercial displaying a fake frog talking through an insurance advertisement. He could barely shake his head in disgust as he'd been through this very thing hundreds or even thousands of times before. Just thinking about a frog with a nail through its back. Useless happenings. Useless occurrences. The apparent need to know what it meant had driven him to drink and drugs on occasion. It was driving him mad before he'd changed his mindset. He simply had to set this paranoia aside. He couldn't physically deal with it because truly nothing had really harmed him. It was as if he were battling an invisible monster or ghost of sorts. He couldn't discuss the feeling of being watched with what he called normal everyday people because they would surely conclude he was "schitzo". People didn't really wanna know how you were doing if you were not doing well. That was just part of life. And although he felt he was doing fine, someone else might beg to differ were he to discuss the everyday weird occurrences that were common to him.

He yawned and stretched out on the couch after setting his coffee down. He truly appreciated coffee. He also appreciated being inside where he wouldn't have to feel "other people" induced agitation. It agitated him for people to stare or spy. He'd had enough of that with the bums in the woods of Tacoma and the Memphis jail.

Drew dreamed and daydreamed to an extreme. He himself didn't find it odd because he lived with it day after day. Every day of his life he dreamed and daydreamed. A lot of the time he would forget that he even had a dream. And sometimes the dreams could be so disturbing that even though he couldn't remember the actual dream he still felt the real trauma – a heavy, devastating trauma weighing down on him both mentally and physically nearly anchoring him to his bed. Like a bout with depression that would normally take years to build, he felt the impact overnight because of a dream he couldn't for the life of him remember. He also got over the traumatizing effect fairly quickly. At the very least he pretended he did. "A fake smile lasts a long while." he'd always believed.

Wallowing on the couch he felt like a pig. He left the couch to take a shower and an extremely small needle jabbed into the tip of his toe just under the nail. It nearly took his breath away. He let a huge breath of air go in place of the would-be roar. The pain was so intense for that moment that right afterward he knew he could take on anything. It reminded him of more pain that he'd endured throughout the years of his life. It reminded him that comfort wasn't everything and that a life of horrible pain could land on any one of us on any given day. And that he should always appreciate life to the fullest. He was able to make light of almost any bad situation because he simply refused to allow anyone or anything to get to him. He was bullheaded and good-hearted. A smile would always be part of his character.

Sitting back down on the couch, he pulled the small fairy sword of a pin from his toe. It hurt but hurt, he knew, was also an inevitable part of life. Fun, fun, fun. He had approximately 70 scars all over his body including but not limited to his head, chest, arms, and fingers. He'd broken toes before and never even knew it until years after they'd healed. Pain for him was a way of life and as simple to him as oxygen. He didn't like it so much that he learned to ignore it. Pain was no one's friend.

Now, his mind began to wander. How did the needle get onto the floor to begin with? He thought he didn't have anything like that in his house. He didn't know how to sew really. He thought maybe it was there when he moved in, only embedded into the carpet. He must have been fortunate to have gone as long as he did without being jabbed. He looked around and vacuumed. He didn't find any more needles.

When he could finally take a shower he noticed water leaking from the side of the shower head. The shower head was loosely twisted on so he tightened it snuggly with his hand. He would have assumed it should have been tight when he moved in. It's not like he would make sure the shower head was on tight before renting. Nevertheless, he'd never seen the shower head leaking until now.

Drying himself off the petty questions floated through his head. "Why was the dadgum shower head loose? Why was there a needle in the floor? And why on God's green earth do I have to put up with this kinda garbage most every single day of my life?" He was sick of it. So, in his own defense, he dismissed it. He didn't wanna put himself in a bad mood the day before he started his new job. He held tight to positivity.

He plopped down in front of the boob tube wearing nothing but boxers. The reception was not only bad but at times so horrible with the timing that it threw Drew into a silent rage. He would turn bright red. Although he wanted to throw the television out the window he managed not to. It seemed like it was intentionally done. He took it personally because every single time he was listening to a news station about something politically important to him the clip would break up at the crucial point of the whole story. There would be no interference all the way up to the point where the newscaster said "police say a man was shot 12 thousand times today because … Back to you, Bob." For a while, it really angered him. But as time went by he humbled himself only to have the same thing happen all the time. He couldn't count on his TV and felt someone had made it that way. "Otherwise, why at those exact moments of audio importance did the dang thing always break up?" Anyway, he would submit to being humbled about it lest he punched a hole through it. He hoped to never catch people playing games with him for fear he might hurt them. His gut told him someone was trying to manipulate his life. On the other hand, why would they? And if not, then why did he feel this way?

He remembered back to when he was leaving Everett, Washington. He'd seen the same double bed dump truck drive by him and get off of the exit up ahead at least four times. It had literally gotten off an exit and back on the interstate at least four times that he knew before he ignored it. He also remembered how a very long and huge train often cut him off on his way to eat or get a bed at the Tacoma Rescue Mission. Drew was without a vehicle and backpacking it around town. He had to cross a particular train track to get to the homeless resources. It seemed more times than not the train never went anywhere but to pull ahead enough to block him from getting from point A to point B. Looking back, he couldn't believe he kept any sanity about him at all. If life was pickin' at him this much then perhaps he should invite insanity in as opposed to having it pry its way into his brain. If he was to invite it in then maybe at least the pry marks might not show. He could mask it so as not to offend anyone.

Glaring at his ceiling in thought he considered how to empty his brain of concern for anyone looking at him. He felt that maybe without that aspect present then he wouldn't have to connect everything else to it, thus making it look larger than it really was.

He remembered his brother being upset when they were kids because Drew was looking at him. "Mom! Drew's looking at me!" Drew got in trouble every time his big-mouthed bratty little brother yelled for their mom. He did think it funny though. His brother getting angry over being looked at was as silly as Drew being angry about people looking at him outside. At least they weren't looking at him within the privacy of his own home. At least there was no physical proof.

Wanting peace so seriously that he was willing to induce amnesia if it meant peace of mind, he lit up a joint. It wouldn't stop the pain but it would allow him to ignore it. The pain from the stick pin was superseded by the pain in his head. The pain of feeling he might be a paranoid schizophrenic or something worse hurt his mind. Feeling that someone meant him harm, hurt him to his heart. He still refused to accept that he'd been taken by his own mind. And he refused to believe someone was watching him with intent to do harm. It was a catch 22 if you will. A dead-end maze. A recipe for a distraught mind. He had to shake it off.

The following morning he started work at the fundraising company. Passing calls all day long and getting to know new faces made him feel a bit peculiar. The job seemed too easy. He could do this forever, couldn't he?

By the end of the workday he was happy and felt a newfound sense of worth. He felt he had everything he needed in life once again. A full-time job, a vehicle, and a pad. He was nearly overwhelmed at how great he felt and decided to celebrate by drinking some homemade wine that he had concocted previously on a rainy day. He simply mixed cherries, strawberries, and bananas into a gallon milk jug along with sugar and yeast. Drinking every day until he blacked out was something he would never revisit. He put a rubber balloon over the top in place of the lid. After poking several small holes in the balloon he sat the jug in the hot water heater closet for a couple of weeks. Presto Strong, clean wine.

He had learned to make alcohol while incarcerated in Memphis, Tennessee at the Shelby County Correctional Center. It was a building first built in the 1800s with roll shut bars that reeked of decades of DNA, hard breath, and suppression. Serving out a three-year prison term he'd grown truly bored. Fighting off attackers and watching his own back wasn't nearly enough excitement for Drew. He had to go and make wine with his lunch. Fruit, bread, and sugar were all that it took to incite a riot. Because of this, he was housed in a high-profile segregation pod where he would stay locked down in a cage for a minimum of 23 hours a day. There he learned to be comfortable. After the initial screaming and crying, thoughts of loneliness and the horror of being confused while suffering in a cage faded, Drew learned to embrace the horrors and even there he managed to make wine.

At home now he drank his homemade wine and immediately felt the need for adrenaline-pumping music. He grabbed his iPod Shuffle and turned up the first song playing. It was an old favorite of his that began with bagpipes and melted into a storm of heavy metal music. He finished his first glass of wine and moved on to the second. By now he was juiced on a variety of music including, but not limited to, heavy metal, rap, soul, pop, country western, and even classical. He learned to experience every emotion possible through alcohol and music. All the emotions being felt during a two-hour period ran a toll on him. So he made the great decision to stop drinking before he did something drastic like getting a DUI. "Yes. Instead of drinking more and doing something stupid, I'll just go for a drive." He'd become emotional.

Drew knew without a doubt that he was perfectly capable of driving without incident after only two glasses of homemade wine. What he hadn't counted on were his brakes going seven minutes into his drive. But they did. They went out and now despite passing a sobriety test, he would have a DUI embedded into his very name.

Breathalyzers didn't lie. Three points over the legal limit on a bac detector were enough to land him in the Clark County Jail drunk tank for about 30 hours or so. On top of that he was facing about eight thousand dollars in fees, fines, and court costs. It appeared there was no justice for a poor man. The costs were the same no matter the poverty level. Enough to drive a man to drink. Again...

He didn't particularly think he should plead guilty to failing to maintain his vehicle simply because he had alcohol in his system when he would have handled the situation the same in either case. His brakes went out and so it was their fault. It just so happened that wine was on his breath, which made a bad situation worse and they called it a crime. Had no alcohol been on his breath, it would have been an accident. "Spill a Coke it's an accident. Spill a beer and you're drunk." he thought with a grin.

Moving on with his life and his new job, Drew noticed the group of people he worked with was segregated somewhat from the other call groups within the company. The other groups seemed a bit more professional as the months went by. He subtly began paying more attention to his surroundings and in doing so discovered that the group he worked with were politely trying to agitate him. There was no other reason he could come up with other than he was being toyed with. His fellow employees in connected cubicles seemed to be often overly nice and bothersome with questions.

Some begged for part of his lunch and others begged for cigarettes. For 10 very long drawn out months, Drew worked what he'd once believed was an easy job. Unfortunately, he was being consumed with an anger brought on by working around undercover crackheads, freeloaders, and even the drunken mentally ill. Why had he been placed to work with these people? Why were these people even being hired on? And why just this particular group? He felt that if indeed this was all just some sort of joke, then he truly wished they would just come out and say, "Smile. You're on candid camera," and be done with it. It wasn't working for him anymore. He knew that he was allowing other people to manipulate him in small ways that really angered him and he didn't like the way it felt. As to avoid becoming another raging, blackout alcoholic, Drew quit the job and felt free again. He didn't care what came next. Life went on. His sanity was far more important than 50 bucks a day.

On his first full Monday of being jerk free, he ventured out to get into trouble. He bought a small amount of amphetamine – the kind you find on the internet that's totally legal. These days dealers sold legal substances on the street corners. This way the charges would be dropped automatically or at worst reduced. Possession of methamphetamine was a felony. Possession of methamphetamine wannabe was no crime. With that also came a wannabe high but a sobering one.

Drew never considered experimenting with drugs as immoral. He considered it minding his own business and self-medicating. He considered it immoral for the government to tell him what he could and couldn't do with his own body and mind. He felt urine tests were the epitome of nosy and didn't believe in Joe Shmoe asking another man for a sample of something so intimate and personal as another man's urine. He certainly was misguided and rebellious.

SPRINKLER HEAD REVISITED

HE SWALLOWED WHAT HE'D acquired and began to feel his mind open wide like a blooming flower time lapse. He could suddenly see the boldness of colors where he hadn't been able to before. He felt a need and a desire to explore anything and everything. Sitting in his home, he opened his computer. He began to look for reasons as to why he had dealt with so much coincidence and near-death experience his entire life.

He began by looking for his own name to see what might pop up. After pages of scrolling, he found not much more than Facebook ads and old lawsuits he'd filed against the prison he'd lived through. He also found mugshots of himself that amounted to nothing more than police photography engineered to make anyone look guilty until proven innocent. Then the bright idea came to him, "Run the serial number on the sprinkler head," so that one less thing would be crowding his mind. Pulling the piece of paper from atop his nightstand he looked up the number he'd tried so hard to retrieve on that drunken day with a magnifying glass. He typed and waited as the slowness of his computer tried to get a clue. He couldn't believe his eyes when the serial number came up as "surveillance equipment". The sprinkler heads were made in the next city over for nursing homes and hospitals. He re-typed the numbers because he truly wanted this to be a mistake. Maybe he had mistyped a number. When it came up the same as before he didn't know what to do.

It was a gross violation of civil liberties. Everything he feared might not be true had just become real. After hours of being as offensive as possible with vulgar music and pushups, he decided to begin drinking. He drank until he was babbling. All the while he cursed the sprinkler heads. He left in drunken disgust and went for a walk. After a mile of walking, he turned back and headed back home. All he could allow himself to do was fall into the bed asleep. The alcohol must have worn off. At three AM he woke up feeling like a million bucks. He rolled a marijuana cigarette in hopes that a few puffs might put him back to sleep. It worked and Drew rested once again. And once again his past re-visited him in the form of a dream.

This time he was 10-years-old. He was trying to collect money in a bucket for muscular dystrophy through a well-known gas station. His goal was two hundred dollars so that he could win a brand new BMX bicycle. The whole thing was sponsored by Jerry's kids. Every time he got close to having a few bucks in the bucket, his stepfather would pull up and empty it into his own lap. His stepfather had gambling issues and had already told him that he hated him. So Drew wanted to give it to his stepfather in the hope he would begin to like him. In the dream he remembered his stepdad's words, "Drew, do you know what it means to hate someone? Well, I hate you.

And I hope you can understand that." Drew was nine when he was informed that he was hated. Now at 10, he just wanted his stepdad to like him and he wanted that BMX bicycle. Although it seemed he was getting nowhere with the bucket, he just didn't know it yet.

Apparently, someone somewhere had been watching because soon thereafter a woman came to his house with her son who went to school with Drew but was in a higher grade. They were well off and had a bucket of their own full of money. In fact, there were two hundred dollars in it. Drew and his mother raced to the Seven Eleven store to collect his brand new bicycle. In his dream, he was as happy as a child could get. It was over with rather quickly but the happiness seemed to linger with him in sleep. A red BMX bicycle was finally his because someone cared enough to rescue him. Someone saw a little boy with a little boy dream and reached out to show him that people did care and that life wasn't really all that bad.

When he awoke his mind was a bit foggy. He didn't immediately remember the night before but felt he wasn't sure if he wanted to recapture any of it. After all, there was never anything worth remembering after a night on the booze. He stumbled to the coffee pot and turned it on before lighting a cigarette. He turned on the news out of what was becoming a bad habit. The news never made him feel good although it did confirm to him that the US was beginning to look like the makings of a police state. He could see it very clearly. And when he posted the clips to social media, all of his "family" and "friends" argued that if these people had followed orders they wouldn't have been shot and killed and that the video didn't necessarily show the whole picture. "Were they brainwashed?" he thought. Nazi Germany came to mind. Follow orders or die.

He went back to the kitchen and made his coffee. While he stirred in the happy parts, his memory gate came open exposing the previous night's events. Despite his commands not to remember, his memory rebelled. As he remembered he also refused to accept it. He didn't even bother to look up at the now infamous sprinkler head. He was traumatized again. Life seemed to have a way of traumatizing him over and over. While he was fully unaware of this fact he only knew that he was disturbed. His head both physically and mentally had been through the works his entire lifetime. Tree limbs had fallen on his head giving him concussion right along with aluminum baseball bats, bricks, bottles, fists, pistols, and windshields just to name a few. Stepfathers and stepfather wannabees helped scar his mind with messages of hate and neglect.

Bouncing from state to state with his mother and her AWOL boyfriend, he hadn't been able to keep any friends for long before the age of 10. In fact, his heart had been broken several times when he made new friends and never saw them again. On many occasions, he'd been taken out of school by his mother in an attempt to escape her then live-in boyfriend or husband. It seemed his poor mother hadn't had much good fortune with the men in her life, but that was another story.

He sat thinking and drinking his coffee. After his third cup, he felt the uncontrollable urge to get out of his apartment. He was disgusted by what he'd discovered the night before. He so badly didn't wanna think about it that he had to leave his own apartment. The very place that he called home didn't feel like home anymore. It seemed the very simple luxury of life called privacy had evaded him.

During his walk, he smoked a little pot to ease the anxiety and discomfort of knowing peace was a long way off. The only possible way to obtain peace in this world on this Earth was to buy your own property. Renting someone else's property would never be truly comfortable for him. He needed his own place away from nosy extremists. He could not believe they were spying on him in his own "home". On one hand, he felt relieved to know that all this time he had been right. On the other hand, it was disturbing to now know that someone actually had been spying on him.

For nearly nine years now, Drew had felt he was part of someone else's entertainment while not knowing for sure if his mind was playing tricks on him. Now he knew he had been right the entire time. In realizing this, he began putting many, many pieces of a puzzle together within his mind. It was nearly too much information for his brain to process all at once. He knew full well that it had all started here in the state of Washington. And he could now look for the answer of exactly "who" the perp was and "why". He would remain patient because he knew that in this life, haste made waste.

He finished smoking, turned tail, and headed back towards his apartment. As he walked in he couldn't help but notice that the sprinkler heads had changed. They no longer had a violet type lens at the tip. Instead, they now appeared to have a thick metal tip similar to that of what holds a watch to a watch band. After all he'd seen and been through in his lifetime, he couldn't find it in him to be shocked. He wouldn't confront his landlord because this had gone on far longer than before he'd lived here. He ruled her out. And besides, if she were involved she would never come clean. He knew he could call the F.B.I. and they would figure it out for him but he decided not to. He wasn't afraid of the beady-eyed little bug of a human who violated him to his core. He would deal with this sub-human entity on his own. In time, what was done in the dark was always brought to the light. He knew this well.

Sitting down at his computer he began to search for everything he could to find out about his name and his family's names. First, he wanted to know if somehow his family was involved. He searched and searched. In between searching, he visited his timeline on Facebook where he told his mother what was happening. She pretty much ignored him. He told his grandmother who questioned his importance in life and why anyone would care about watching him of all people. She seemed to dismiss it. He mentioned it to his aunt who merely asked him, "What kind of drugs are you on now?" He dismissed her as not being of any help and moved on. While he searched he thought back to how a head shrink in Tacoma had deemed him suffering from psychotic hallucinations and mania. He'd made a quick visit to the man while he was homeless in Tacoma to try and get assistance. It had worked. The state had given him money—a small amount for a couple of months—but it hadn't helped. The feeling was still there. He knew that feeling would haunt him no matter what mental health therapist he counseled with. Talking about it with people only frustrated him because he knew that they didn't believe that he felt what he thought he felt. In their eyes, he would be merely another mental health patient who couldn't distinguish fantasy from reality. Another product to push through the system. A nut that had been mentally affected by prior drug use and alcohol.

He searched and found music on the internet. Maybe tunes would relax him a little during his internet search. He didn't enjoy searching for himself because he felt it a bit narcissistic. Plus, his mind was faster than his computer, which was aggravating. When a song came up he looked at the cover. The peculiar thing about it was that the face on the front of the album looked like his brother who lived three thousand miles away. Drew saw that this was a picture of his brother with makeup and funny looking hair. He was wearing what appeared to be a broken pair of glasses with a feeder tube attached to them. His brother did, in fact, use a feeder tube because he had cancer in his jaw. The picture wouldn't save and he didn't know how to capture it for proof that this was happening. So he grabbed an old cell phone and snapped shots of his computer screen. He'd captured the picture and it wasn't getting away. He sent it to his mother through messenger. She never responded. Because she hadn't responded he assumed she must know something about it or think he's crazy. By the same token, he couldn't see his mother starting a spyathon on him. Why would she want to humiliate him? She wouldn't even help him when he asked for help as an adult 20 years back. He'd truly hoped it wasn't his mother watching him.

Anything Drew did that was offensive was originally meant to offend a Washington stranger whom he felt was obsessed with him. Originally, it was supposed to scare them off or drive them out of hiding. It eventually became a language through which he could say, "UP YOURS. I FEEL YOU STARING AND YOU ARE A MANIPULATIVE PIECE OF GARBAGE!" Conforming to playing a part was highly draining. He felt he had lost another piece of himself somewhere along the way into his nine years in Washington.

He also found a backdoor through a social media account that showed him another account connected to his own. It was listed under Drew Truman. It was connected directly to his page but he couldn't get in except through several other people's pages – a "backdoor" if you will. Once he was in he found his way back into the internet where he could click onto a website that went directly into his page. He didn't understand why someone would hack his account. He only knew now that it had been done.

His social media account had been hacked. His life in his home had been watched by God only knew who. He'd lost his job and his car. Drew was definitely not enjoying good fortune. Still, you wouldn't know his pain by talking to him. Through it all, he maintained a good wholesome spirit about him. He reflected a positive attitude out from the dingy mirror called life. No matter the situation, he knew in his heart that it could always be worse. He also knew that despite it all he was glad to be alive.

By midnight he'd surfed the web so much that his eyes were hurting. He felt as though he'd been staring into a flashlight for hours. He also felt exhausted. It was all nearly too much to put together. After all, he had years and years of peculiar people and happenings to go over. So incredibly tired from the mental beating he'd taken, he laid down and stretched out for sleep. This time he didn't even dream. His body lay motionless in the fetal position for six straight hours before getting up to pee. He relieved himself before going back to bed. He switched sides and slept a few more hours before rising from his bed for coffee. Another day of questions weighed on his mind. It was another day in which to fit puzzle pieces together through his mind's eye. Coffee and the news were always first. First, take care of your head a friend once said. Looking back on his life, he tried to imagine what he could have done to make someone so interested in his private life. He stared at the news blindly while his mind drifted to another time.

CHAPTER

FAMILY AND CONFUSION

HE FOUND HIMSELF THINKING about his family. They'd gone through life in poverty so it didn't make sense that his brother would be financially capable of this trickery. Someone was trying desperately to influence Drew to believe that it was his family toying with him. He knew better. It would take a lot of money and power to do things like moving a train in front of him like clockwork. Or to dub another picture into a secure website and onto an album. Too much wasn't adding up, at least not quickly enough for Drew. He was overjoyed to now know it hadn't been his imagination running away with him. But he was frustrated at the new file of questions it brought to his already overloaded mindset.

Drew had never met his father. His mother said she left him because he was too strict. She explained that when he was little, his father fed him peas and when Drew threw them up his father force fed him his own puke. She also said that his father jerked his arm out of its socket once while snatching him from a high chair. But she also told him that she'd been raped by seven high school football players and honestly couldn't be sure that one of them wasn't his real father. The whole "real father thing" was up in the air. His mother once had the idea that Drew was somehow hung up on knowing who his father was and it seemed to anger her. Although curious, he was never hung up on any of it. It really didn't matter to Drew one way or another. He didn't suppose it would make a difference in his life if he did know his father. He'd looked his father up once before more or less chickening out on wanting to meet him. He thought perhaps his mother's account of what his father did to him was perhaps a little fabricated and never really took any of it to heart. He was certain his father would tell a different story entirely were he ever to meet him. But all this was neither here nor there because he had ruled out his unknown father as having anything to do with the game playing. Was it some sort of intervention? Was it an experiment? Was it reality TV?

Who was the question he needed answers to now. If he knew who, he could most certainly figure out why. He couldn't see someone intervening in his college-level drug experimentations that had taken place his entire life. He wasn't even close to being as badly addicted as he once was with alcohol and drugs so a drug intervention would be a little late. His grandmother had told him point blank that she didn't know what was happening. She was a born-again Christian and Baptist churchgoer. She also held a special place in Drew's heart because she had always been there for him when he needed or wanted help. From the beginning, she had always been there as his "Gramma". She was a wonderful lady who he knew without a doubt would never lie to him and therefore she was off of the list of suspects.

He only had a handful of friends in Memphis that he'd kept up with and was sure none were capable of or even had enough heart to pull a stunt like spying. There was but one man he thought capable but that man was supposed to be resting in water where his ashes were freed – his grandfather.

His grandfather was an inventive man. He'd basically invented the first computerized telephone, although the company he worked for took the credit. He also assisted with engineering the first satellite and subcontracted for the NSA. In his retirement, he repaired CAT scan machines and enjoyed travel. Drew was doing his last prison stretch when he got the news that his grandfather had died. He could hardly believe the news in his Gramma's letter. His grandfather had been in perfect health for a 72-year-old man the last time he'd seen him. It didn't make any sense considering it had begun as a hip surgery. He had to rule his grandfather out too while keeping in mind that something didn't quite seem right about it. It had a hint of something sour about it but he had to explore all other avenues before fully dismissing the idea that his grandfather would fake his own death. Drew was expected to believe his grandfather had suddenly got Alzheimer's and within a few years couldn't recognize his own family and then died of an infection.

He had pretty much ruled out everyone he knew in and around Memphis, Tennessee. It left him nowhere to look but under his nose. He'd heard of a movie that involved a man's life being watched but had never seen it. He wondered if his behavior nine years ago had been so outrageous that it warranted viewing. He couldn't imagine what he'd done upon entering the state of Washington all those years back that started someone watching. The very watcher that forced him to change character in a subtle yet barbaric attempt to force a self-righteous sneak out of the cracks.

The news had long since seemed to play in the common coincidental area of his life. Sometimes he thought deeply about things such as politics and justice. He even spoke aloud to himself in the "privacy" of his own apartment. And often he noticed the news covered stories that he may have had questions with the day before. Or they covered a story on something he'd researched on the internet earlier in the day. The news always had something ironic to say. So he thought to himself, "What if this goes that far up? What if, in fact, more people than I actually know are watching me and playing me for a fool on television or YouTube for money?" He was absolutely positive that the idea sounded completely insane but he was running out of avenues. Out loud he pretended to be talking to himself. He said, "I'm afraid of scary clowns. Why have I never told anyone?" He was shooting in the dark at an experiment. He wasn't afraid of scary clowns in the least. However, if someone were at least listening then they may later make reference to clowns. He thought it had to be worth a try.

The following morning Drew turned on his television. The very first story airing after the giant pile of commercials put an extra little thump in his heartbeat: "A scary clown was spotted in Portland, Oregon." This was only 20 minutes from Drew. The report displayed a picture of a clown about to walk into a mobile home. The news reporter tried hard to make it sound serious. Drew was overwhelmed with a new excitement that he didn't really want but had no choice but to accept. He was happy to now know that his life had been manipulated and that he could pull himself together and rest assured that it wasn't his sanity slipping but the actions of a controlling culprit – someone else that wanted to be the authority. He was confident that there was more to it than met the eye regarding his opinion of what was happening in his life. He was certain that the cameras had "gone away" at least for now. But he was also certain that someone had been listening to him whether it be God or a nosy jerk. Either way, it was divine that he would never again have to question his own sanity. Or so he thought.

In the weeks following his "private" clown statement, a rash of scary clown sightings flooded the news and every reporter seemed as serious about them as a heart attack. There were no reports of them doing anything illegal yet it became part of a growing concern across the United States. What must the Micky Ds clown think? What was the fascination with the clown life and why were people growing tense about it? He knew the whole world hadn't heard him say that he was afraid of scary clowns. Surely the entire world wasn't playing tricks on him. Were they?

He looked back on when he thought it all started and he remembered instances when odd things had occurred. He remembered one night when he was homeless in Everett that he walked up to a guy he'd met earlier that night named Sean Slicer. Slicer was an arrogant yet cool guy. He told Drew he went to college and joined the military. Drew was usually a good judge of character and could tell whether people were being honest or not. He could tell that Slicer was, in fact, well-educated and that he may well have been in the military. Slicer was cunning. He posed no threat and interested Drew but seemed to be acting out of character and trying too hard.

When he walked up, Slicer cut him off as he was pacing in the middle of the sidewalk. Slicer was very polite and seemed like an all-around good guy. He asked Drew if he wanted to come in and smoke some glass with him. Drew had already done some earlier. Twenty bucks got him through a couple of days of having nowhere to sleep. He merely marched the streets and he was fine with it until he had somewhere to sleep. Drew had once met Slicer while buying glass from a dealer.

Drew only hung out with Slicer for maybe 20 minutes. He thought it time to go when Slicer had asked him in a whisper to go outside and see if his girlfriend was sitting in a nearby blacked-out car. A first glimpse at the car out the window showed Drew the car had been parked for some time and there was no one in it. Being the gentleman he was, he checked it out for him anyway. He came back in to get his jacket and let Slicer know she wasn't out there. Slicer's voice was back to normal when Drew returned and he wasn't whispering anymore. He seemed sober and not at all like the addict he presented himself as.

When Drew left Slicer's place he noticed right away that his jacket was now dry and it smelled like it was freshly cleaned. It had been wet from the rain and it stunk from his body odors. At that point, he remembered someone going out of their way to give him the jacket at the homeless mission. It was a black woolen type hoodie but inside the hood was red. He wondered if he'd been given the hoodie to mark him so people like Slicer would spot him. Slicer was a slickster. Drew saw straight through the act but couldn't figure out his motive or intent. He would come back later and explore a little more who he was and what he was really up to.

Drew returned to hang out with Slicer for over a month. During that time, Drew saw clearly that Slicer wasn't really smoking but he had some good stories and some good hallucinogens that he slipped into Drew's beer. Drew knew it but never mentioned it. Drew sometimes entertained himself by watching other people think that he was stupid. It was fun to see them thinking they were so much smarter than him. He learned how people used this process. People didn't mind being themselves if they believed they were smarter than you. At that point, the mask came off. Drew had a cute, dumb look about him that intensified with his goofy smile and respectful mannerisms. People often saw an opportunity to take him for granted. Half the time it worked and half the time it did not. This time, Drew would be thankful for the hallucinogen. He'd started using acid when he was 12 and knew the taste. He would have taken it freely had Slicer just offered it to him. Slicer attempted to brainwash Drew once into going to rehab after he was sure the drug had kicked in. Unfortunately for Slicer, Drew was onto it and merely playing along. Drew left for rehab but he marched straight to the liquor store.

He had met Slicer through a dope dealer named Gabby. Gabby was an odd person who sometimes told Drew to meet her at the police station to sell him dope. He knew something wasn't right with her either. Drew could pinpoint some of the people involved but he couldn't pinpoint the chump who was in charge of it all.

He'd also met the girl who had presented herself as Slicer's girlfriend. Her name was Charity and she was very nice and attractive. She had once told Drew that she used and even had a pipe but he still could not be sure that she was being completely honest. "Was she pretending too?" he thought. She once allowed Drew to spend the night at her friend Katie's house. He thought it was nice. He'd slept on the floor while she slept on the couch. Katie struck him as an extremely attractive woman who was very polite and slightly talkative. Before Drew went to sleep, Charity offered Drew a small paperback book to read. It was called "High School Sweetheart" and on the cover was an animated picture of the girl he'd just met. He didn't quite know what to make of it. It seemed coincidence and irony were slapping him in the face more times than not. Today would be no different.

He thought also of a time outside of Everett, Washington in a casino with his then-boss Randall Gothis. Randall was a man who liked living the high life despite not having the means to do so. Often, his paychecks were late because Randall was "in Vegas" and hadn't signed them. Other excuses included, but were not limited to, "running out of check paper", "checks were printed from a closed account" and "Randall is very sick".

On this night in particular, Randall had caught up on his bills and was playing the big shot. He gave Drew a hundred dollar bill and told him that if he won he could pay it back. Randall showed Drew how to bet on the crap table. He told him basically to buy the chips and that he would show Drew where to put them on the table. Drew did exactly that. During every roll of the dice, he won something. He knew this by the way the rest of the people at the table were looking at him. The overhead lights seemed to put Drew in his own personal spotlight. He felt an energy that was focused purely on himself. He felt like it was coming from the people at the table and it felt strange. Within 20 minutes, and before Drew could even figure out what was going on, he had won over three thousand dollars. He and his boss left at that point. Another funny thing was that despite the fact that his boss walked, talked, and appeared to be rich, once they were in the elevator alone he changed. He desperately asked Drew to borrow three hundred dollars even though Drew had just watched him win big money. It didn't make sense unless he'd been playing a part in a sinister scene.

As Drew continuously put the pieces together, he found himself no closer to knowing what was going on than before. He thought about Tacoma for a moment and remembered seeing someone drive by him on a bicycle that he could have sworn was his Uncle Stan. He also saw a lady jog by him once that looked like his grandfather's wife, Maddy. He remembered the angry look in her eyes but at the time he thought it must be yet another coincidence. He saw look-alikes of his brothers when they were younger riding bicycles. There were look-alikes everywhere and he had to train himself to ignore them. He saw a look-a-like of his friend from Memphis too except he was made up to look Chinese. At the time he'd wondered if the drugs he'd used had eaten holes in his brain or the alcohol was killing his brain cells? He remembered quickly dismissing these thoughts before again concluding something weird was going on. He knew that although he was undereducated he was above average when it came to intelligence and trusted his brain more than this. He also realized that there were people who look like other people and more so when we move to another climate.

CHAPTER

MORE REBELLION

Many odd things happened to Drew during his first nine years in Washington. So much so that he couldn't remember it all at once. It was just part of his life that he'd learned to deal with. He'd once seen a man walk down the road opposite him with a bright colored shirt that read, "Leave or it will never stop" on the front. The back was blank. He thought perhaps it was personal and meant especially for him to read. He hadn't enjoyed feeling that he may be paranoid. So he entertained the brighter side, which was that he was not.

Drew knew without a doubt that the government and the media had long portrayed marijuana as a dangerous poison that drove people crazy once they consumed it. He knew that drugs didn't actually pose nearly as bad a threat as they said and drug problems were mainly caused by police arrests. A small percentage of users died but the millions that were affected every year were only due to arrests. People could always pull out of drug use. Pulling out of a justice system that was built of hypocrisy wasn't as easy. Had they not been arrested then perhaps they would have gotten that nice job. If they hadn't gotten arrested they might not be homeless now due to court costs, fines, fees, and penalties. He also realized that America was considered a superpower because they had so much money as a government that they were above the law. And the reason they had so much money was because they stole it from their own citizens by way of over penalizing for drug use, amongst other things. Drugs could do damage only when consumed in excess. And one couldn't tell Drew any differently because he knew this from hands-on experience. People caused problems and not drugs in the grander scheme of things.

He felt anxious to piece it together but he kept running into dead ends within his mind. If the last nine years hadn't driven him insane, then perhaps trying to piece it all together would. He thought about everything he could remember. He remembered the policeman who'd meant to arrest him in Everett for peeing in an alley and being in possession of what the officer thought was a drug pipe. The officer told Drew he was going to jail and Drew laughed at him because jail there would be the Hilton in comparison to southern and east coast jails. However, the officer's field supervisor pulled up and ordered that Drew be released for reasons unbeknownst to Drew. Again, Drew had been left with a giant question mark above his head. Why had he just been freed?

Another time during his homeless stint in Everett, Drew had tried sleeping on top of a building he'd once worked and lived in. It was more or less a storage room just under the roof. The building was at the corner of Wetmore Ave. and Everett St. His first night or two he was comfortable. He was able to relax. It may have been the second or third night there when he felt he was being watched. Immediately, he felt stressed and the urge to let the looker know that he didn't approve. No one ever showed themselves no matter what he did.

One day, while in the storage area, he heard sounds like that of an alien gerbil. It was as if some sort of creature were running abroad amongst the upper storage area. Drew was angered that the watcher wasn't just watching anymore but now playing childish games with him as well. He didn't believe in monsters or ghosts or aliens. It had to be a human monster. The only kind that existed.

He played this game over and over until it drove him batty thinking about what he must look like to "it". He tried many times over to analyze the situation but never drew any sure conclusions. No amount of drugs could take him from reality. Reality was also embedded into him. He knew his Maker and his Maker kept him sane through it all. Obviously, he was human and couldn't manage all by himself. It would have been far too much for him to handle on his own. What he'd been through, he wished on no man.

Another aspect that he had to take into consideration was that not everyone was playing games with him. When people played games with another human being the entire time they were around, one could start to believe everything was directed towards him or her when, in fact, it was not. Questioning everyone's intentions would be exhausting. He would have to learn to roll with the punches. Pretending life was normal he would try and keep himself at least moderately humble.

Still sitting in front of his television, Drew decided not to think about this anymore until maybe later in the evening. It was too consuming and draining. He had to move on and enjoy life. He couldn't stay stuck in this otherworldly way of life. It felt gross to him in so many ways.

No sooner had he decided to stop thinking about it, the thought forced its way back in. Drew wondered briefly if the military or some experimental entity were maybe experimenting with him by manipulating his life in so many ways. He also wondered if perhaps someone were trying to set him up or slander him. One name came to mind when he thought of the word slander. Alice.

He'd met her at the collection's agency when he was in Everett. He'd also lived with before he left. She was a near look alike to the actress Jennifer Aniston but there was, of course, something strange about her as well. She didn't look like a man but something about her seemed to throw him off. He never put his finger on it but he'd kept his distance from her. When he'd met her, she'd told him a story about her runaway cat named Slander as if she were setting a foundation in the back of his mind to build on. She explained slowly how cats needed to be pushed or driven back into their territory. That once they were lost in another area, they stayed in it. They often ventured too far from their territory and got stuck in another. She emphasized this to Drew in a manner that made him question if there was an underlying agenda. She seemed dead set on getting Drew to understand how much "Slander" meant to her and how badly she wanted the feline back. It was as if she were trying to hypnotize him into thinking he should go home like Slicer did about the rehab? Go back to the south where he came from? What was she really saying? Drew never for once believed she had lost a cat named Slander. He felt she'd been instructed by someone else and was breezing through a sort of script. Either way, it didn't matter. Drew dismissed it just as he dismissed everyone and everything else that seemed strange to him. He dismissed it, as always, to a file in his head in no particular order.

In his bathroom, he washed his face. He shaved and brushed his teeth. At nearly 45-years-old, Drew still had all of his teeth and had never had any issues with them. He'd been warned years back that drug use would rot out his teeth. He chuckled to himself because he also now knew that users only lost their teeth because they didn't brush their teeth, didn't eat right, and worried all the time about getting caught. Of course worrying, not eating, and not brushing would result in tooth loss. Especially so if there was added anxiety about the police catching you and either killing you, beating you, or throwing you in a cage with wild animals. Yeah. It was true. Drugs did ruin lives but not by using them alone. Drew felt he'd outgrown drugs for the most part. The thought of the taste made him want to puke. It was nasty and although he wasn't a common user anymore he didn't knock others for trying to outgrow it too. To each his, her, or its own.

Halloween was coming and he hoped it would go by smoothly without drama and chaos. Once he enjoyed a Halloween party at his grandmother's house out near the woods. His mother, aunt, and uncles worked hard to make a sort of outside haunted house. They made monsters from papier-mâché. They engineered scary pop-ups and made their own spooky music. It would have been scary to Drew looking back if he'd not already been used to dealing with fear. He felt a sense of sorrow in knowing he feared nothing and no one. This wasn't how he thought life would be. He clung to the near-excitement of the Halloween party because he knew in his heart he may never feel it again.

When he was done brushing his teeth and cleaning up, he left for a walk. On his walk he thought more about it. He remembered noticing things change shortly after arriving in Washington. Yet when he looked back on his life he remembered the irony of events in his life when he'd lived in Memphis. He remembered that in Memphis he'd tried to escape life by using an overabundance of cocaine. For a couple of years, he'd been on cocaine. When he left the south, he decided cocaine was behind him. He'd rather be sober than on that garbage any day of the week. What made him look back was remembering that peculiar things happened to him in Memphis as well. Things such as finding a one hundred dollar bill on the sidewalk while on his way to buy 10 dollars in drugs. Things like being pulled over by the police for driving without a license and not getting a ticket or going to jail despite the fact that the officer saw drugs on the floor. Perhaps it started there but he wasn't sure. He was sure that he wasn't out of touch with reality. He questioned whether a paranoid schizophrenic would question their own reality. He questioned a lot but came up with nothing useful. He dabbled in cocaine a few more times in Washington before closing the drug off completely. In recent years, fact had become stranger than fiction and he didn't need drugs to help make life strange. It was strange enough already.

He'd walked for a couple of miles before getting tired. He sat down for a rest and took a look around at the nearby park. It appeared as though it might turn out to be a beautiful day despite the invisible problems in his life. There was sunshine with highs in the mid-sixties.

He stared into the trees remembering another time in Everett when he'd been at a park with a bench in front of a lake. He'd sat there discretely crying to himself about things unsaid. He was sad for a moment or perhaps always had been and didn't recognize it. He released his sadness through his eyes as that is where it had come in. No one had been around. He felt comfortable crying there. He remembered buying drugs from Gabby and some other people later that same day that were also there. They were finishing a conversation about a guy at the park who was crying like a sissy. He remembered thinking to himself, "Are they talking about me? Is this just more coincidence? Again?" But he knew he'd been alone that day on that bench at the waterfront park. He remembered also having thought to himself, "There's no way they could be referring to me because I will whip all their asses right now if they think I'm a joke." He'd kept calm and ignored the conversation's end. It wasn't his business and best if he kept it that way.

There wasn't much going on at the park in Vancouver. The birds sang and the trees danced in the wind. He saw a homeless woman with a huge cart full of all of her belongings. She looked like she'd been living this way for many years. She was literally screaming at invisible people who didn't seem to want to leave her alone. He could totally relate. She continuously said out loud while looking down at the sidewalk, "Stop it, you guys! Cut it out!" He felt sorry for her. He thought that maybe someone used to play games with her until she lost her mind. Maybe even the same games that were being played with him.

When he left the park, the sun was shining when suddenly it began to rain sleet very heavily. The sleet lasted for at least 10 minutes straight. This reminded him of another aspect of his life that he didn't want to entangle with the rest when sometimes divine intervention played a role in his life, which he could mostly separate from human manipulation. Although, sometimes he wasn't entirely sure. Sometimes he wondered if someone wasn't setting up situations in his life to intentionally manipulate him into thinking it was divine. He had long since known how evil people could be. People were capable of evil even with the best of intentions in mind. He couldn't trust anyone as a friend right now because it was too risky. His gut had been right most of his life and now he was learning to go with it. Trusting people whom he'd known better than to trust had often cost him money and jail time amongst other things.

When the sleet stopped, the sun was shining very brightly and the streets, sidewalks, and park grounds were covered in white. It was absolutely beautiful. He was thankful for it as he remembered how horribly the sun had treated him in Memphis near the Mississippi River. One could shower, get dressed, and leave an air-conditioned apartment dry but bend over to tie a shoe and sweat poured from one's head. That kind of weather made it hard for Drew to think. It also invited ice cold beer and drove him to drink.

Drinking had both saved his life and cost him. He knew alcohol was terrible. Yet every now and then he still reached for it. In his older years, he had all but shaken it completely. Drugs used to follow alcohol but no longer did. It occurred to him that he'd matured enough that he didn't need drugs after alcohol any longer. If he did have the occasional drink, he stayed in the privacy of his own home away from people as much as possible. He used to love getting drunk in the snow near a campfire with people he once thought friends. However, they were more like fair-weather friends. They'd always been his friend if he had alcohol and drugs to offer. Outside of that, most of the kids he'd grown up with hadn't really remained friends. They ignored him on Facebook. He didn't entirely understand but he wasn't gonna force anyone to communicate. He figured that if they didn't care then why should he?

His Facebook account had friends and family who didn't agree with his views so they ex-communicated him in a sense. No one liked his posts or seemed to agree with his views on crooked, violent police departments, and his controversial outlook on government. He never meant to upset anyone with his posts. He merely wanted everyone else to see another side of things that it seemed they refused to look at. There was always another side to it. Sometimes the whole picture changed when viewed from another point. Sometimes another point of view made better sense than the most obvious scenario.

Later at home, Drew began Googling clues he could think of and came across various websites as a result. Many he did not click on because his computer was slow and so was his patience. And besides, he really didn't know what to look for. He left his computer to get himself a glass of tea. When he came back, all the names and small websites he'd seen before would no longer come up. He concluded that someone had hacked into his computer but he didn't really care. He'd done nothing illegal and he had no financial information to hack into. He was at the point of caring less who was watching. He was done looking for them. But only for now. For now, he wanted to forget. He smoked some pot, ate some cookies, and fell asleep.

When he woke up, he lay in bed deep in thought. He remembered a time when he'd both smoked and snorted dope to look for a reaction from the watcher. The only reaction he'd gotten was a neighbor banging on the wall, which he chalked up to them hanging a picture or something. The funny thing was the knocking came precisely as Drew leaned down to snort. Often times, strange things did occur when he was high. At some point, he thought someone was trying desperately to make him think he was so incredibly high that he was hearing and seeing things. He counted it out because it happened even in sobriety.

The riddles and puzzles in his head were interesting yet annoying at times. He tried not to think about it but somehow something somewhere was always there to remind him. Coincidence never wandered far away. Neither did irony.

"What is a normal life?" he thought to himself. What would it be like if he didn't have to experience a world of annoying coincidence? He'd have a life of privacy. A life of respect. He had never known what life in that realm felt like. It was alien to him. The only life he'd ever known was a life of feeling less than. He felt less than while being monitored in jail cages and he was feeling less than in freedom. He could only be thankful that he was alive and not in a state of torture. He'd adapted to being watched most of his life but never enjoyed it. He despised people who watched and pointed fingers. Stone throwers and hypocrites were many. He thought that if perhaps people lent a hand instead of pointing that somehow it would be a greater place to live. "It gets greater later," he thought.

That evening, Drew went shopping for groceries. He could barely get around the cart traffic. People seemed to wander aimlessly to whatever packages attracted them at that moment. They showed no regard for anyone else around them and seemed to care less who's way they were in. "Me! Me! Me!" he thought. Greed ruled over common courtesy here in the northwest. Or at least it was more noticeable here than where he'd come from. People seemed to have no common courtesy or sense of being hospitable. He thought perhaps they could all use a good old fashioned Tennessee ass-whippin'. Violence, from his perspective, made people in violent areas more respectful of fear and retaliation. Rude people often ended up bloody and beaten. While he didn't entirely agree with the violent ways of Memphians, their ways were quite effective. He'd once seen a man knocked out at a grocery store because he'd been rude to a little old lady. A man shoved the elderly woman's cart out of his way as he barged down aisle 12 of the neighborhood grocer. A homeless man saw this, ran up the aisle full speed, and cold-cocked the rude guy. He hit the jerk so hard that he buckled up and fell on a pickle jar display. He didn't regain consciousness until the E.M.T.s arrived.

His idea was to get in and out of the store as fast as possible without upsetting himself over the solipsistic jerk in front of him who didn't think twice about blocking an entire aisle with both cart and body. It felt like a percentage of the shoppers were being intentionally bothersome but he humbly brushed their rudeness off as a part of their lives that they had no control of. Sickly, hateful people. Poor wretched people who took joy in aggravating other people. The same kind of people he thought might go as low as spitting in someone else's food. They were inhabitants of the Earth there to exercise and test the patience of real people. They were people who lacked soul like orange cones in the street meant to be driven around.

Making it out of the grocery store was a relief. The unfortunate agitators were now nowhere in sight. Bless their poor hearts. They only get by. They never get away. Being a rude and selfish person would surely get anyone just what they deserved.

At home, he knew his days were numbered before the rent and utilities were due. So he took full advantage of the comfort at hand. He sat and thought to himself, "There must be a better way." Working for people who made life harder wasn't living. It was just short of existing. He couldn't go back to playing the games because to him it no longer was a game. It had become a problem, for lack of a better word. A problem that left him leery of people. Being leery of people created more problems such as in gaining employment. Employment he knew, however, didn't always mean working with others. Perhaps he could slide into a job somewhere working unsupervised and by himself. It was definitely something he had to think about. Homeless or not he would always need a way to pay for his livelihood. It certainly wouldn't pay for itself. His grandmother had always told him that where she was from, "If you don't work you don't eat." He thought it a little humorous within his delinquent state of mind that his Baptist grandmother would say this considering she worshipped Jesus Christ who fed the multitudes while not ordering a single soul to work for it. He imagined to himself for a moment hearing Jesus Christ tell the multitude that he would not feed them bread and fish unless they worked for it. Drew thought it humorous. He truly loved his gramma.

Resting again, his mind wandered. He daydreamed of the hard times past and how they were inevitable. He took comfort in remembering times others thought hard. He recalled a time as a young boy in Texas when he was so hungry he could eat a horse. He, his mother, stepfather, and two brothers were all inside a makeshift tent of sorts with a package of unopened raw hot dogs in the middle as if the tent floor were a dinner table. A large tree branch held up the blanket roof. It seemed to him as a child to hold very well right up until the rain came and the drops popped on his head. A Texas State Trooper came to the tent and told his parents that they must leave because there was a flash flood warning. Reluctantly they did leave. What comforted him about the whole situation was that he knew that a hot dog was coming soon and he could not wait.

Drew grew fond of food and cooking as the years went by. Cooking became one of his favorite past times. It was not something he could easily do while homeless. Raw hot dogs he could always do. They could be eaten in virtually any situation. All you had to do was bust a pack open, slide one out, and get to chompin'. You could even use a bun and mustard. It was all good. He loved hot dogs. They were reliable. And tasty.

He drifted from hot dog thoughts to thoughts he'd sometimes rather not remember. Thoughts like being beaten to a purple welt with a leather belt that would maim an elephant by a man who'd foster fathered him when he was six years old.

Thoughts like falling from the roof of a meter shed and onto a gas meter balls first when he was seven. Thoughts of pain once inflicted. Pain so horrible that, blended with the taste of fear, felt to a child like a ride to hell. Remembering pain and fear inflicted upon him throughout his younger years helped him to cope with current pain. Or so he thought. At least it kept him prepared to endure it should the need arise. Pain and death were inevitable parts of life that took time to get used to. He dealt with it on his own terms.

Turning on the news he saw police were now shooting and killing people who videotaped them. America seemed to be changing but not necessarily for the better. Terrorists in other counties were lining up people and cutting their throats as a common way of life. The presidential election seemed to be a battle of tooth and nail between Donald Trump and Hillary Clinton. Most people voted Republican simply because the Democrats were snide and sneaky. Or so it seemed to Drew.

CHAPTER

DREW FEELING SORRY FOR HIMSELF AND MORE CRAZY

DREW WONDERED IF IT were right for him to protest subjects like police brutality and poverty and overall government corruption. His family had often let him know that they didn't want to hear about his crazy life or his near extreme views. His mother once asked him on Facebook if he was capable of extremism. She showed what seemed to be a genuine concern that Drew could perhaps conform to killing people to make a point. Drew, in turn, became concerned for his mother. He couldn't figure out why posting news clips of recent murders committed by the police seemed extreme to her. After all, he merely re-posted what was already right in front of him on Facebook. He clicked share and that was it. His aunt ridiculed him in the same way. She talked to him like a stepchild about posting videos of police and police departments murdering people. Drew was in his forties by now and had no tolerance for ignorance. It emotionally confused Drew that his own family, whom he thought stood for something, were telling him not to. He'd seen his mother protest in her younger years. He couldn't figure where she got off. Everyone else pretty much ignored his posts. It was as if none of what was horrible with America mattered to any of them. He appeared to have nothing in common with anyone he thought he knew, according to his Facebook communications. One of his brothers felt the need to prove he was smarter than Drew all of the time and the other wasn't entirely honest. Drew felt like he was in a world all by himself. He had to get in where he fit in. He just didn't know the right people.

He opened an internet sales account and began selling items he bought from local thrift stores in order to bring in currency. Twenty dollars of merchandise sometimes netted him two hundred dollars in profit. It was a nice gig up until someone slandered him and accused him of selling bogus merchandise. He had a good feeling that someone had called and intentionally targeted him for whatever reason. He had one complaint whereas other sellers had accumulated several complaints. It only made sense that someone interfered again with his livelihood.

He'd grown simply sick and tired of having his life manipulated by an unknown origin of nothing. He remembered back to a time in Memphis, Tennessee when he signed a satanic contract and thought nothing of it…

Some 20 years ago, Drew was hopping and skipping along on his way to work for a pizza store. He had no car or bills. He just couchsurfed from girlfriend to girlfriend. Listening to his headphones, his shoes bounced along to the aggressive music. He wasn't a Satanist and didn't really believe in the devil. An acquaintance had once played the music and he really liked the heavy beat. Because he was always walking he needed music to march to and so he bought the cassette tape of a satanic album.

As he marched to work, cutting through a gigantic church on Union Avenue in Memphis, Tennessee, he noticed an old van, possibly a narrow Volkswagen van, almost bird-dogging him in the parking lot. As he got to the end of the parking lot, the van cut him off and a pretty girl poked her head out the window. She looked about Drew's age, had her hair tied back and a nose ring. When she poked her head out of the window she asked Drew, "We were just wondering if you'd like to join our church?" Without hesitation and in a sense of weird desperation Drew said "yes" before he even knew what the name of the church was. Likewise, the girl slid open the side door immediately. Once in the van, she explained that their church was the church of satanic something or another. He didn't particularly care what it was called. His only concern was talking with this attractive woman he'd just met. He was not afraid.

Being the ladies' man he thought he was, he was more than happy to oblige to get a smile out of a beautiful woman. He explained that although he was on his way to work he wasn't in an extreme hurry. They drove to what they called the Crossroads at Avalon and some street running along a Piggy Wiggly grocery store in midtown. When they pulled into the parking lot they were facing a dry, open sunned, four-way stop. There in front of them was an old antique store called Rare Finds. The place appeared to be out of business and used for storage. The girl pointed at the window, which boasted an old clay or cement statue of a giant goat head. From that point, she explained how Drew would be selling his soul for power under Satan.

"Okay this is how it works," she explained. "You will pick a time limit for the contract which ranges from six years to the rest of your life. You will sign the first contract with a pen and the second with your blood." Then she told Drew that he needed to repeat after her some mumbo jumbo about worshipping Satan through music and otherwise. Afterward she told him to repeat "natas si retsam" three times which spelt "Satan is master" backward. When it came time to sign the contract with a pen, she realized they didn't have one and asked Drew for one. He did not. The girl almost seemed to panic until she spotted a pen in the parking lot. She got out to pick it up and got back in. "See?" she said, "he helps you out when you need help," as if to say the pen in the parking lot was a blessing from the devil.

She finished up by informing Drew that she worked at a topless bar and that was where members of the "church" met up. She handed Drew a get in free card good for five years along with contracts of his own to recruit others. According to her, each contract that Drew had someone sign would bring Drew more satanic power. Drew signed the contract first in ink and afterward with his own blood by pricking his finger with a needle. When the signing was all said and done, she dropped Drew off at work. Drew never saw her again as he never visited the club.

That same day, Drew returned home to his girlfriend whom he did not tell about his earlier experience. Days went by before his girlfriend found the contracts and threw them out. That same day they had an argument about where he got them before making up and moving on to their usual drunken partying. As she sat "Indian style" on the large bathroom sink applying makeup, she shouted to Drew in the other room, "Man this sucks that we only have 10 dollars." Drew, listening to his boom box while downing a 40-ounce beer shouted back over the music in arrogance, "Don't worry about it. Satan will take care of us." His girlfriend shouted, "What?" And he shouted, "Never mind," back to her. He somehow felt an extreme sense of guilt after making the comment. He washed it down with more beer. He couldn't believe he'd said it but he had.

Later that evening, he and his girlfriend set out to a bar and grill. At the bar, they could afford a pitcher of draft beer, a game of pool, and a couple of jukebox songs. This would have to do as they had no more money. A couple of blocks down the road, Drew felt the strangest feeling come over him. Like a dark cloud of quiet, Drew could have heard a pin drop on the sidewalk had one done so. The wind completely stopped and not a car or soul was in sight. This felt very awkward as it had just been a somewhat breezy Friday night in downtown Memphis and they'd been near a strip of bars. Everything seemed still as if time had actually stopped as they walked up the sidewalk towards the bar. Up ahead of them was what was best described as a small tornado of paper debris. This set off alarms within his head that screamed that something abnormal was occurring. There was absolutely no wind blowing, yet up ahead debris was spiraling. He looked at his girlfriend who did not seem to notice anything out of the ordinary. As they got closer to the whirlwind, they both realized that the debris wasn't debris at all. It was money: three hundred dollars in twenties. They both hurried to scoop it up before it could get away and before the night ahead could get away. He wasn't entirely sure why or even when he'd blacked out but when he came to he was at a topless bar sunk down into a soft recliner. Immediately, he remembered finding the money and reached for his pockets. He found 30 dollars and three separate 20-dollar pony packs of cocaine. He darted to the bathroom to sniff the healing powder that would inevitably take him out of his tiresome alcoholic slumber.

He had, in fact, experienced an odd multitude of fortune with women as well as money for a time thereafter. Women began to hit on him left and right. He met friends that liked him so much that they gave him money without him even asking for it. He saw things that made him wonder if all of this sinful fortune was a result of signing the contract. He once sat behind a building in the middle of the night asking the devil to show himself if he were actually real. He said out loud but not yelling, "If you're real, Satan, then send a blonde and a brunette around the corner." As sure as he spoke, two women came around the corner of the building. One was a blonde and one a brunette. They passed him by with a light giggle. Something was happening but he didn't understand it. He could hardly believe his eyes. He could hardly believe any of what had occurred in his life since the signing.

When Drew finally realized that the devil did indeed exist, he couldn't help but realize that God existed. He knew God who made Satan was the Almighty and that there could be only one true God. So, then, what business would he have in worshipping the weaker of the two? It stood to reason with Drew that evil was not of him nor was it how he planned to live his life. Drew was completely incapable of being evil on his own. He felt like somehow he was racking up a bill with Satan. He wanted nothing else to do with the thought of a satanic contract.

You could say Drew found God while visiting Satan. Although Drew could never be said to have lived like a saint. He would always know his Maker. Drew would never forget how Satan picked him up on high and then dropped him on his head. It seemed God took an approach rarely seen to change the beliefs of a young man with a huge heart. God afforded a young man who never had guidance, a path to transparency through Satan himself while keeping him under His protection. God used Satan as an example so that Drew could see his own reality. Drew began to understand this through the years leading up to his current life in Vancouver, Washington. He currently entertained the thought that maybe the people of the Satanic church were stalking him and playing games as a sort of penalty for not attending their church and moving to Washington.

Whatever the motive and whoever the culprit was offered far too many possibilities to narrow it down to one yet. On the other hand, he preferred to move on with his life. He refused ever to hold onto anger. He preferred to hang on to hope and forgiveness. Anger was a fire best extinguished upon ignition. If he let it build it could cause issues. Issues he'd had enough of.

Enjoying yet another beautiful day in Vancouver, Washington, Drew made his court appearance on the DUI that had totaled his car. Merlinda, his attorney, advised him that the prosecution was offering him two days in jail and a suspended license for 90 days, not to mention umpteen dollars in fines and court costs. His attorney advised him that the prosecution were threatening to charge him with reckless endangerment as well if he didn't agree to sign the plea bargain right now. As sick and tired as Drew was of the justice system, he felt it in his best interest to bow down and kneel before the system once again. So he took the backstabbing once again from a so-called "attorney".

Despite it all, Drew was still bored with his life. He was always expectant of something interesting happening because, in fact, it usually had. He thought perhaps if he could maybe surprise life for once instead of life surprising him, then things might get better. He imagined holding a crack dealer hostage and forcing him to smoke crack at gunpoint. That might surprise life a little. Or maybe suing the show "Cops" for attempting to influence the American people that it was okay to be harassed once you'd submitted to a consensual acquaintance initiated by police officers. Or maybe he could win a million-dollar lottery ticket and use it to change the world. Drew wasn't sure what to do with his life next. By now, Donald J. Trump had just won the presidency and people everywhere across the nation were protesting his victory. Hillary Clinton's followers were crying on TV and assuming America was doomed. Drew could join the protest but to his knowledge protesting had never solved anything. Especially the kind of protesting involving holding up a sign and chanting. This Drew saw as a complete waste of time and money. Wile E. Coyote never got anywhere with a sign but smashed. War was the only way to change things once the government had gotten this bad. It was inevitable but he didn't think the American people had had enough yet. As long as they were holding signs instead of their government accountable, justice would not be possible. Chanting a complaint and holding a sign was a lost cause. Either start a nationwide petition and put cool paper on their bottoms or start a revolution. No guts no glory.

People across the US protested by the thousands. Five thousand people protested the election somewhere in California and more in other cities elsewhere protesting black lives matter. People protested the building of pipelines across Indian reservations and burial grounds. Others protested about immigration policies. People even protested the protesters. The country was slowly growing more and more chaotic and losing more and more control of their freedoms it seemed.

People were uptight and worried about anything and everything in general. One could only imagine how other less fortunate countries saw the good ole U.S. of A. From what he could see in the media, other countries including the UN saw America as a giant bowl of fat, greedy, knit-picking homosexuals. Attack was eventually going to be inevitable. The UN had just condemned the United States' policing policies against its own people. Police in Canada had killed a near total of two hundred of their own citizens over a course of 150 years, whereas police in the United States had killed nearly four hundred citizens in a matter of only 115 days – an outrage in comparison. Drew was beginning to think that maybe the citizens should police themselves. That would cut government liability to zero. It would also make nearly everyone rich. Without the judicial system sucking the people dry for every mistake they made, money for the people would be abundant and crime would slow to a crawl. Drew didn't want to feel superior in his thinking so he often dismissed most of his thoughts on politics as per his own entertainment. He didn't have the credentials he thought he needed to possess in order to introduce his somewhat radical ideas to the general public. And besides that, he knew the American people were far too divided to listen to the political ideas of a virtually uneducated, unemployed Memphian from the backwoods state of Tennessee who had a criminal record. No one on his Facebook account really seemed to care about politics. He was determined to find a way to spruce up life. He hadn't found it yet but he was sure he would. Wondering who might be watching him had grown tiresome. So had politics.

Bored and a little upset about it, Drew dropped to the floor and began a rigorous push-up workout. He did Diamond style Marine pushups by sets of 30 then 25 then 20. He did pushups until he couldn't do anymore. He could feel how swollen his muscles were and he liked it. It felt great. Like an accomplishment, he felt high from it. Knowing that he would see the results almost instantly motivated him. As a juvenile delinquent, he had learned fast in life that muscles mattered. When he was 11 he had an old rusty bench in his backyard along with a bar but he had no weights. So he began by bench pressing two old tires by looping them on both sides of the bar. It was a start. By the time he was done going to prison, his size had doubled. His chest, neck, and arms showed the most progress. He'd gone from a beanpole to a giant. Yet he never really knew how big other people actually saw him. Until recently he never thought he was a big guy. He always felt a physical equality around other people and never a superiority complex. But being aggravated by people seemed to have driven that innocence away from him. At 40, he'd begun to realize that he looked very intimidating to other people. His therapist informed him that smoking too much pot could make a man look psychotic. She never said he himself looked psychotic but in conversation about marijuana she brought it up. "Beauty is in the eyes of the beholder," he remembered thinking.

After his workout, he showered before laying down to relax. He turned on a talk radio show where people shared stories about strange things like encounters with angels and Grim Reapers standing on the side of highways. He found the stories interesting only when they sounded like they themselves believed what they were saying. Their excitement excited him. He felt goosebumps form up and down his arms as he listened to a story about an aircraft that a group of people had seen deliberately flying into the ocean as if to enter an underground world. They claimed to have seen this occur on more than one occasion but in the same area. Drew considered the possibilities and came to the conclusion that either the story was bogus or the government was, as usual, hiding things from its citizens. Aliens were completely out of the question as far as Drew was concerned. He knew the devil existed. In turn, he knew God was real. And if God was real then so was His word. And Drew was almost certain that he'd read in the Bible that God created Adam and Eve, not Starman and Steve.

As he started falling asleep, he remembered frolicking with his little brothers a time long ago in the backseat of a car. They had been picking on one another and adventuring over the fact that their stepfather told them to keep their heads down or they would go to jail if they were seen. Their stepfather had to make a late night stop by the topless bar and had no sitter as their mother was working. All three were under the age of eight at the time and enjoyed playing hide-from-the-bad-guy games. They rarely got to play at night but on this night they did. He loved his younger brothers and he missed them. But no way was he moving back to Memphis empty-handed. He wanted to accomplish something. Anything..

He eventually fell asleep. When he woke up he felt a feeling best described as a question yet he didn't know what the question was. Maybe he'd had a dream about something traumatic and was in a state of semi-shock? It was a feeling of loss. He felt like a dog might feel if its head were turned sideways in question but without being so excited about it. It bothered him because he somehow felt it important to remember but couldn't for the life of him. It was a little exhausting so he tried his very best to forget about it. It had happened before but not often.

Trying to get his head together he made himself some coffee. Drew wasn't a martyr by any means. He'd never once felt sorry for himself. He'd never once blamed his past for who he was or what he'd done. On more than one occasion Drew had been told matter of factly by other people how difficult a life he'd had and that he wasn't entirely to blame for being the irresponsible person he'd always been. He never accepted within himself that anyone anywhere was to blame for anything in his life. He was fully aware of the fact that he made his own choices in life and that ultimately no one was in charge of fate. It was all part of a larger plan. Then he remembered.

In his dream, he was in a bed, which lay in a row with many other beds. It was a fictional juvenile facility that he'd never been to. All the boys in the bed corridor were lying in bed, flat on their backs with a piano wire wrapped around their two big toes to join them. In his dream, he must've fallen asleep because when he woke up again it was because an authority figure within the confines had slammed two cymbals together loud enough to make Drew jump and cut his two big toes off. Then, of course, he woke up.

This dream was not a reality that he ever experienced but rather a story told to him as a child by another stepfather. In fact, it was the same stepfather who'd once asked Drew if he knew what it was to hate somebody. When Drew agreed, looking to be accepted, his stepfather told him simply, "Well, I hate you, Drew. I can't stand you."

Drew couldn't forget the jerk. And although he never hated his stepfather back, he did wonder, looking back, how a man could be so mean to a child. Drew had definitely portrayed the problem child. Playing with fire and stealing were nothing to be proud of. His stepfather made sure to humiliate him every chance he got. Countless times in his early teens Drew was forced to "sit on the couch and don't move" while the same stepfather that forced him to smoke pot when he was nine smoked pot in front of him and played Nintendo. If Drew did something really bad he got spanked butt naked bent over the bed by the monster. He was often whipped so hard that he had two-inch-wide leather belt welts up and down his legs and buttocks. It sickened Drew even more as the monster pretended to have compassion by analyzing his welts and asking him if he was okay. Later in his teens, Drew caught the man running through the house to hide the fact that he was dressed like a woman. He was clad in high heels, a long white, large wedding dress, and a big white fruit hat to boot. He hid in his bedroom for a portion of the day. Drew actually felt bad for the man. Here was the man who called black guys the "N" word to their faces and the tough guy who ran a hot workshop of black male employees, wearing a dress. The mean stepfather with a twist of lime and sugar. Drew had always known something different was going on but could never put his finger on it.

Drew had known since he was a little boy about the "weird" magazines under his stepfather's bathroom sink. That never stopped Drew from opening the cabinet door because most of his magazines were straight pornography of men and women. He'd learned to ignore the rest as none of it seemed natural and it partially scared Drew. He'd also seen the rubbery, realistic looking penis that appeared to be dirty with a flaky brown residue. As a younger kid, he didn't entirely know what to make of it. It was not only disturbing to him but confusing as well.

He'd once questioned his mother along with his brothers about the things their stepfather possessed. She left him unsatisfied with an answer he knew she didn't even believe. "He has a fascination with silk, you guys." She basically shunned them as one would expect any mother to do in just such a situation. Drew was young but he hadn't bought the answer. She couldn't explain and it and make it alright. One day, Drew had finally gotten even with his stepfather. He and his two brothers told everyone his stepfather knew about the dress, the dildo, and the whole nine yards. If that humiliation didn't make them even, Drew didn't care. He wasn't out to get even in the first place. He just couldn't believe that the tough guy with the other side had the gall to talk to the employees he supervised in such a blatantly disrespectful manner. Besides, Drew would never have gotten to know any of these people as friends had the stepfather not forced Drew to spend the day at his work. Choose your battles wisely.

Drew's life wasn't about his stepdad. Drew's life was about Drew. He truly believed that someday he would serve a purpose in this world. Blaming his past for his current life wouldn't make any sense when he'd always felt optimistic about life. He always felt that it would get better. To Drew, there was nothing to blame anyone or anything for. Life was fine. Rich or poor it would always be there and why not always make the best of it, at least as far as you could. His mother had always told him not to blame his past and he could never figure out what she was talking about. Then, one day as an adult, he thought she must have blamed her own past for something that was currently going on in her own life. Drew laughed at the idea of blaming anyone for anything at this point in his life. He'd always taken his own charges and sometimes for other people too. He would always love his mom, albeit she looked angrily at him every time he saw her. She was a very intelligent woman yet had been codependent on abusive men for a time in her life. In his teens, Drew spent his life running. There was a sense of relief in being out on his own. He would still miss his mother and his brothers. He loved all of his family including his stepfather who cut out the face of his real father in the only picture Drew had of him. Despite the fact that he told a young Drew that he hated him, despite the fact that he forced Drew to smoke pot as a child causing him to cry, and despite it all, Drew couldn't help but see that the man had fed and clothed and housed him for a number of years. In essence, he had protected the young Drew. His stepfather didn't know it but Drew had long since forgiven him for anything and everything. Now in his later years, Drew held nothing but respect for his stepfather. They say time makes the heart grow fonder. Drew hadn't seen nor heard from his stepfather in well over 20 years. He hoped someday they could patch things up.

Drew thought about his uncle. He remembered way back when he was a boy that his uncle showed him a magic trick over a bowl of water. It had been a trick to splash the whole bowl of water into Drew's face as a joke or horseplay. Drew remembered laughing but his brother balled like a little baby. They had a fun uncle. Their uncle took them out to the woods and played on the vines and in the valleys. They enjoyed playing in the mud and leaves. They threw dirt clods at one another until one of Drew's brothers' feelings got hurt again. His brothers were younger than Drew by one and two years respectively. His uncle was the closest thing they had to a father. Drew appreciated the wholesome times in his life such as drinking whiskey around a campfire with friends or playing with his uncle and brothers. Those memories would never fade. His life now was minus the headache of losing friends to disagreements or money issues. Being a loner had its perks. He nearly hated not being able to help a friend in need. To add to it, sometimes he didn't know who his true friends were until after he gave them help. Fake friends in fake need often came and went. That happened up into Drew's thirties until he finally picked up a personal Ph.D. on profiling good people and jerks. With no friends, he didn't have that problem anyway. He'd learned enough by now to keep his distance from most people as much as possible. In his experiences, other people always seemed to have some sort of underlying agenda. He always ended up being the friend that helped. No one had even considered helping him during the few times he'd felt distressed. It seemed the whole friend thing wasn't getting Drew anywhere but being used by fair-weather friends.

Drew had slowly become a loner. Not because he didn't like people but because he couldn't trust them. As much as he would like to trust again, he couldn't help but remember where trust had got him most of his life. It had got him hurt. He had finally touched the burner one too many times and he was tired of being burnt. Logic found its way into his life and it wasn't going away. The part of his heart that wanted to help others was there and it was very strong underneath a mental "ball and chain". Perhaps one day he could release it and begin to trust once more. For now, there was no place for it. Drew's trust had been betrayed since childhood and up into his 40s.

Days went by and oddly nothing strange or ironic happened. If it had, Drew tried hard not to notice. He wanted change. He felt that he was maybe missing out on something more in life. And that part of himself was fading because of it. He was beginning to realize it wasn't healthy to be antisocial and he missed having people pretending to be friends until they got what they wanted. He missed taking a chance on finding real friends and having no place for it hurt. Aside from the fake factor, he had to deal with those friends who actually had potential but insisted on disapproving of Drew's personal actions like smoking pot and cigarettes. When trustworthy friends started trying to manipulate his life by telling him what he should and shouldn't do, he strayed away from them. Drew's idea of a friend was someone who liked him for who he was and showed true concern in conversations by expressing their own opinions without prejudice towards his. Someone who didn't constantly need a favor right after becoming friends. Someone who wouldn't backstab for personal gain and could keep a secret. He was loyal and always would be to those kinds of people but they were few and far between.

THE RENT AND OTHER
CRAZY CONCERN

COUNTING THE DAYS DOWN before the rent was due, Drew enjoyed the peace of his apartment whether being watched or listened to anymore or not. He had paid for privacy and he was going to have it whether he had to pretend or not. Clearing his mind he rolled himself a joint. He was thankful that he had one. Anxiety was getting to him lately no matter how positive he was. Pot numbed his anxiety just enough for him to maintain his anger at times. His anger was produced and fueled mainly by watching news of atrocious people, including the government, who took advantage of the smaller people. If he didn't watch the news his life might have been different. Closing that door could very well open another positive door. But by the same token, being informed could prove to be lifesaving in the event of say a predetermined earthquake or the coming of a deadly storm or world war. The way it was going anything might happen at any time in the USA. People were now even protesting the homeless being homeless. If all of the protestors across the US united, then one might need to hear about it before that great riot began. Riots, terrorism, and politics dominated world news. Syrians were being attacked by ISIS and seeking asylum in America and Europe. The population was growing by the day and rent prices were going up. More and more people were becoming homeless every day. Things weren't getting better. They were getting worse. Camping outside was nearly illegal. A police state in the making on one hand and a jar full of hope in the other.

Protesters protested the homeless by explaining that they had too many aggressive conflicts and confrontations amongst each other on the sidewalks where their tents were set up. The people who owned homes in the area wanted the homeless tent bandits out. They expressed fear and disgust. What they never took into consideration was the fact that some of these homeless people living in a tent on their block once also had homes until their greedy, bloodsucking landlords raised their rent by 35 percent. When they couldn't pay their rent because their bills had gotten beyond their means, they tried working while living on the streets with high hopes of bringing themselves back up. That didn't work for them either because now people didn't want to smell them at work. Now they were jobless and homeless and standing by their tent on your street corner. What a shame and, at times, through no fault of their own. People didn't seem to care for other people anymore. It didn't seem to Drew that anyone had enough compassion anymore to simply put themselves in the next person's shoes for maybe just a moment. It wasn't his perception that was changing. It was the world around him that was changing.

Drew had once been made homeless because he'd refused to sleep with his 70-year-old landlady. She was a nice looking woman for 70. Drew could tell she'd once been a very beautiful woman. He'd been late on his rent when he was 19 and Ms. Maloney had said in a slower anticipating manner, "Now, Drew, maybe there is something else you could do … (eyebrow in the air)... ah, but maybe I'm too old for you. I'm not as young as I once was." Drew had quickly changed the subject. The following day his locks were changed and all his clothes packed. As beautiful as Ms. Maloney was for a 70-year-old he simply couldn't bring himself to do it. Besides, he would never have known how to initiate such a transaction at 19.

Drew never came on to the ladies. The ladies always came on to Drew. He feared offending them were he to ask them out. He didn't want to be labeled a "creep" for making an unwanted advance. And they were far too beautiful to him to scare away. And hurting people's feelings wasn't a thing on his list ever. When he turned 19 women came from every direction. He was a virgin up until then. In one week he'd gone from virgin to having slept with five ladies. He felt like he'd finally hit the jackpot. The girls practically raped him whenever they felt like it. Drew didn't mind. He was a pushover for girls. And of course, he was young then.

Drew's life in Vancouver, Washington was not entirely boring but things had begun to slow down a bit. The weird stuff had begun subsiding a little mostly, he was sure, because he wasn't interacting with other people. It was a nice break but he understood that soon he had to get back to interacting.

He got himself a job with a credit reporting agency for three or four months before quitting. He was tired of giving everyone in the office the satisfaction of clapping when he came in five minutes late. He couldn't seem to make it to work on time because the buses were either a few minutes too late or too early. It seemed to Drew that it was orchestrated. There was no way he would believe that the buses could by mere coincidence cause him to be five minutes late every single day. He loved the job because he enjoyed beating out the educated collectors. Drew only had a sixth-grade education but always posted that he'd graduated high school in order to get jobs and feed himself. He thought somehow that lying in one's own defense in order to survive was acceptable yet unmentionable. "Fake it till ya make it," he'd often proclaimed to himself.

He didn't entirely believe in many of the worldly things that excited most people. He figured bigfoot couldn't possibly be real considering no one had ever found any remains. Vampires and werewolves were null and void although as a kid he did get scared watching werewolf movies. The last time he'd been scared while watching a movie was at his gramma's house half surrounded by woods in Drummonds, Tennessee. He was using his uncle's old room. It was late at night and the wind brushed the tree branches up against the house. At the same time, he was watching the scene where the little boy looked over at the scarecrow just before its head turned to look at him. It was a little creepy. At this moment, Drew heard noises outside. Lately, he hadn't seen many really scary movies. He wasn't usually impressed with them anyway. Maybe it was because reality had numbed his attraction to scary movies. His past reality had been far scarier than any movie he'd seen. Being beaten, watching people get beaten, being homeless, and shivering while trying to sleep in the rain, seeing people hurt animals, and the overall wear and tear from life's unexpected direction had all been much scarier than any movie. Movies had nothing on real-life hatred.

SEAN AUGUSTA RENNER
AND ELECTRIC GUITAR

DREW SAT DOWN TO watch a movie about a 17-year-old kid who challenged the devil to a guitar playing match. The devil used a Memphis guitar player to fight against the kid but to no avail. The kid eventually won and they lived happily ever after but only after taking a lot of chances along the way. Drew grew up with a guitarist who was just as good as any other. Some even said he was one of the best. Sean Augusta Renner was his name. Guitar playin' was his game. He was also an electrician by trade. And rumor had it that when he played his guitar, electricity flowed from his fingertips straight into the strings, thereby amplifying the beauty of his music. The story went that he'd been shocked so many times while learning the trade that a certain part of his soul held on to the electricity. Drew wished that had been true of him in their younger years. Had Sean played like he did these days, then Drew wouldn't have minded waiting on Sean to hurry up and get done playing so that he could fire up that hostage marijuana joint. Drew thought it a hostage joint because Sean held it hostage until he was done showing Drew what he'd been practicing lately. It was almost painful at times. But, eventually, Sean became an expert and people paid to hear him play his guitar. He also stopped getting shocked by electricity and went on to become the proud owner of his own electric company. Drew would have done well to follow suit but did not. He watched other people become successful as he stood in place. Sean Augusta Renner took first place amongst successful childhood friends. And he hadn't even visited the crossroads.

When the movie was over, he stepped out for a breath of fresh air. He also had a cigarette. Smoking like a broken stove, he took in the cool beauty of Washington. A smell brought to mind a time when his mother was working at a greenhouse and he'd fallen through the roof. He'd been a somewhat mischievous child and climbed up on the greenhouse roof. The good old days of a time spent in Texas. How could he ever forget Texas?

Sometimes he remembered doing things in public that would have embarrassed his mother. Like a time when he was six years old and had an extreme case of poison ivy itch on his testicles. He found himself outside with a hairbrush scratching his testicles before he realized he was in public. These days looking back he couldn't understand why he'd done half of what he did as a youngin'. He'd burnt down a house his family was renting back in the seventies when he was a five-year-old. Or, at least, he'd taken the blame for it. He and his brothers were sticking toilet paper into the red-hot coils of a wire heater and then waving it out and throwing it under the bed. All three brothers were doing this but Drew was more than a year older, which labeled him the responsible culprit. The fire chief's face and gigantic helmet had etched into his mind forever as he told young Drew how bad it was to play with fire. Drew and his brothers went on to play with fire for years afterward before growing bored with it. Before it was over, however, Drew's parents held his hand close to the flame of a lighter in an attempt to exercise the pyromania out of him. It certainly scared him knowing his stepfather that hated him was holding a flame near his hand. Yet it did nothing but make him fear authority that much more. By that time he was done with playing anyway. They didn't realize that the lighter they'd caught him with was for smoking not lighting fires.

His parents or guardians, usually not including his mother, always seemed to come up with new ways to punish him. His mother never knew. A few of his guardians or stepfathers liked to force him not to eat dinner and to hide the punishment from his mother by pretending not to be hungry or to hold his arms straight out for an hour or more at a time or until he couldn't do it any longer and was crying in pain. Sometimes paddles, switches, belts, and rubber racetrack pieces satisfied their need to make him cry. Perhaps they had all grown tired of his constant smile. His mother had once told him that he hardly ever cried as a baby and that he was all smiles. Regardless of whatever happened, Drew boasted a smile even to this day that wouldn't go away in the presence of people. He liked them but again, had grown leery through the years. Who could blame him? He'd been through it and back, time and time again.

For now, he would take life day by day until he knew what to do. Survival was enough. He had to figure out how to make money. He didn't too much like what currency stood for but he grasped the simple truth that he needed it to survive. He understood more so later in life how imperative money could be. In a day and age where it was illegal for a man to live off of the land without asking and paying another man first, money ruled. Being financially embarrassed posed its own threats.

CHAPTER

FORGET ABOUT THE PAST, WE WILL REMEMBER FOR YOU

Enjoying a day of wandering and trying to come up with ideas for work, Drew passed by his local park. People enjoyed walking their dogs and picking up their poop, although some left the poop to lie there. He thought how nasty some of their homes might be. From his experience, people who didn't clean up after their dogs lived grossly in their homes. He'd seen homes that were covered in cockroaches from roof to floor and cat and or dog feces trod into the carpets. That combined with no air conditioning and a 120-degree humid August day in Memphis created a smell not like death but of the evilest of life. It smelled perhaps the way a demon would smell, with rotted flesh that had a sulfuric edge to it.

Others just hung out in the park. Today he just passed it by. He headed to a local Vancouver collections agency called DZS Financial. Drew filled out the application and submitted to the background check. He headed back towards home with confidence. Drew had never applied for a job and not gotten it. His charm and well-spoken southern drawl fit well with his sharp formal attire. He always won them over during interviews. With a sixth grade education and nothing more than personality and street smarts, Drew was able to convince employers on a personable level that he was the man for the job. All of his felony theft crimes were over 10 years old and in another state. It would show clear. Even though he did not have a high school education, that lie would never come out because he'd taught himself how to speak on an intellectual and educated level. And no one questioned a high school diploma if your English was good. Had he been tested for math skills he may have fallen short.

For the next few days, he waited on the hiring phone call. Before he knew it four days had gone by and still no call. People often tried to explain to Drew that he should look for a job elsewhere until the one he'd applied to called. He never understood why they felt the need to explain something so simple to him as if he were mentally challenged and didn't understand how to get a job. Those people he assumed merely didn't believe in his being confident in his ability to gain lawful employment. Drew never worried about not getting the call because he always had. People either didn't understand that or thought he might be bonkers.

On the evening of the fourth day, he received the interview call. He grabbed the interview by the horns and ran with it. He was hired. As he walked home, the hop in his step spoke volumes. He hopped and skipped all the way home like a 13-year-old on his birthday. In two days he would be seated at his new desk and again be employed for the near one-hundredth time in his life. Keeping the job always presented the challenge not getting the job. That was easy for him.

Turning the key he realized his front and only door was already unlocked. He entered quickly but with caution presuming he may have to apprehend an intruder. He also kept in mind that he may possibly have forgotten to lock it. In his blind attempts to humble himself, he always made sure to remind himself that he wasn't perfect. He'd seen enough of himself to know he could be slightly forgetful at times. Sometimes it was very difficult to remember priorities in order because so much data was cramming his head at one time.

No one was in his apartment and nothing looked suspicious. He closed his door and indulged in the comfort of his bed. He turned on his TV and flipped through the news channels and the movie channels. Nothing really looked interesting to him. He'd already seen "A Clockwork Orange" too many times to want to see it anymore. And besides that, he first watched it when he was 12-years-old. At 12, everything sunk in but the things that truly mattered to him didn't include this movie. He really didn't like how the villain was always drinking milk because he loved milk and didn't want milk involved in such a nasty movie. But then he was 12 at the time. Around that time he'd also viewed other movies such as "Caligula" and "I Spit On Your Grave". None were movies he'd ever want to see again.

Again, with nothing interesting on television, Drew resorted to the news. Today's news was about the same as any other day's news. A policeman was acquitted of murder charges after having shot an unarmed man to death on bodycam. It was the usual bureaucratic bull hockey. Policemen got off the hook for murder all the time because they reserved secrets and dirt on the department. The general population thought this was just a conspiracy theory, which in Drew's eyes showed mass ignorance. The country was doomed to the confines of a tyranny. They were under the thumb of the new Uncle Sam. The government was no longer working for the people. It was now quite the opposite. The people were at the mercy of their own government. The horror of it was that they invited it. They insisted that it was still the American way. Better not burn a flag or risk suffering the repercussions. The people were quick to attack anyone burning a flag in protest but very, very slow in recognizing that soldiers had fought and died for the right to burn that very flag in the land of the free. It was not very patriotic but legal nevertheless.

The land of the free seemed to be becoming the land of the rich and poor. If you had a neverending supply of money, the crimes that entailed fines weren't even a bother. You had to pay to break the government's rules. If you had no money then suspension of privileges and cages were in your future. That was if one decided to speed while driving or drinking in public. The typical misdemeanor charges didn't really affect the rich. There weren't very many millionaires in jail. Millionaires with good lawyers could get off the hook for murder. Money was worshipped as if it were God Almighty. Families stabbed each other in the back for it. It turned good men bad. It was a necessary evil.

Later in the week, Drew reported to work at DZS Financial. He sat down at his new desk and began to do his thing. Forty-five minutes into his job, the heads in charge waved him into the office. They showed him mugshots of himself on PDX.com before asking him to explain. Drew explained that it was a case that was very old and that they shouldn't have pulled it up. He'd already passed the background exam and in Drew's eyes, that should have been enough. Nevertheless, he was fired and told that they couldn't have someone with a mugshot online associated with their company. Drew decided to give up on corporate America. He'd decided that he would not look for the American dream by working for Joe Schmoe the hypocrital discriminator. Screw that mess. He had to come up with a better way.

He entertained the possibility of writing books for a living. He didn't have the documented proof of education but he was smarter than the average bear. He'd been told as a young kid that his I.Q. was amongst the top 30 percent in the entire world. He remembered thinking that they were blowing smoke up his derriere. He'd been told by so many adults that he was a "dumbass" and "stupid" that he'd begun to believe it. He thought it was a trick to get him to do better in growing up. One couldn't tell by Drew's actions that he was in fact as smart as he was. Once he graduated to the seventh grade, his trouble with school really began. He failed the seventh grade four times because he'd developed a new found hobby called skipping school and getting as drunk as possible. He had been in so much confusion and pain as a child and still, he felt the need to smile. If felt better for him to smile than to frown.

He also thought about driving for someone except for the fact that he had a fresh DUI charge. That idea was out the window. Perhaps he could go back to working Labor Ready. It was a daily paycheck but one in which he'd most certainly have to work with a less friendly sort of people. People who would pretend to be boss when in fact they weren't. Rude people who seemed to have no consideration for those around them.

People upset him to the point of drinking. As optimistic as he'd attempted to be over the years about working labor jobs, they always involved negative people. Those sort of people bothered Drew even when it wasn't him taking the flack but someone else. He didn't like watching people being treated like dogs or even talked to disrespectfully. It both saddened and angered him.

Drew sifted through his options before nodding off. An hour into falling asleep, his mind raced in and out of a cluster of dreams that seemed to last for an eternity. Some of the dreams made no sense and others were past incidents. In one dream, he was somewhere between one and five-years-old and his foot was swollen so badly in the small clear rubber rain boot that it had busted open inside. The entire clear boot that once showed his naked foot was now nothing but red as the blood pumped out of his busted skin. They had to cut his boot off to get it off of his foot. In a flash, he was in another dream. This time, he was again very young. He was suffering a severe asthma attack and laying in the back of his mother's station wagon as she rushed him to the hospital. Just as quick as that dream began, he was onto the next one. This time, he had climbed 20 feet up a tree that had no limbs. He was 11 and getting smarter by the day. He'd almost fallen and instead managed to survive by sliding down the branchless tree using his forearms. When he hit the ground his arms were "on fire" for lack of a better phrase. Within a week, both of his forearms were a mess of puss and blood. They eventually scabbed over but the pain lasted for some time. His mind moved on to bits and pieces of a time when he was a teenager and had broken into his ex-boss' trailer at a trailer park he also lived in. His boss had fired him without reason. Most likely he did have a reason but Drew hadn't been given one. Drew, in his desperate state of financial crisis and teenage confusion and sautéed in alcohol, decided to use his situation as an excuse to break into the trailer and steal the water jug full of quarters, dimes, nickels, and pennies. He dumped them into the man's pillowcase and took off. He had assumed he'd gotten away with it. A couple of weeks later, Drew had been walking down the road on his way to do a suitcase of laundry when his ex-boss pulled up and offered him a ride. Awkward was the word.

Drew accepted the ride and made small talk with the guy as if nothing had ever happened. The man asked Drew if he wanted something to drink because he had to stop at the service station for gas and make a quick phone call – cell phones hadn't been invented yet. Drew wasn't particularly thirsty and replied with a "no, thanks". The man went in. Drew was slightly suspicious but also knew to worry would only make it worse. When the man got back into the truck, he asked Drew if he minded making a stop with him at city hall. Drew assured him that it was fine and that he was in no hurry. Drew did not know what city hall was at that time. When they arrived at city hall, the man got out of his truck after assuring Drew that he'd be right back. Drew sat dumbly smoking a cigarette as his ex-employer came back with a sheriff's deputy.

"Drew, do you mind if I have a look in your suitcase?" his old boss asked.

In some surprise, Drew said, "Yes. Of course. What's going on?" Drew had nothing to worry about. He had already spent most of the change after having exchanged it for cash. The man wouldn't find any change so what on God's green earth was he looking for? Drew thought he foresaw his old boss looking stupid to the deputy because there was no evidence. Drew already felt remorse for what he'd done to the man and now he was going to feel worse about it because his boss was about to look stupid for accusing him.

The man sifted through Drew's dirty clothes twice before shaking his head in upset.

"What did he expect to find?" Drew had wondered.

The sheriff's deputy looked very uncomfortable as well and advised the man to move on and forget about it.

The man stood over the clothes now with his hands on his hips shaking his head in humble disgust. "One more time," he said to the sheriff's deputy as he bent down for another search.

Just as he flipped through for the last time he came up with a pillowcase. "This is my pillowcase."

The deputy turned to Drew and asked him, "Is that his pillowcase?"

Drew was glad it was over and confessed to everything. In turn, the man didn't show up for court. Drew was released 30 days later.

Drew swapped over to dreaming about the bits and pieces of other burglaries he'd once committed. He'd once worked for a man pressure washing for two months before finally realizing he was never getting paid. His girlfriend of the time was nagging him to death about getting paid. His boss continuously gave him the runaround about not having yet been paid by the clients. He'd been literally stuck between a rock and a hard place while waiting on his boss to show up one morning. On this particular morning, his boss was already half an hour late whereas he'd never been late. As he waited in giant rubber boots for a boss that appeared to have abandoned him, he noticed two ladies in an apartment down from his leaving in a car. They seemed to be rich older women. Once again, out of desperation, Drew walked up to their door and kicked it open with his back. He began searching through drawers frantically before realizing there was no money, jewelry or guns inside. Within five minutes he was taking apart a stereo system and sitting pieces of it by the door right along with a pillowcase full of booze. It was all by the door and ready. He had one last piece of the stereo system to pull before leaving. As he pulled the last piece, he heard keys in the door. It shocked him with surprise. He would never have assumed that they would be back in six minutes the way that they had been so nicely dressed. But they had. They were coming in and there was no other way out of the apartment. No back door or windows. He was screwed. He ran quickly to the bedroom and slid under the bed. When the ladies who were presumably mother and daughter came in he could hear them panicking in the other room. He could hear them saying that whoever it was must be gone now. They looked through the house and saw no one. They called the police and summoned other people in the complex to ask them if they had seen anyone coming or going. No one had seen anything. And then he heard an individual saying, "You should check under the beds." The lady insisted whoever the culprit was had already gone. Again the male voice suggested to her to check under the beds. After about the third time of hearing this, the younger of the two older ladies came into the bedroom and lifted the blanket to look under the bed. When she saw Drew she gasped as she put her hand over her mouth. She jumped back and up before exiting the room. Then Drew heard nothing but silence. He had no choice but to get out from under the bed and man up. As he walked out the front door with his chest poked out and head held high in defense, he now saw all of the people there. Not daring to confront any one individual, he walked tall right through them as they formed a line on both sides of him.

Drew spotted two would-be heroes who ranked him in size coming down the stairwell. They weren't paying attention to the small crowd of people gathered there who were so scared they couldn't speak. The mother of the lady who had discovered his whereabouts stood there with her hand over mouth just as her daughter had. Only she muttered quietly while pointing at him, "I know who you are." Drew's mouth had a mind of its own and he attempted to distract them before high tailing it out of there. He said to the woman, "Calm down, lady. I'll check for you." At that point, he moved with stealth around the corner of the building and ducked into the bushes because he knew the two bigger guys would give chase. As he suspected, the two men flew past the bushes and around to another area. Drew jumped up and darted across the freeway and viaducts before landing in a suburban neighborhood of middle-class houses that all looked the same. He saw a police car and just missed it as he hit another corner. A bit further down he saw a friend he'd grown up with working on the roof of a house. It was his buddy Alph. Alph had once saved his skin in school by getting rid of a starter pistol that was in Drew's locker. Drew's other buddy had put it in there and someone had snitched. When the time came to search Drew's locker, the principal found nothing as Alph had already thrown the gun on the bedroom roof. Drew knew nothing of any of this until after the fact.

Drew had five bucks and offered it to Alph as pay for a nice ride out of the area. Alph said, "Hell, that's beer money," and proceeded to climb down from the roof. He got Drew where he wanted to go without even knowing the trouble Drew was in. As they drove from the area, Drew noticed the helicopters buzzing about in search of him. Three days later they caught him at a laundromat smoking pot.

Drew began breaking into houses when he was a child. It was not to support a habit and not to capitalize but only because he was extremely curious and extremely bored. He had no guidance because all of the men in his life were undesirable and he held no high respect for them. All he had was a very busy mother who sometimes wasn't there. The rest of his time was spent trying not to make whatever man was there upset.

In another burglary when Drew had gotten out of prison for the first one, Drew had met a girl who worked at a pizza place. He was introduced to her by another jerk named David when he and David were spending the night with the girls at their father's apartment. Their father was a truck driver and currently in another state. David went upstairs with one of the girls and closed the door. Drew kinda felt like a tag along. As he and the other girl sat downstairs watching television he felt a little nervous and out of place. They sat on separate couches.

The girl made the statement, "Well, I'm going to bed." She glanced at Drew and moseyed on up to the other bedroom while leaving the door open. Drew wasn't sure it was an invitation so he didn't try it. He fell asleep right there on the couch. The following morning the girl told Drew that he could have come up the night before. He felt awkward and the need to get drunk. When they left and went their separate ways, she went to work and Drew came back to break into her apartment. While he was searching through her father's belongings for money or jewelry, the girl came home. This time he hid in the closet. In just a few minutes she left again. At the time it hadn't felt creepy to him. Looking back now, he felt horrible about it and couldn't understand his actions. He was now a completely different person and ashamed of his prior way of life.

Drew had then gathered what he could and walked out. He was caught three days later. He did more prison time and this time he realized it was wrong to take anything from anyone ever. He began to realize that this was not who he was. He began to put himself in the shoes of his victims. He didn't like it and finally changed the behavior that had been blind to the feelings of others. In his late twenties, he'd finally started feeling compassionate and not victimizing people. He'd not only victimized others by stealing from them and invading their homes but he'd also seen too many people victimized and it hurt him to his heart. He'd been wrong about what he'd done and thought and he wanted it to change. He would no longer victimize innocent people.

Drew was a bit of a different person after two three-year prison stints. He had no way of knowing that again he would commit burglary when he came out. Another man had again worked Drew without paying him. So Drew got drunk and kicked the jerk's door in to take what was owed him. Drew stole thousands of dollars' worth of jewelry before being caught again three days later. Another prison stint came and went. Only this time, instead of three years he was sentenced to seven years. He completed four and a half years of the sentence by doing hard labor before he was released.

Bits and pieces of dramatic lifestyle raced through his brain as he lay motionless in his dreams.

CHAPTER

GUILT AND CRAZY

DREW FELT SINCERE GUILT for the life he'd lived in the past and couldn't for the life of him figure out why he'd behaved the way he did in his younger years. He would never burgal anyone ever again. He was done living in close quarters with hatred and violence. Hatred and violence were all prison was about. It was disgusting to him. It rehabilitated no one and took lives. It was merely a money machine that boosted the government's own personal economy. It did nothing for the people but sucked them dry and taught them to hate or how to be a slicker deviant. Prisons were somewhat of an abomination in Drew's eyes. They were immoral and needed revision. Vengeance is mine sayeth the Lord. Judge not, lest ye be judged yourself. Although there were dangerous people in prison who should, by all means, stay there, there were also people that blended in as sort of a filler for state governments desire for funding from the federal government. This included drug dealers and petty thieves or a hack that owed the state money. They were all mixed in together as if all were equally dangerous. Why should a financial status be a reason to put a human being in a cage? The government was too big for its britches and needed to be taken down quite a few notches. It would never be taken down if people stayed divided against one another. Unity was the only way to achieve it and as he could see in his mind's eye, Uncle Sam was slowly shackling America by dividing them into groups. If it was too complicated the average idiot would understand this was a conspiracy theory and nothing more. Drew believed he could trust his brain more than that. Yes, disappointment ran through his dreams whether he liked it or not.

Drew's night of weird dreams probably only took seconds but they felt like an eternity when he woke up. He was emotionally and mentally drained from the dreams he'd endured. When he woke up he wanted to go back to sleep but he couldn't. So he smoked some pot before going back to sleep, now free of dreams.

The following day he got as wasted as he could in an attempt to forget about the life he'd been running from for years. He didn't drink on a regular basis anymore and didn't realize that he couldn't handle all the alcohol he once could. It was hard on him and left him feeling sickly. So sickly that he wanted nothing more than to not feel this way. His brilliant drunk brain introduced the idea of copping some methamphetamine as it would sober him up almost instantly. If he could find it without being arrested by the self-medication police he'd be doing great. Then there was also always the getting ripped off factor. If someone ripped him off he'd be doubly angry. Half the time he attempted to buy drugs from people he didn't know and he was ripped off. That was enough of a reason not to try and buy drugs but a drunken state was not a place of much logic.

Drew managed to buy 10 dollars' worth of amphetamine and get back home safely without being caught and trapped in a cage. He rolled it up in a square of toilet paper and swallowed it. Within minutes, he felt like a million bucks. It was worth every bit of the 20 dollars he'd paid for 10 dollars' worth of dope. Or was it?

The horrible drunk feeling felt as though it had never even occurred. Drew's ADHD also vanished right along with his drunken stupor. He felt on top of the world. Now he could actually think and focus on whatever was at hand. The only problem was that he couldn't focus on one thing. He was now focused on everything. And while he could focus well on the thought that came to mind, this thought was interrupted by other thoughts. The extreme focus from one thought to another got him nowhere but an escape from reality. His priorities were completely out of whack. He knew that using drugs wasn't ever going to ease his pain. He also knew that his use of substances was a mere experiment he'd started as a child to help him understand drugs like this weren't the answer. It was an experiment that would soon be over. Experience had taught him well that there was no escape and that life needed to be grabbed by the horns and not feared. Fear was a sin and fear was the first to go. Running from it would have to stop.

He was thinking of a time in Tacoma when his short-term superpower focus began to kick in. He remembered staying in a cheap motel one night when a caravan of white trucks and vans checked in and took every available room as if they were filming a movie and had just gotten into town. Their license plates showed they were from California. Then thoughts shifted to a time in Seattle at a bus stop late at night when he came upon maybe 20 or so elderly people who seemed to all be healthy for their age, all with white hair, and all facing to the left in sync. For a moment, he thought they had appeared as if angels. At the time, he entertained the idea that they might be actors considering the mass of weird things he'd already seen in Washington. He was truly amazed by something no one else may have even seen. Something that to another individual may have seemed like just a bunch of old people waiting for a bus and nothing more.

Another thought came of a time when he'd seen his dead friend's girlfriend at a train station in Everett. She'd stared right into his eyes and he'd known something was very wrong. He'd known well before then that something was wrong. In a sense, he'd always known something was wrong. His mind seemed to be compiling evidence that somehow seemed to defend his sanity. Being watched so much as a child in juvenile detention and adult jail had imposed a sense upon him that he was unaware he had until his middle-aged years. However, knowing when people were watching you wasn't a necessarily pleasant state of mind. In fact, Drew thought it sucked.

Shifting to another thought, he remembered thinking he'd seen his brother near the train station in Everett as well. But he couldn't be sure. All he was sure of was that he'd seen one person in Everett who did not belong there along with many look-a-likes of his so-called family and friends. Someone was watching him. The drug forced his mind deep into reality even though it was said to induce an escape from the very reality he was facing. It didn't make any sense and it didn't matter right now because there wasn't much he could do about it. Still, he felt an uncontrollable urge to understand why. So his mind shifted again to a night in Seattle when 10-12 crackheads approached him at once from all different directions to ask him if he needed anything. He felt that they weren't acting on impulse nor were they really trying to get crack but to agitate him. He badly wanted to know who sent them.

For nearly 36 hours, he put bits and pieces together in an attempt to build one small piece of a jigsaw puzzle. He searched his computer for clues and thought and thought about what could be happening in his life. He came to many a conclusion but none added up completely. Strange things began once again to happen such as loud noises outside in the middle of the night made by the voices of strange people. One night a woman was singing in the adjacent apartment at 2am. This was definitely an intervention in his life. Perhaps someone somewhere was trying to get him to wake up and snap out of his old life and into a new one. To him, that would be understandable from someone who genuinely cared about him but unacceptable from a stranger. And unacceptable for a lying family member. And then, maybe someone somewhere enjoyed making a mockery of him. He simply did not know. But he knew life wasn't about him and surely not many people were interested enough in his life to play any such games. Surely they had something better to do.

This would be the last time he ever used a mind-enhancing drug he swore to himself. He thought to himself that maybe it would be okay if it were just him and God. But it wasn't. It was him, God, and millions of finger-pointing humans. He didn't need it. And it could only cause problems for him. He would move on with the rest of his life without using hard drugs. He now intended to drop both drugs and alcohol from his life completely. Marijuana would keep its place for now as an anxiety medication. After all, it was completely legal now and far safer than Valium or Xanax or opiates.

CHAPTER

MISSY

Months of sobriety went by before an ex-girlfriend contacted him on Facebook. Her name was Missy. Missy was a five-foot-tall Korean girl who wore her hair short and had big, brown, and cute eyes. Unlike Drew, she had a high school education. She reminded him of a dumb blonde valley girl at times but they got along fine. She was bubbly and the two of them never argued. What's more, he found her to be the cutest girl he'd ever known. She loved to be cuddled and Drew adored that part of her. At five-foot-tall and 110 pounds, Missy looked younger than her age. She'd always been loyal to Drew in the past so the two of them hooked back up as basically husband and wife without the certificate. Missy came to Drew's and moved in while Drew took care of the bills. For a time, Drew did whatever work came his way. That stopped when Missy got herself a job that she enjoyed at a five-star hotel. She gave Drew the relief he needed in order to begin writing books. He was thankful for his Missy. He loved her and he needed her. Missy would fill in Drew's heart and leave room for no other.

Drew and Missy met in Everett, Washington at a labor source. She was pregnant and the father a no-show. Drew felt the need to protect her and her baby by helping to keep her nourished and safe from predators. He hung around without the expectation of having sex with her and at his own cost until the two finally did click. When they met, they merely partied together until they went their own ways. They didn't part on bad terms. They were friends that merely drifted apart. But now, they were together again, off the drugs, and planning everyday life together. Missy would now get to experience the same oddball life that Drew had endured, at least since he'd been in Washington.

Drew went on with life, as usual, experiencing coincidence day after day. By now it was merely part of everyday life. He no longer questioned why. He no longer fumed from the ears because of anger and confusion. In a way, he'd dismissed what had so badly bothered him. People like that weren't worth a rise in blood pressure. Watching the news on police violence wasn't either. And although he still enjoyed watching the news with his reunited girlfriend, he refused to allow it under his skin any longer. There truly was nothing that he himself could do about any of what made him furious. He now understood that and felt that he could move on through life without the bumpy ride of anger. Or at least now he could control it.

Just when everything began to go well, Drew realized his clothes had been cut. Several pairs of his pants and shirts had very small yet precisely cut square holes. On top of that, there were holes punched in his straw hat with what could have been either a screwdriver or a pencil from the looks of it. He didn't know what to make of it. Angry for a moment he moved on to wonder why and who could hate him so much as to break into his home and tear up his clothes? He moved on without holding on to the familiar bitterness he'd already let go of. He remembered the Mexican neighborhood he'd lived in as a child when he and his family had returned home to find a note on the door explaining that the house had been flooded.

The water pipes running through their home had been deliberately sawed in half. San Diego hadn't proved to be the ideal hideaway at the time for his stepfather who was then A.W.O.L. from the military. The Mexican people did not want any crackers in their neighborhood. They made a point of expressing it. Drew wondered if the motive presented by the un-sub was the same as it was back then. Did someone want him out? He couldn't grasp why and so he dropped it.

It was a Monday and Drew was scrolling through his social media when he came across an app that boasted it would show you what you would look like if you were old. He double clicked for giggles. Why not? he thought. As the app loaded, he lit his cigarette. He pulled in a drag and exhaled with a sigh of relief. He'd always truly enjoyed the taste of a cigarette. It made him smile.

When the app produced a four-picture profile of what he might look like in his fifties, sixties, and seventies he totally expected it would be cheesy. He anticipated a ghost of grey hair and a few fake looking wrinkles. What was not anticipated was the oldest picture of him being a picture of someone else entirely; someone in a judge's robe with a pic of a face that could be of his biological father.

The picture of him representing his seventies would somewhat shock him. He hadn't expected what he believed to be a picture of his 61-year-old father. He felt certain that this was a picture of his father who he did not know. And even though he'd never seen a picture of his father at this angle, he saw the very familiar facial structure that he saw in his mirror every morning. He saw his own smile in another man's face.

He'd never seen this picture until now but he was almost certain he wasn't mistaken. He also kept in mind his that desperation to get to the bottom of an eerie mystery could influence his thoughts. Maybe deep inside he wanted to think that all this time someone who cared was trying to influence him to do what was right. Maybe he wanted to think that it wasn't an enemy or a stranger who had taken an interest in his personal life. He simply wanted to be positive about his life. The thought of it all being for nothing did not exist in his mind. It could knock but it wasn't welcome in. Perhaps this was why he once was so angered by the videos of police shootings. While trying to be positive about everything in life, his eyes had accepted the negativity of the violent videos where his mind wouldn't. He couldn't make anything positive of the videos and it truly angered him. In his current state of mind, he was far more lax. And although the weird stuff came and went he no longer entertained a mental uproar. He was somewhat at peace with the fact that he was under some kind of surveillance by an unknown source. He'd always felt that with his Maker anyway. He would never be completely alone. If no one else, the Man upstairs was watching.

When he pointed out the odd and coincidence happenings to Missy she seemed to blow it off as if it were nothing. As if it didn't add up to anything. But the more often he brought it to her attention, the more she too began to see it on her own. Much of the nonsense he dealt with was now via computer. Since he'd stopped using uppers there'd been no more scratching at his walls or floors. No more cords drug through the hall or the kitchen. If he were being watched, they weren't being obvious about it anymore. He wondered if whoever it was had strong personal issues and beliefs about drug use and they were forcing it on him, like the way an unwanted Mormon knocked on your door. Or it could possibly be an anti-tobacco group. Someone who protested the actions of others so extremely as to break the law to feel that they'd completed a mission. Someone who personally felt justified in their actions because they been told so by another bunch of idiots that they could do no wrong. Just because a million people told you that you were justified in doing something controversial didn't mean you truly were justified by any means. It just meant there were a million other people just like you. Just because the people of North Korea believed Kim Jong Un did not have a rectum did not make it so.

Lately, he'd been thinking about small things that popped up in his mind just before they happened. For instance, he often awoke with a song in his head. It was usually a softer, uplifting song from say the 70s or 80s. On one particular morning, he woke up a song in his head. He couldn't figure out why but he had to pull it up and show it to Missy on the internet. Later that day he was taking a walk and singing the song to himself when a passing jogger shouted back at him, "Hey, I just downloaded that song. Right on." It didn't surprise or upset Drew but it opened doors all over again in his head. Or perhaps it merely shone light through doors that were already open. And it could have been simple synchronicity.

Other instances included thinking about something just before it was said on the radio, TV, or social media. Missy knew he was telling the truth because he'd spoken of things to her just before seeing or hearing them. She wanted to tell him that she thought perhaps he was experiencing discernment. But she wasn't sure. Missy was merely along for the ride. She grew on him and he on her. Despite the fact that she was working a job and supporting him, she did not mind. Drew had taken good care of her in the past. She was grateful to him and he loved her so. Now he was grateful to her as well. Side jobs at labor companies every so often reminded him why he needed to work for himself.

On January 26, 2017, Drew was in good spirits. He woke up to coffee and more news about people protesting the election of Donald Trump as President of the United States. It seemed to be a womanathon of crying and complaining about how they lost the election. Drew didn't understand what the protesters were trying to do. The election was over and it was a done deal. Perhaps they all felt misunderstood. Drew certainly didn't understand but he was also beginning not to care either. He himself had no money or power yet in this world. And no one he thought he knew on social media ever had much to say on the topics. He decided to leave it with God. He watched as a guy named Devin skied off of a cliff by accident and with a camera attached to him. When the guy finally hit the bottom he was still alive and not even hurt. What was odd was the fact that Drew had just daydreamed about falling from a great distance and surviving by sheer faith. He questioned how and where the fall could occur and imagined being able to get up. The news segment was nearly what he'd imagined to himself the day before. Again, it made no sense to him. He'd often created scenarios in his head. He wasn't yet entirely sure why.

After the news and coffee, he set out on foot to check on buying a car. Between what little money he could hustle through labor and what Missy made they could afford something cheap. He bought a white van with tinted windows. It was a nice, medium-sized passenger van that could seat eight people. It seemed all good but for one small problem – when he turned on the stereo it took a couple of seconds before the sound would come on, all except for the nearly hidden sound of a telephone dial tone. If the van's stereo issue wasn't weird enough when he got home later a Facebook friend sent him a link asking if it was his link. Drew had never seen the link before until now.

The link was displayed only as YouTube with Drew's name and 257,000 views. It was actually connected to Drew's own profile pic. When Drew clicked the link he was told that he was being blocked from a malicious site for his own safety. The message later disappeared and in its place was a triangle with an exclamation point. It was gone. When he messaged his friend back, he found she wasn't his friend anymore. Needless to say, she did not message back. It was as if she knew she'd made a mistake by mentioning something she shouldn't have. He wasn't surprised. He pretty much had an understanding that he was limited to what he could do on his computer by design. It wasn't because of the service. It was because someone somewhere was at least partially in control of his computer. They had to be.

He remembered a time not so long ago when he'd crossed the bridge into Portland, Oregon where he'd had an active warrant for a probation violation. He'd been high and drunk without a care in the world for days. He got off the bus at Jensen Beach where he was going to buy himself some cheaper cigarettes than what was available in Washington State. He exited the bus and began to walk towards the tobacco shops. Halfway to the store, he saw two police officers pull in behind the McDonald's restaurant. To be safe he turned around and headed back towards the bus depot. Almost immediately, the cops rolled up on him for business that Drew wasn't entirely ready for, although his mouth seemed to be.

CHAPTER

A NARROW ESCAPE, PORTLAND
AND MORE CRAZY

"Aren't you that guy in the wanted ads?" one cop asked.

"Wanted ads? No," Drew replied. When the officer asked for Drew's identification Drew told him, "No. I need to speak with your supervisor."

"Why?" the officer replied.

What came out of Drew's mouth next would not only surprise him but it would save his life from another time stint in a brutal cage of violent, needy idiots. Behind a deep exhale, Drew jumped off the cliff so to speak when he spilled words from his mouth that he didn't even realize he was capable of. "Officer, I am not a suspect in a crime nor do I fit the description of a suspect in a crime. This is not considered a consensual acquaintance. I wasn't loitering or soliciting and therefore you have no legal reason to stop me and ask for my identification. I need to speak with your supervisor."

In return, the cop informed Drew that because he didn't consent to a request to produce identification that he, the cop, could still legally detain Drew pending permission for transport.

Drew knew the law and he agreed. But he never once thought he was capable of communicating the way in which he did. His mouth just seemed to move on its own. It seemed to get him out of trouble without any thought. It had to be help from above. He later read that God could speak for you through your own mouth. Looking back, he knew he was incapable of talking that way. Once Drew was in cuffs, his wallet was removed from his back pocket and his ID forcibly produced. Drew was placed on the sidewalk in cuffs next to one of the officers while one officer got back into the vehicle to contact his supervisor.

After a few moments, the officer got out of his car. He proceeded to uncuff Drew while telling him, "Okay, here's the deal. You seem like a pretty smart guy. My boss told me to release you and to give you this piece of paper that pretty much says that you can't come back to Oregon. If you do it will be considered trespassing and you will be arrested."

Drew's heart felt like it fell on the ground because you see, the probation warrant was the least of his worries. Drew, in fact, was in possession of an eight-ball of methamphetamine and a small amount of marijuana at a time before it was legal. He couldn't make it back to the bus stop fast enough. Once on it, he never looked back. The time in question was during a homeless, carefree, drug-using stint. A time when Drew simply felt the need to explore. A need to be free and do as he damn well pleased. That very same evening, he sat out near a bank that had a spot to charge his phone. He was pretty well lit with half of the eight-ball left. He'd gone into his backpack to find something when a sheriff's deputy pulled up on him.

The deputy parked and abruptly exited his vehicle as if he meant business, only to say, "Hey, watcha doin'?"

Drew's drugs were sitting right next to him but the deputy turned his back on Drew as if to clean out some garbage from the passenger's seat of his car. Drew could hardly believe this was happening. He put the dope in his mouth quickly before realizing it was too big a bag of dope. The officer seemed to almost purposely give Drew the opportunity to put it away. Quickly, Drew pulled it off his mouth and put it straight into his pocket.

The officer turned around after what seemed to be an eternity to tell Drew he couldn't stay there because it was beginning to rain and but he could go underneath the awning of El Presidente, a small Mexican restaurant. Drew was beginning to understand even before then that someone up there was seriously looking out for him and had for quite some time. He sat under the awning thanking God and wondering what to do next. He simply didn't know.

Drew was also privately very grateful to the sheriff's deputy for letting him slide. He was certain the deputy was cutting him slack but hadn't understood why. Whatever the case, Drew had avoided a cage twice in one day. He'd endured all of the excitement he could take. During those days, he'd played it a little too close and was already deciding to drop it all. His consistent need to revisit a drug-related mystery had begun diminishing.

He wasn't an addict. He was not in denial. He was somebody who stepped out there into a life less traveled. He had a curious and immature mind. His young, lustful life was rooted in rebellion. He was a sinner and a grinner. A bad kid with a golden heart. A product of the southern ghetto he still held dear to his heart.

To make a long story short, Drew wondered if the years he'd spent living in the twilight zone could be partially attributed to the police in some way. Oddly enough, he and Missy had a conversation once about the law on headlights and whether or not they were supposed to be on during windshield wiper use. During their conversation, Drew noticed a police officer three cars back in the opposite lane. He pointed the car out to Missy as a joke and said, "They're comin' for ya." That was about the time Missy said, "See. He doesn't have his lights on." He nearly wished she'd never said it because at that moment the officer turned his headlights on. They both enjoyed a laugh until the officer abruptly turned his headlights back off again. Drew felt strongly that the officer, in fact, was listening to what they were saying and his smile faded to a look of concentration. Missy saw it as nothing more than coincidence but Drew knew better. He felt strongly that there was more to it than met the eye.

Those few instances weren't the only reason he half-expected police to be involved. He was pretty sure he'd set off some red neck cops in a really bad way in his earlier years in Memphis, Tennessee. He'd once called 911 on an officer who threatened to throw him in jail if he didn't get off of "HIS" street. Drew had actually been on his way to buy cocaine and a couple of whoppers from Burger King. He was meeting the dealer at the very payphone that he called 911 from. Drew was homeless then too and not in the mood for any bull. He got the officer suspended for three days. Drew didn't feel a bit guilty for smacking the officer's pride square in the face. The very same officer had once threatened to break his girlfriend's arms and legs. And besides, he felt he was doing nothing more than minding his own business. He didn't feel any man had the right to tell him what he could and couldn't do with his own body.

Sometime after that, strange things seemed to happen but back then he wasn't looking for connections. Police seemed to back off of him. At that time, he felt that it could be a calm before the storm and that his ass might soon be grass.

Aside from the headlight blinking incident, the only questionable thing the police had done as of late was getting behind him for a few minutes and then doing U-turns. He figured they must have known what was going on. But he still felt like they weren't the "mastermind" behind it. There were still far too many suspects. And he didn't personally know any of the policemen in Vancouver, Washington and had no beef with them. To his knowledge, the police here were the real police. Beatings and shootings by cops here were unheard of. He held respect for them here in Vancouver.

Drew continued to live his life despite it all. He was scrolling through the internet when he found more blogs about Drew Truman. He thought to himself, "What a joke." It was supposed to be about some sort of knock-off from an older movie but he'd never seen nor heard of it. And when he read about it there was never enough detail to amount to much of anything. He still wanted to and was left with no choice but to assume they were talking about someone else. Yes, despite everything he'd seen, he refused to accept that it was himself they spoke of. After all, that would be highly illegal. He couldn't picture someone risking prison to spy on him, of all people, unless they were making millions exploiting him there. And if that were the case, then he expected that someone would have already come forward to rat the perp out. People were naturally snitches and gossipers so it just didn't add up.

All of this brought him to the semi-conclusion that this had all been someone's idea of an intervention. That he wasn't, after all, an infamously popular person but the intended victim of a long game of manipulation mostly through his home, his computer, and his recent vehicle. Perhaps someone intended to make Drew believe the world was watching his every move when they were not. People had their own lives to live. Drew knew he was doing nothing that would entertain anyone. At least he didn't think so. He now only needed to know who was doing it and why.

Often Drew regretted how he'd lived his past. And although it weighed on him a little, he'd always been able to drop it at his Maker's door for disposal. Everything in his life had happened for a reason. Even his mistakes were all part of a grander scheme.

That day, he reflected on a time in Everett, Washington where regret had made a swift attempt to smack him in the face. He remembered hanging out with Slicer and how he wasn't even smoking the dope that he was feeding Drew. He recalled seeing Slicer flick something from his fingers onto Drew. Drew did not indicate he'd noticed because he felt sorry for Slicer in a weird sort of way. He felt the need to allow Slicer to feel as though he'd gotten away with it. But following the flick of Slicer's hand, Drew began to itch as if something were crawling all over his body. He knew it was strange that someone would actually go through the trouble of even putting bugs in their hand to throw on someone else. But by the same token, someone had indeed gone through an awful lot of trouble already. When he left Slicer's place, he went to the hospital to let them know that someone had thrown either bugs or some sort of powder on him and that he was itching all over although he could control his need to scratch.

In the doctor's office, a nurse asked if he'd been using meth. Drew replied bluntly, "Yes." She began to inform him that meth crept out of the bloodstream and rose to the skin to make the user itch. Drew laughed at her because he knew better. On his way out the door, another nurse was leaving. As she held the door open for him he distinctly heard her mumble under her breath, "Let's go, bug boy."

CHAPTER

FRAYSER AND JASON

Drew remembered a time when he'd been walking down Old Benjestown Road in an area of Memphis he'd grown up in called Frayser. Frayser was full of redneck, good ole boys and had a reputation for breeding badasses such as Drew and a few of his old friends. Fist fighting was common amongst youth aged from 16 up to 60. They had an angry sort of way to deal with one another. On one summer night as the sun vanished behind the trees, Drew thought he was walking on a barren road that few cars drove down. Within seconds of the sun disappearing, darkness fell on the entire mile-long area engulfed in surrounding trees. As he walked along, he could barely see what was two feet in front of him. That's how dark it was. It was literally like what one would expect to see in a scary movie. At that point, he could see no visible cars within the mile or so long perimeter.

When he was halfway down the road he felt a freedom like he hadn't felt in some time. There was complete silence aside from a frog and a cricket. It was very peaceful. At that very moment in time, two bright headlights blasted him in the face. Maybe 10 feet away was an Impala that looked similar to a police car. Apparently, it had been sitting there waiting for him to get closer. A couple of seconds after the headlights appeared, the vehicle accelerated towards him in a way that screamed move or get hit. He ran out of the way and it nearly hit him. He saw another car pull up that also appeared to be an Impala. A large black woman emerged from one of the vehicles and said, "You da one who t-boned that truck. I know it was you." The lady was dressed in what appeared to be police or security guard clothes with blue pants and a white button down shirt with a badge. Nevertheless, he wasn't about to hang around and let them run him over so he made a blind dash into the Benjestown woods in an attempt to save his own life. He did not know what the lady was talking about. He hadn't had possession of nor owned any vehicles in years. He was a walker.

As he ran through the woods, it was dark he couldn't see in front of his face. Within the first 30 seconds, he ran face first into a tree and fell flat on his back. He got back up and continued a bit more carefully while still tripping over wild vines. The woods were also thick with the hungriest mosquitos on Earth, not to mention water moccasins, coyotes, and strong poison ivy. Right now none of that mattered. The object was to get away from the crazy security guard lady who was trying to murder him. When he finally got to his childhood friend Jason's house, he noticed the police were there.

He'd moved in with Jason months back after serving a prison stint at S.C.C.C. Jason owned his own tree service with the name left to him by his father. People respected him for a number of reasons that included but was not limited to burning down crack houses, beating up every jerk at a party at once, taking care of his sister's kids and his mother, and riding his motorcycle like a daredevil banshee. He was a well-known good ole boy and Drew's lifelong friend.

Drew continued to sit across the street and watch until the police left. He sipped on a small bottle of Jack Daniel's Whiskey he'd kept in his back pocket. He'd started drinking when Jason had paid everyone on his payroll right in front of Drew while assuming Drew would be okay with waiting. He made his way across the street where Jason began to inform him that the police were looking for him because of a hit and run where someone had t-boned a truck. Jason told him that someone had described him to a "T" with curly black hair, set back eyes, and a baseball cap worn backwards. Drew explained to Jason what had just occurred on Benjestown road and that he was guilty of nothing of the sort. Jason and Drew went for a ride that same evening when Jason suddenly pulled a huge knife and held it to Drew's guts. He wanted his friend Drew to come clean and not lie to him. When Drew told Jason simply that he had nothing to do with it and why would he lie to his buddy about something like that, Jason realized he was telling the truth and lowered the knife. Drew was glad they had an understanding but he was crushed inside that his childhood friend had held a knife to him as if Drew were something or someone fit to be played with. Inside, his hurt turned to anger. He felt disrespected. Drew wasn't scared of Jason. He cared about him. He thought it best to drop it. He laid down to bed but could not sleep. The bitter taste of both Jack Daniel's whiskey and this disrespect kept him awake and wallowing in dreadful anger. Drew wanted to get up and go out but he couldn't afford to because Jason hadn't paid him. Instead, Drew stole some money from Jason's cousin who was laying on the couch in the next room. Drew crawled on the floor like a drunken snake to steal the money. At the time, his emotional state made every excuse in the world as to why it was okay. Drew would soon realize how not okay it was.

Drew went out and, of course, used more drugs and alcohol before finally sobering up to the reality of what he'd done. It felt as if he were another person and he couldn't believe he'd stolen from his buddy's cousin. All of his prior anger had shifted now to himself. Before he knew what was happening and how to get out of it, Jason and his baby's mama found Drew. They took him out into a house in the Memphis woods while pretending that everything was okay. These were the very woods in which he'd escaped from the Impalas the night before. Jason beat the breaks off of Drew with an ax handle. His arm poured blood and meat from his tricep. After the beating, the two forced Drew into the back of a pickup truck at gunpoint where they drove Drew across the bridge into Arkansas. They entered a very large and secluded field where they told Drew to get out and face down on the ground. They were going to shoot Drew and asked him where he wanted it – in the back or in the head. Drew ignored the question because he knew his brother would never have a part in shooting anyone. He also knew that they were merely pretending to have a gun. They ultimately left Drew with the warning not to come back to Memphis. Drew barred none and once they were gone he made his way back up to the bridge and headed back into Memphis. Once on the bridge, the police showed up with an ambulance. Someone had called in about a badly beaten man and now the authorities were involved. An officer asked if Drew needed to make a phone call after he explained he'd fallen from a three-story roof. Drew accepted the policeman's cell phone and immediately called Jason to inform him that he'd fallen from a roof and that authorities were assisting him. He wanted to simply reiterate to Jason that he wasn't going anywhere but back into Memphis despite the ass whoppin' he'd endured. Drew wasn't a sissy and definitely not a quitter. He would take another ass whoppin' if need be but he would fear absolutely no man.

When Drew got into the ambulance, the paramedics explained to him that the smaller bone in his arm was broken and that he would need surgery. Apparently, the smaller broken bone in his arm was the reason that the muscle was protruding from the back of his arm. When he arrived at the regional medical center in Memphis, he was almost immediately sedated. Before he nodded off, the doctors told him they were waiting on a bone surgeon to arrive. When Drew was awakened at 3:30 am, a nurse advised him that he was okay after all and that nothing had been broken and he didn't need surgery.

"Am I in the Twilight Zone again?" he'd thought to himself. He was busted up pretty bad. He could hardly believe nothing was broken but it was true. Twenty home run licks to his arm from a fiberglass ax handle had merely broken the skin and pushed out muscle but not one fracture or break. Between assailants, Impalas, and his brother he'd nearly lost his life within a 24-hour period once again. Death seemed to chase him relentlessly but to no avail. Drew felt he deserved the beating. He couldn't stand himself at the time either. Drew would remember Jason forever as a brother.

However, back in the present, the only dangers he faced were those of the idiotic car driver who nearly pulled out in front of him while traveling at only 40 miles per hour. He and Missy couldn't believe that in one day and all within an hour, five people had nearly pulled out in front of him causing him to brake. He was still able to control his anger even after five near possible wrecks. He thought, "There's absolutely no way that I am going to die of high blood pressure after all the near-death situations I've already surpassed." Life hadn't brought him this far to die of a stroke, a heart attack, or a car wreck.

CHAPTER

FEELINGS

DREW DIDN'T WANT TO dwell on his youthful offenses but the regrets hurt the most. And although he'd once lived by a "no remorse no regret" attitude, he still felt portions of guilt and supposed he always would. He felt guilty for burning down his mother's house when he was five. He felt guilty for the things he'd learned as a child because of temptation and curiosity. He could relate to how Adam and Eve must have felt after having eaten the forbidden fruit. He understood none of it could ever change because it had already been done and seen. One could only acknowledge one's guilt, learn from it, and lay it to rest. Drew believed we were born to rise up and not to live in shame or disgust. Wrong turns were inevitable. And so was finding one's way out of a wrong turn. In fact, he couldn't think of a time when he'd taken a wrong turn while driving and not been able to find his way out of it and back on the right path to his original destination. Whenever does someone drive down a dead end road without ever turning back?

He also felt remorse when he remembered the times he had degraded himself with drugs or because of alcoholic intoxication. He felt sorry for ever having victimized anyone for his own selfish and personal gain. He felt sorry for what victims of his thievery had once felt because of him. He felt sorry for not having hugged his mother goodnight on the very nights his brothers' did complete with kisses. He was sorry he'd ever lied to his grandmother in order to get money for alcohol and or drugs. He was sorry she's had to endure his lies while restraining judgment because she loved him so. He felt sorry that he knew she knew he was lying and yet he persisted. He was sorry still to this day that he'd thought it was hilarious that his younger brother knocked his own tooth out while violently chasing him with a hammer all because Drew changed the TV channel from "Tom and Jerry" to the "Little Rascals".

Remembering was all Drew could do to analyze some of his situations. He lived life far too fast to focus his attention on the now. He merely collected information and stored it for analysis on a later date. Less distraction occurred in his abode. There he would put things together within his mind's eye, especially during times of rest.

He thought of how the city had been working on his driveway for months now. "What the hell were they doing?" he thought. On one hand, he didn't care. On the other, he found it odd that wherever he seemed to reside people were doing what appeared to be major construction and or upgrading. He had to be very careful of what he included in his mysterious equation because he knew some things were just part of ordinary life. Whereas five cars may have pulled out in front of him, two of them may actually have done it out of spite leaving the other three vehicles as accidental and part of everyday life. Not everything in his life was manipulated. Only a portion.

For some reason, the workers in the driveway reminded him of the guilt he felt for running off with a friend's car because his friend was smoking crack with his money. At the time, he'd felt justified but in his older age, he felt bad for Todd Micheal Watkins. He'd given Todd his money to hold so that he wouldn't smoke crack with it but Todd turned around and smoked crack with it himself. "What a world," he thought. He thought it would be nice to maybe one day find him and make amends.

He knew many a person he'd like to make amends with but he didn't yet have the resources to do so. There weren't many but the few there were seemed now to matter to Drew. Years afterward, his life had begun to slow down enough that he considered the people in his past that he'd somehow taken advantage of. Drew hadn't realized that one day he might actually care. He felt he must be finally headed in the right direction because he'd begun to think with his heart instead of his scarred mind.

A homeless person approached him as he got into his van. He decided that giving them the time they needed to possibly pull a con was out of the question. He would ignore them. Whereas, before he had given the homeless change or dollars, he now decided not to entertain that sort of giving. At any time, one of them might be in possession of illegal drugs and any policeman could stop Drew and accuse him of buying or selling drugs even though his heart had been in the right place. They wouldn't want to hear his side of the story considering Drew had a criminal record. Small situations could become big situations in the public eye especially when police arrived and amplified the least of problems. What they said seemed to stick as if they were the holies amongst a naïve population of simps. He wished the world weren't so gullible but it was. As it were, Drew didn't need police trouble nor did he need to meet an aggressive panhandler whom he might have to kill or fight off. For their own safety, Drew stayed away from beggars. He'd seen people in Memphis ask for money and then start going off because you had not given them enough of a percentage of the amount they saw you pull from your pocket. Those kinds of people had no room anywhere near Drew. Today, that sort of situation could anger Drew just enough for him to see red and blackout into a UFC fighter. Of course, it might also hurt his back a little in his older age.

Nearly two months after his DUI charge and one day before his next court appointment, Drew finally spoke with the woman who would be "representing" him as his attorney. Everything seemed fine until he showed up for court the following morning. His attorney was now advising him that he would have to do one more day in jail and that if he didn't plead guilty right now, the prosecutor was going to give him an additional charge of reckless driving. "Am I being coerced right now?" he thought to himself as she continued trying to convince him that signing the plea bargain was what he needed to do. He told her screw it and take it to trial several times while she convinced him that he was guilty anyway because the breathalyzer proved it. He finally accepted that he was doomed but not without giving her backlash by emailing, amongst others, the Bar Association and the Board of Professional Responsibility. Drew knew how to play the legal "screw you" game. He knew how to shoot back when necessary using nothing but communication. Paperwork, phone calls, and emails could assure others would always know that this attorney truly worked for the prosecution. Her agenda was a paycheck and status quo. Defending someone was absent from her needs.

When he came back to do his day in jail, he was put into the Clark County jail in Vancouver, Washington that boasted quite the evil area code of 98666. The dorm he was housed in was a nasty two-story dorm that smelled of urine, dirty socks, feces, and hopelessness. He could see that the young men inside were being held down by the system and didn't see much hope in life other than one day being released from the custody of a disgusting county government. The walls portrayed feces paintings and past unappreciated meals. The urinals were literally caked with urine residue a half-inch thick. It housed the least threatening people he'd ever seen and was more disgusting than a chicken dumpster behind any chicken shack in Memphis on the hottest and most humid of days in August. He let it be.

Drew was a fighter and what angered him more than someone trying to bully him was someone trying to bully someone else. He was also a lover and believed no one should ever be forced to live this way. He did not care if the whole world ousted him because of it. He for one would stand up for what he thought was right. This meant minimizing his own mistakes in order not to be recognized as a loud mouth hypocrite.

Lately, he'd taken his behavior into consideration and chosen to moderate it. With alcohol on its way to being nothing more than a figment of his past, he could most certainly move on with life and get answers to the questions crowding his mind. Questions like:

"Why is that lady across the street staring at me so intently as I sit in my own parking spot smoking a cigarette?"

"Why is the television addressing a topic that I was just considering?"

"Why does my vehicle seem to run better today than it was yesterday?"

"Why do I always feel unwanted attention?"

"Why are irritating people part of my life no matter where I go?"

"Why on earth did no one ever tell me that bed bugs weren't just a before bedtime jingle?"

Ever since that day at the Everett rescue mission when he had pneumonia and the bed bugs introduced themselves into his skin, he would hold a special place in his memory for them. As if being sick enough to hallucinate weren't enough, the bed bugs had dropped down on him from the wooden upper bunk. As they fell from their crevices, they sunk into his skin and he felt disgusting as if he were being raped. It was on a list of the most horrible moments of his life tucked away in a violet file, rarely to be opened. He'd felt extremely violated and was near death enough to hallucinate. He felt helpless and trampled, on the teetering verge of insanity, and so exhausted he couldn't even try to fight them off. At least 40 times throughout the night, during nightmares, they dropped and sank inside him as if somehow feeling his vulnerability. He'd once again come under attack and been incapable of defending himself. He felt helpless and violated, more so than he thought he ever had before.

Drew watched a show about women snapping on television as the show introduced an inmate named Monique. Ironically, Monique had been his housing jailer in Memphis, Tennessee at the Shelby County jail during Drew's stint in administrative segregation. She sometimes deprived the small pod of high profile inmates their two hours of recreation, phone, and shower time. She'd killed her police officer boyfriend and stuffed him in the trunk of his car. She even got her teenage son caught up in helping her to hide the body. But because she knew as much as she did about the corruption within her branch of the system, she only did two years of jail time. In this show, she cried about the banquet TV dinners she was being forced to eat three times per day. Drew could hardly believe he was seeing real justice right there on the television in front of him. It tasted good but he felt it wrong to feel pleasure from justice. He wished a caged life on no one. People should only be in a cage when they were violent. Not otherwise. It was an immoral practice found largely within the U.S. Monique should have by all means spent the rest of her life in prison had the system been truly just but it was not and she received only two years.

He laughed it off before turning the television off. And then he visited one of his favorite past times: cat napping while daydreaming. He daydreamed of times when he was a little boy lying in bed hoping Mom wouldn't get up and make him go to school as her 70s radio alarm went off. One of the songs that used to play ran through his head, "She Ran Calling Wildfire" and another "Nobody Gonna Slow me Down. I Gotta Keep on Movin'" followed by "Tell 'em That it's Human Nature". It was a good time for music back then.

Sometimes, he could remember good clean areas of his childhood but they were few and far in between. Growing up without a real father had taught Drew to think for himself; that to him was an upside of being a bastard's son. Although it would have helped to have a leader in a father when he was growing up, he appreciated being able to think for himself and not having to rely on someone else to tell him how to think.

Drew often did everything in his power to assure himself that he was thinking logically. It didn't matter what he felt true about because there were always people who disagreed on the most obvious truths; it might be his mother today and a stranger tomorrow. In any case, he was often left to question himself. He was beginning to learn that this was his life and that no one on Earth should be able to change what he believed in as an individual human being. No one should ever be allowed to change what the mind of a moral man perceived. Drew was very respectful of other people's beliefs and learned at an early age that it was often better to listen than to speak. It was often better to show concern as opposed to "constructive criticism". He began learning that his views on politics, religion, what makes people mean, and life, in general, didn't really matter to anyone but himself. He reckoned he'd felt that lonely feeling long enough to move on from it. It simply didn't matter what anyone else thought because people were always divided and people had their own views. You could say it was part of Drew's lifelong problem. Trying to get other people to at least pretend they understood where he was coming from had proven unfruitful and meeting people like himself seemed even further away.

As he shifted from daydreaming to sleep, his mind slipped to a time when he was a young teenager of 13-years-old. His friends always pressured him into doing something illegal with them like drinking whiskey, stealing cigarettes from the store, or even stealing cars. One day they'd convinced him it would be cool for him to steal a very small three-wheeler. All he knew was that the number 70 was written on the side. He didn't even know how to crank it much less drive it. Drew jumped up over the small hill behind the cycle shop where he saw not one employee or mechanic in sight. He stealthily grabbed hold of the small three-wheeler and dragged it back over the hill with him. When it was off of the lot and the coast was clear, his eight other friends all at once showed him what to do as they cranked it for him. Drew felt a freedom that he'd never felt before as he was in charge of a vessel for the first time ever. He rode like the wind down the sidewalks of highway 51 until he was able to cut into his rural playground behind Westside High School. Behind him, his ill-willed friends ran to keep up with him as they also wanted the turn they felt they deserved for their assistance in committing the crime. He jumped off quickly as he'd had his fill. He'd also not forgotten that sometime before this he'd accidentally run a bigger three-wheeler into a fence, crushing his leg in between the two. He didn't go to the hospital because he didn't want to get in trouble for it. At that age, he knew that pretty much anything he did to bring himself attention was trouble.

Children seemed better off seen and not heard, at least in Drew's case. The dream wasn't long at all. When it was over, he drifted to a different dream. Drew now dreamed in a sort of foggy haze in remembrance of the friends he'd gained and never maintained contact with after being released from the correctional centers. He felt within his heart that he'd met some genuine friends during his younger life of incarceration. Most of them were black men. Although his childhood was filled with a somewhat pro-white population, his later twenties on through into his 30s were mostly accompanied by a pro-black population. He'd felt at times that his black friends and acquaintances were truer to him than his white friends and family had been. Drew had once gone so far as talking with the accent of a southern black man as to better communicate with his black friends and brothers. He stopped doing this one day while incarcerated because he didn't feel he was being real. He admired and respected his black friends enough to keep it real with them and be his true self. He would just have to speak less country white boy and more plainly to assure he was understood by his friends. Drew often helped his friends with legal paperwork and letter writing so clear communication was a necessity. In his dream, the faces flashed by him with only brief cuts of casual conversations; real friends sharing life within the confines of immorality. Not even a dungeon meant for true animals could hold back the companionship and dignity of real men.

The dream left Drew feeling drained when he awoke. He felt somewhat sad but uncertain why. And then it hit him. He felt sad because he'd been so consumed by the mere thought of being released that once out the gate he'd in a sense left his friends behind. He couldn't even remember names enough to look them up. How could he have been such an insensitive jerk? He shook it off. He had to move on. "He didn't like the feeling so why entertain it?" he thought. Lessons were learned and the damage was done. He felt it unlikely he would never see any of these men again and there was really no sense in entertaining a regret over what was just part of life. People came and people went. Having the wisdom to move on was what was more important to Drew. Once again, he had to remind himself to put his feelings in his back pocket and sit on 'em. He'd learned this from his lock-up buddy "Big Ced". Cedric Jones was a friend. A friend whose name he hadn't thought of in years. A name he still hadn't yet recalled to this day.

While Drew acknowledged the lost friends, he didn't much entertain the dark side of being incarcerated. He'd once been attacked while lying in his bed after lights out by a group of Gangster Disciples who were merely playing with him and honestly meant no harm. Drew didn't understand and when they snatched him off his bunk he began sticking as many of them as he could with a rubber jail security writing pen. It wasn't sturdy enough to have hurt any one of them but it may have stung a little. It was enough to let them know he meant business. Suddenly, the playing stopped and the 40-man dorm grew silent. They set him down rather gently. Drew could tell that they were completely shocked by his reaction and that they truly meant him no harm. They actually liked him and like innocent children, assumed it was okay to play. Drew had hurt their feelings and he felt it. Immediately he felt sorry for how he'd reacted but he didn't feel it an appropriate time to apologize lest someone think he was a punk. The leader of the pack told the rest that they should whoop Drew but no one ever did. He lived amongst them in the same dorm for more than a year afterward before being transferred to another housing unit due to a drop in classification. He'd survived the "Thunderdome", as they called it, long enough before being written up as less of a security risk by the administration.

Darker times in prison included, but by far weren't limited to, random guys walking up and smashing him in the mouth to initiate fights, watching helplessly as 10 inmates or more beat another inmate or turnkey nearly to death, seeing inmates die as officers ignored their pleas for medical attention, and being fed half-raw chicken and rotten lunch meat when you were already starving because breakfast just didn't hit the spot. Drew had a little help for a time from his grandmother who sent him commissary money so that he wouldn't be hungry until her friend told her not to help him anymore. It wasn't even important that the guy made his jail time harder than it already was; he'd done his time and survived. Drew didn't doubt for a minute that the guy was merely living up to his name and somehow getting paid to assist his grandmother into making Drew a "more responsible person", but that was such a very long time ago. Drew had become a responsible human being, albeit he had no job. He'd become responsible enough to make dinner and maintain household chores. And although Missy loved him enough to live any way that Drew chose, Drew lived it responsibly by budgeting what little they brought in.

He knew that if he had a full-time job too that they would have more money but he had deep issues with people that he first had to deal with. He'd learned that he could only pretend to like someone for so long before he had to leave or let them know that he didn't like their behavior. Letting them know would create an assumption of threat and most likely wouldn't be tolerated on most work sites. He'd been verbally abused by most of his past employers for being a dunce at one time or another and had, over the years, grown intolerant to people who spoke to him with brutal authority. He wanted that kind of person to know that they held no power over him.

Months went by and Missy seemed to enjoy housekeeping in her hotel job. She loved her job which helped ease Drew's burden of guilt for not having worked in so long. Missy was fed up with the kind of friends in life that weren't really friends and thus stayed social only with fellow employees and Drew. With that in mind, it stood to reason that she avoided city buses at all costs. She had no license to drive and never had.

She relied solely on Drew to take her anywhere she wanted to go. And despite Drew's recent DUI, he'd applied for an ignition interlock device and had permission to drive despite the fact his license was temporarily suspended. As long as he blew cleanly into the device, he could start his vehicle and go anywhere he or Missy wanted to go.

Drew was Missy's everything and she his. And although more money would be nice, he was thinking long-term. He wanted to find out what he was good at and he still wanted to know the answer to his questions. He didn't want the questions to interfere negatively with his life so he mostly put them to the side, in the company of a peripheral eye. While he tried not to focus too much on them he found himself drawn to them at times. He refused to allow anyone or anything to take over his mind and somehow sometimes that's how it seemed. It seemed sometimes he was in shock from storing so much information on a mystery that he couldn't even remember what all the fuss was about. It felt as though it was an overload that would short circuit at the thought.

Drew wondered and thought a lot about what to do about he and Missy's future retirement. He knew at times he could be a bit slow but he also knew without a doubt that he would come up with and implement a solid solution eventually. Drew was never in a hurry. He knew he had no control over what life brought him day by day. As many times as it seemed he'd actually escaped death in his lifetime by what most would consider being dumb luck, he couldn't help but understand that something much, much larger than himself was in control of his life. Time had nothing to do with it. Nor did money. In Drew's eyes, being in a hurry to chase money wasn't worth losing one's peace of mind. Running around like a chicken with its head cut off in a rat race wasn't his idea of truly living life. It seemed more like the path of the power hungry than anything else. He surely wasn't fond of the power hungry and the manipulative. The very thought of living that way day to day as a way of life was repelling to him. Drew wanted to make a living doing something he enjoyed doing. The only power Drew ever longed for was the power of freedom. The freedom to remain unattained and fearless. The freedom to live out his own life the way in whichever way he chose. The freedom not to have to defend his views on life. The freedom to learn about life without the opinions of hypocrites or their rule. The freedom to be Drew.

Drew knew that some of these freedoms could be bought with enough money but with money also came more problems. Problems would always be part of life. Drew saw it as inevitable. When he grew weary of thinking about what to do for money, his mind shifted to a time when he had absolutely nothing and had still found peace eating from a garbage can and nearly being dumped into a garbage truck while sleeping in a dumpster.

Somehow, it had always worked out for him. When things did work out for him he often still felt as though he didn't deserve it. Therefore, he would always be thankful. Drew was thankful that there were real policemen out there who protected the handicapped and the elderly. Policemen who protected the weak or those who needed help. He was thankful that we the people had a system known as the constitution that often superseded state and local laws that were unjust. He was thankful to be in the presence of compassionate people. People, who showed within their very body language, a respect, and consideration for their fellow man. Drew was thankful for the old black lady had taken him into her house to help him in Memphis, Tennessee. Drew was thankful that he understood something greater than himself was and always would be in complete control of everything. And that no matter how hard we treaded water we would never get where we wanted to be unless we recognized that our arrogance in believing that we were fully in charge of our own lives was lifted. The truth was none of us knew what day and time that plane engine might or might not drop from the sky turning us into paint. None of us was expecting that home invasion where our wives were raped in front of us just before we were murdered. Not one of us was truly in charge of our own lives.

Drew had a horrible earache and couldn't think because his ear hurt so much. He had free government insurance and decided what better time to use it than in the emergency room. It was almost unbearable and he needed relief. He was a bit skeptical of doctors and hospitals because they'd often kept him in pain for long hours before helping him if they even helped him at all. Today a physician's assistant and his three assistants all worked together on torturing Drew by taking a water syringe to his ear in order to "clean the wax from his ear to obtain a better view within the canal". For six hours he endured the uncomfortable stay. For a shorter period in between, the staff continued to take turns gouging in his ear and blowing water at high pressure. By the end, he was screaming because it hurt so badly. An entire side of his head felt like a giant slab of concrete attached to his face. They finally gave up and told Drew to go to the local grocer and buy some spray to soften the wax in his ear. When he had to ask for pain relief they simply told him to go buy some Motrin. Drew left the hospital disgusted and in pain. In fact, he was now in more pain than he had before he'd gone in. It reminded him of the pistol whipping he'd once gotten for trying, in a drunken and blacked out state, to kick a south Memphis drug dealer's motel room door open. The dealer knew Drew all too well and forgave Drew the next morning because it had been totally out of Drew's character.

Drew could have just bought some whiskey to relieve his pain but he had no further interest in the "alcoholic" state of mind that once took his freedom. Marijuana would have to do. Marijuana was something Drew often used instead of the pain and anxiety medications that were rarely prescribed to him. Besides, what the doctors prescribed was physically addicting, whereas marijuana was not. Although it didn't completely get rid of the pain it did help with the anxiety associated with pain. At least he would not be left to go crazy, no thanks to the physician and his assistants.

Drew smoked from a water bong to intake the pot more easily. He breathed far better than the average person who'd smoked for 36 years of their life. Drew began smoking pot when he was nine years old. He'd walked in and seen his stepfather smoking with his younger brothers. But before he could get back out the door, his stepfather forced him to take a hit. Drew cried and tried not to have to but he was helpless. He took the puff that he was ordered to take. Despite the fact that he'd broken a promise to his gramma that he would never smoke, he smoked because he'd been afraid. And for five years after the incident, Drew stole his stepdad's pot. One could only imagine how he felt about his stepson by the age of 16. Drew stayed grounded most of the time because of it and thus frequently ran away from home.

Smoking posed no problems for him as he was moderate. He listened to the bong as he pulled smoke from it. It sounded somewhat like a snorkel, he thought. Cute yet disgusting to the anti-marijuana advocates of today's and yesterday's societies. His earache issue began to subside. As the relief came, he shifted once again to a daydream of past experiences. He thought it funny remembering his grandmother telling him to go out in the yard and find her a switch to swat him with. He'd been a smart little toddler and brought her the smallest twig he could find. Of course, she had immediately let him know that it wasn't big enough. She took him by his wrist outside to get a switch appropriate for any wise old grandmother to get her point across. As soon as she'd loosed his wrist, Drew had taken off running around the yard before she finally caught up to him, hurting his feelings more than his behind.

In the same pattern of thought, he remembered doing the stupidest toddler things like putting toilet paper into the bathtub before pouring shampoo all over it. He remembered hiding in his mother's closet to jump out and scare her but not being able to because she'd begun to undress. He remembered feeling the sudden change of complete innocence when it turned into a what-have-I-gotten-myself-into frame of mind. He also thought about when he'd stolen a pinch of Redman chewing tobacco only to find out it was as disgusting as the swallow of vodka he'd stolen days prior. He'd been a mischievous little boy but never once intended any harm to anyone. Curiosity and lack of guidance turned the mischievous little boy into a criminal yet without a complete criminal state of mind. And while he no longer even entertained the thought of ever taking anything from anyone he still felt a layer of remorse for having ever stolen anything from anyone. He also knew that although he'd changed, the eyes of society would forever refer to him as a criminal. At least, that was what was written within the system.

Some people didn't like the fact that Drew rested no judgment on a man or woman because of their color. Some of those that he'd grown up with didn't particularly like the "colored folk" but Drew didn't care. When people talked against blacks or Mexicans to him, he merely heard them out before finding a way to change the subject. He felt there was nothing he could do to change their beliefs once racism was embedded within them. All he could do was avoid conversation with them so that he wouldn't be at fault for escalating a situation by debunking an angry redneck's racial views. Drew wished his redneck friends and his racially divided black friends could all come together and forgive one another for the sake of humanity but in his heart, he knew it wasn't possible for many. And for them, his heart ached.

He did have a love for people but a lack of trust in most. His better judgment had always told him ahead of time what kind of people he was dealing with but he'd always found a reason to ignore it. In these times, he was more than alert and aware of people's underhanded intent. He could read it about them in every twitch of the face and every movement of the body during the conversation. These days it didn't take long to see where someone was going with their communication or even the lack thereof. He felt a sharp sense of know when was intended to be a victim. He knew that nipping it in the bud before it could grow was the best way to handle this type of person. Cutting them off as soon as something lead to them imposing a burden on you when you hadn't even known them that long created a peace. Entertaining the pressure of what people were trying to sell you was an invitation to more issues. Cutting communications was much smoother than being tricked or pressured into something you didn't want and later tried to find a way out. Drew felt this true whether in reference to friends or business. It seemed he was rarely able to offer people help because everyone he'd met would be asking for help shortly into a "friendship". He couldn't entertain the thought of enjoying helping someone in need because everyone he came across either begged or tried playing games in order to capitalize. As Drew often thought to himself, "You got the right game but the wrong man." Drew wasn't the one going for the okey-dokey anymore. He recognized a vulture in disguise when he saw one and lately, in his more mature years, it seemed they were around every corner of life.

After having completed his DUI jail time, Drew now had to work free of charge for the county of Clark in Vancouver, Washington. He had a grand total of eight days work to do. Drew was thoroughly overjoyed with the idea of working for free again. Nothing made him happier than to push a wheelbarrow full of wet tree bark and sawdust up four blocks of mole torn and muddy grass hills over and over again all day long until his muscles busted from his shirt like the incredible hulk. In truth, he hated the very idea of slavery.

The idea of being forced to work for the profit of another repulsed him so much that he nearly hated the men in charge of him. But when he met them face to face he couldn't hate them because he knew that they too were slaves to a job some of them didn't want. It seemed Drew was completely incapable of hating anyone as an individual but that didn't mean he didn't have a temper. He felt anger for the justice system and how negligent it was in concerning itself with people's lives. He saw that justice was green, not white or black as it once was. The system had gone from racial discrimination to financial discrimination. No one else it seemed would back up his beliefs as an individual. No one he knew would agree with him and to him, it didn't matter. To Drew, right was right and just because the whole world was throwing stones on national stone throwing day didn't mean that Drew didn't have his own prerogative. He understood morality, whereas the system was incapable. The system was corrupt. He would do what was necessary to get them off of his back with every intention of never dealing with them again as a defendant. Staying away from the wrong people, he felt, was key.

Lately, ants had shown up in Drew and Missy's apartment. Mold had begun to grow on their ceiling. The apartment was kept very clean. No food was left lying around and it was often bleached clean but the tiniest of ants began traveling the kitchen sink and bathroom sink. Five at a time were killed within a full day so they weren't much of a problem but Drew couldn't help but wonder if they had been somehow planted to get a reaction from him. The mold appeared mostly after the shower had been run in the bathroom. And though Drew wiped it off with bleach, it always seemed to come back. He was sure the mold wasn't meant to purposely inconvenience him. He didn't think he'd ever even met anyone hateful enough to purposely try and effect his and Missy's health either by the negligence of not reporting it to him before rental or inducing it otherwise.

Together they saved enough money to buy themselves a small $100 flat screen television set. They brought in the television set and replaced the huge dinosaur of a cube TV with the smaller more practical version. In the process, Drew was able to push the 350 lb. monster into the other room they rarely used. Drew never liked it anyway. He felt that at one point someone had taken it apart and put some sort of video streaming or listening device in it. Why else would it be tampered with in the back when he'd gotten it brand new? It was clearly busted up in the back as if it had been taken apart. And Drew didn't like the constant interference he encountered while watching it. The gigantic TV was a headache best left behind.

The two enjoyed their television set for a little while before Drew stood for a stretch and a breath of fresh air. He went to the door thanking God for the little things in life like a working television set. He opened the door to find a freshly folded sheet of paper taped to it. The paper informed him that his rent was going up $225 after next month's payment. He didn't get angry. He didn't even complain. He simply sat back down to decide what to do next. He decided it was wrong to jack someone's rent up by such a high percentage all at once. Where his rent had once been $825 per month, it had now jumped to $1,050. He felt he at least deserved the lubed version of highway robbery.

You could maybe raise the rent by $100 at a time but not all at once like a slap in the face. He planned to move out but was almost certain it would show to be difficult if someone were trying to break him and or play games with his and Missy's lives. The same people who told the police that he'd just crossed the bridge into Portland at one time could call every apartment complex he tried to rent and slander him by showing them old mugshots and presenting some scary story. He thumbed at the idea of buying an RV complete with all the necessities of living. He could get a used one delivered for five to 10 thousand dollars. He and Missy were good at saving money and could nearly afford it. Besides that, the lot income for parking it would be much, much cheaper than paying unreasonable rent to a kisser. It seemed most of their money went to basic survival and rent.

Drew felt that the rent hike was personal. He didn't want to think that way but it appeared that way in his mind's eye. It almost felt as though someone didn't like the fact that he'd gotten a new television set and decided to plot with their possibly existing coconspirator to raise the rent. He thought perhaps he would present this to a lawyer. He really needed a good lawyer and from another state excluding Washington and Oregon.

They already weren't to be trusted by the dozens. Trusting local attorneys for a local complaint could backfire as obviously the business or person you sued also had an attorney who probably socialized with your attorney. This kinda made them friends. An attorney who didn't know the local defendant's attorney was far more likely to get something done. Drew had a lot of experience in watching how attorneys worked from his years of incarceration. They too were human and capable of deceit. He did not want to be screwed by the person he hired to screw someone back for the screwing they gave Drew to begin with. That might set him off and Drew always did everything in his power to keep from being set off. Drew was simply tired of people screwing him around. The hospital workers, the apartment rental management, and his DUI attorney had all done something to make his life harder despite the fact that he counted on all of them to make it easier for him. It was no wonder that Drew didn't feel comfortable around people. So far most of the people he'd met he could have done without.

And while this all felt personal to Drew, he knew that holding personal feelings against something that was currently beyond his control could only make it worse. He would again opt out for the positive point of view and run with it. The positive side of Drew was that whether he was eaten alive by pit bulls or burned alive with gasoline, problems would eventually all come to pass. Drew was willing to experience anything at this point in his life. A countdown to a bullet in the brain wouldn't cause him to miss a heartbeat. Spending the rest of his life in prison for protecting a friend or loved one would always be amongst the many possibilities of death before graduating from this beautiful earth of unholy people.

Drew and Missy continued to live with a positive and somewhat humorous attitude on life. When they encountered strange things they merely laughed them off as someone's misguided attempts at playing games. As the days passed, odd things occurred on a regular basis. It was only when it came to playing with their livelihood that Drew got upset. Aside from that the childish games meant to agitate Drew, the rest meant nothing to him. He was currently working on his road rage. He was now used to people playing games with their automobiles. He could deal with those games. He couldn't deal with people trying to take his or Missy's money.

And so, Drew began to search for a recreational vehicle. As long as it had a shower, a toilet, a kitchen, and somewhere for them to lay their head they would both be thankful. Living in something that actually belonged to them would be a freedom neither had experienced. There were thousands and thousands of RVs to choose from and choosing the right one was the only issue. Time would tell. He'd once tried to buy a Camaro in Vancouver and someone had intervened. The guy that he was set to buy it from flaked out really bad and said he couldn't be there to sell it because he'd cut his leg open at work. If that had been the case then the guy most certainly would have maintained contact had he really wanted to sell the car as advertised. He'd also tried to sell his van once and the guy actually took the for sale sign out and said he would be back with the money. The guy had every intention of coming back. Drew knew these things. Only he never came back which Drew thought perhaps to be another intervention in his livelihood but at the time he'd chosen to let it go and live his life. Focusing on revenge wasn't living. Especially when you didn't know who you were trying to get back at.

Drew sat down to the news with a fresh cup of Columbian coffee. He savored the rich aroma. He rolled himself a cigarette and listened as reporters talked about the usual: officers of the law not being charged with the murders they'd committed, men who "identified as women" protested that they wanted access to the women's bathrooms, and President Trump claiming the president before him had spied on him. It was all a load of crap to Drew. He turned it back off as he enjoyed his coffee. He thought that there must be more to life than all the strife presented by the media. He sat in silence as he wondered why people couldn't all just get along. Why did black and white people have to hate one another? What was wrong with the world? Where could he find peace of mind?

Drew went outside to smoke his freshly rolled cigarette when an odd feeling struck him. Suddenly, he felt again as if he were being watched. He glanced to his left on this foggier than average day in Vancouver, Washington when he saw what appeared to be two legs standing under the layer of fog.

The legs he saw were of someone standing with feet spread apart within the thick fog as if they were holding some sort of object on top of their shoulders like a bazooka or a large video camera. It was his neighbor's yard so he dared not investigate lest he was charged with trespassing or attempted burglary. He knew how mean people could be and how discriminative the law was. He'd been charged with both in his younger years and knew all too well that if he were ever charged with such that it would stick. For now, all he could do was simply wonder what they were doing hiding in the fog and who they were. And that's all he did. Wonder. When he was done smoking, he went back into his apartment. He prepared baby back ribs for his and Missy's dinner. Since he had no job he made sure he pulled his weight by cooking gourmet meals for the both of them every chance he got. Drew and Missy had an understanding together and got along well. He catered to her every need. And she his.

As always, when Drew cooked he remembered things from the past. He often drifted off in the memories while he waited for the water to boil or the grease to heat up. Now he drifted off to an evening long ago when he'd abused LSD. He remembered that the one thing that stuck out most to him was seeing true colors that he'd never seen before. Drew was color blind but acid allowed him to see color far more fully than he had before taking it. He never saw anything that might be a hallucination while under the influence of such a drug. It seemed to merely enhance his ability to think. And it kept an odd smile on his face. He'd known that too much of anything wasn't ever good and eventually discontinued use of it. The first time he'd ever used it, he and Jason were shot at by a man who called his El Camino a truck.

LSD, JILL AND MORE PEOPLE

HE REMEMBERED COOKING HOTDOGS on broil in the oven the way his stepfather liked them cooked. He remembered watching closely with the oven light on as portions of the outer layer of the hotdogs began to explode as the heat cooked them. This was something that normally he wouldn't notice but now it was the focus of his attention. LSD was quite the experience yet one to be left alone and only remembered. Besides, if drugs and alcohol could offend his neighbors in any way then he felt it best left alone. Life truly wasn't so bad that there was any need for escape anymore. Drew felt good about life. Yes, despite the fact he'd narrowly escaped death on far more than one occasion, been traumatized, and been toyed with by unknown assailants for years, he felt optimistic of things to come. He didn't care if his cup were half full or half empty, just so long as there was a drink within the cup. Preferably a non-alcoholic drink. He looked back on his bar-hopping days and he realized he's been a complete alcoholic. He remembered Jill.

Drew had met Jill at a bar called the Beer Joint in good ole' Memphis, Tennessee. He sat at the bar for some time before Jill approached him. When she did approach, she spoke to him in a very suggestive way that made him feel wanted. She did this off and on while she played pool with another man. At last call, Drew decided in his super drunken state to ask her if she wanted to come back to his place. He mentioned he had pot at home and she was there. She was a beautiful, blond-haired, blue-eyed woman. He honestly couldn't believe at the time that he'd gotten such a beautiful young woman to walk with him for four miles in the rain at three o'clock in the morning.

When they finally got to his room at a house he rented on Garland Street in midtown Memphis, they smoked pot and did what one would expect of two very young adults. They were intimate strangers. Two people still searching life. Over the following morning, they ventured on the bus to Jill's house where Drew would stay over for a couple of nights. The first night they drank and smoked before enjoying the newness of one another's company. It felt good to Drew. It appeared to feel good to Jill as well. Exhausted, Drew went to sleep with Jill in her bed. A couple of cats wandered around the domains of her half of a duplexed house. When Drew woke up, Jill was walking around the house butt naked. She seemed to enjoy listening to Drew's tape player, which included one chaotic heavy metal tape. But it was three o'clock in the morning. Why wasn't she in bed sleeping with him? He sat up a bit to look at her. When she noticed she had his attention, she quickly came to him and explained to him that it was time to take his medication. She tried to give him Prozac from a bottle prescribed to her as well as Thorazine. He took them into his hand from her as he realized what he hadn't before – Jill was psychotic. He pretended to take the pills with water to keep the smile on her face, It was far too late at night to be walking home when he could enjoy the company of such a beautiful woman whether crazy or not. He went back to sleep and assumed she would continue to entertain herself long enough for him to get some sleep. After a few nights of hanging with Jill, Drew needed a break. So he went home and forgot about her for a few days. He came across some acid blotter days later and decided to pay Jill another visit. Acid had also worked as an aphrodisiac for Drew. He'd basically come over just to have sex again. After all, she was very beautiful at 26 years old with a thin feminine build and a beautiful smile.

Jill answered the door with an extended, "Hi Drew! Do you have some weed?" Drew said he did with a smile from ear to ear like a dumb ape. Once inside he noticed Jill was already naked and sitting in a chair. He began to rub her leg and she invited it. He was definitely in the mood for physical intimacy. The fact that she was too made it overwhelming. He was very ready to take her into the bedroom and have his way with her when all of the sudden a brick smashed through the living room window. "Come out Jill! Open the door!" the deep voice of another man shouted. "I know all about you and who you are Drew!" The voice continued. Drew turned quickly to Jill who simply said with a sigh, "That's my husband," as if he were a fly that just wouldn't go away. Drew hollered out to the man that he wasn't coming to the door because he was not going to be put into a position of seeing a jail cell tonight. Just as he finished his sentence, Jill grabbed him by the wrist and directed him into her bedroom with her hubby at the front door. She told Drew to have sex with her right now. Drew couldn't believe she was not worried about him being out there but he obliged anyway as she bent over with the side of her face touching the bed. He could see headlights leaving the driveway from her bedroom window, which put him at ease. Drew went home the following morning and got drunk while he reflected on what had happened the night before.

Drew re-visited Jill's house again weeks later when the neighbors informed him that she had run out into the street naked and fighting police before being taken away. He never tried to reach her again after that. His bar life continued for a short time after that. He met Tricia at a small Irish bar across from a lesbian bar on Madison Avenue called the Madison Flame. Drew actually moved in with the nurse's assistant after meeting her and having wild sex the same night. He didn't like the fact that her place smelled like all six cats that lived in her home. She wasn't the most sanitary person he'd ever met but he was willing to try and make it work. He worked with an electric company as a mere "plug" and even brought a van home at times. One day, Drew decided to clean Tricia's house up and even make it smell good. When his new brunette with big brown eyes showed up he was eager to please her with her newly cleaned home. He didn't have so much as a clue that she would be angry by what he'd done.

"Why did you clean my house? Oh, my things aren't where I put them now and it will be hard to find anything. I can't believe you did this!"

Drew could hardly believe his ears. She was complaining. He was speechless. She hadn't thanked him for cleaning up all of the Siamese cat poop everywhere on magazines and under couches and for cleaning up the layer of cat hair spread throughout the house. She merely complained. Drew got drunk. He couldn't win for losing. In those days, he was so fed up with life that he really looked hard for escape whether by drinking or any other means possible.

Weeks later when he'd found the $650 diamond ring in the bottom of an empty jewelry case he was rewiring for a large jewelry store he started to realize that Tricia wasn't who he wanted to see every day. When he found the ring he'd pocketed it. Looking back he couldn't believe a jewelry store could make such a mistake. He took the ring home and gave it to her. Days later she was acting like a cat in the water for what seemed like any reason. Then he asked her where the ring was. She screamed at him that she'd lost money when she was gambling and had pawned it for $160 to pay her debts. He'd had quite enough. The following morning while Tricia was at work, Drew called his brother to come to pick him up. And just as it had seemed to always be with Drew, Tricia came home early before Drew's brother arrived. Drew stood on the front porch with bags next to him completely caught off guard. She got out of the car with what appeared to be a true concern in her eyes. She seemed almost sad. She said, "Where are you going?" Drew said, "Out of here." She responded, "But why? I love you. I don't cook for people I don't love. I wouldn't be with you if I didn't love you." As Drew's brother pulled up, Drew told her that it wasn't going to work. The next thing to come out of her mouth would be the last thing he ever heard from her. "You're not gonna give me any money?" That last request was enough to cool down his guilt a little. The truth was that she had a gambling problem that he'd at first been totally unaware of. And that she had never really cared about him in the first place. It was only about the almighty dollar.

Another girl he'd met was during his crack smoking years was named Jamie and another extraordinary looking young woman. He lived in a huge drug house with her on Stonewall St. in Memphis. He thought back to an evening that he was invited to a private cocaine party in West Memphis Arkansas with Jamie and her nurse friend. The reason it stuck out in his mind was because during a good portion of this sorry excuse for a party, Drew just sat back and waited to get high while

Jamie's nurse friend continued to poke Jamie with a needle. She seemed to be missing the vein until Drew realized that by poking Jamie with the needle she was enjoying herself. The nurse girl was being sexually aroused by causing Jamie pain with the needle. That's what the whole thing was all about. Drew was the unwanted third wheel he assumed unless the nurse was waiting on Drew to initiate a sexual advance. He didn't know what to do but ride things out and see how it fell. After hours of needle poking the party was over. He'd split up with Jamie because she was too wild for him. He couldn't have held onto her if he wanted too. And cocaine brought its own problems.

Another younger woman he'd hooked up with in Memphis was Jessica. He'd met Jessica while in the back seat of a car on the way to a party. He had been drinking and was full of confidence. Not to mention the fact that he was a lady killer. The ladies loved his curly locks and big blue eyes. He'd started by rubbing his fingers against her outer thigh and while neither made eye contact they knew that the feeling was mutual. The guy on the opposite side of her had no idea what was about to transpire between the two. When the five people pulled up to the party, Jessica told three of them to go the door in front of them where the party was. She then turned to Drew to make eye contact for the first time and said, "And you are coming with me?" She lead him into another apartment where again he had meaningless sex. Later he found out that she was part of a racist skinhead group and that she wanted to recruit him. He ditched her quickly. He wasn't racist nor could he understand putting so much time and effort into being hateful to other people. He'd seen blood too many times and it was always red. Drew was familiar with what blood looked like.

He stood in his kitchen thinking about the choices he'd made during his lifetime and where they could have gone very wrong. He was thankful to have made it this far in life. It was only now in his over-the-hill years that he began to understand he had some sort of purpose in life. He believed what that purpose was would not be revealed to him until the time came. If it meant dying to save the life of another then he would accept. He somehow didn't feel it fair that he had been given so many chances at life where others appeared to have had none.

Drew continued to cook in his kitchen while he remembered times when he had no kitchen or anything of the sort. Again he felt thankfulness wash over him leaving goosebumps behind. Goosebumps because he lived in south Memphis for a time in an all-black neighborhood where he sometimes ate from a BBQ dumpster at night.

He'd met an old black woman there who had sometimes helped him out with food and shelter. Her name was Mariom Weador. She was a funny who he enjoyed drinking Colt 45 beer with out in the yard on hundred-degree days. He would make beer runs for her in exchange for beer and conversation. Weador was a humorous old lady and fun to kick the bobo with. She had a small speech impediment, which sometimes made it difficult for Drew to understand what she was saying, but in time he learned her language. She once asked him, "You ain't no fabay is ya?" Drew had to ask her what she was talking about several times before he understood that the word she was looking for was fagot. She wanted to know that he wasn't gay because she didn't too much fancy their gay outlook on life. Drew assured her he was not a homosexual.

He once sat out in Weador's yard with her drinking beer and having a merry old time when a very long old metal car pulled up to her neighbor's house. Three black men jumped out of the LTD monster of a rusty car carrying what appeared to be assault rifles. They leaped from the vehicle and ran into the neighbor's house and were back out within minutes. Weador assured Drew it was a drug robbery and that they personally had nothing to worry about. That very same day, Drew noticed what appeared to be a squirrel sitting in a tree. The questionable issue for Drew was that the squirrel had been in that very same spot and in the same position on other days past. He began to wonder at the time if the squirrel had long since been dead. He looked up as far as he could and focused. He noticed the squirrel seemed to be perfectly healthy and had its eyes open. He began to throw things at the frozen squirrel. He threw rocks, sticks and even a Colt 45 beer bottle. The squirrel never once moved. The neighborhood in question was a high drug trafficking area in south Memphis. Drew wondered whether it was actually some sort of surveillance camera. It was far too hot outside that day to concentrate too much on the squirrel that wouldn't move or fall from the tree. By day's end, he would be good and drunk and would have forgotten all about it.

Drew's brain jumped from south Memphis to north Memphis in a matter of seconds. He jumped from his 30s all the way down to when he was 12 years old and had broken into a gas station. It was a hot August night and he'd thrown a tire rim through the window of the garage at 2am and then taken off down the street on his bicycle as to see if there were any silent alarms. Once the coast was clear and no police arrived, he proceeded to climb in the garage window and steal wine coolers and Marlboros. He bicycled cases of Seagram's wine coolers and cartons of Marlboros and Newports all the way to his and his friends' hideout in the woods before sneaking back home to his parents' house by 3am. Drew did this three times over the course of a year. Each time he came back he saw that the windows had been boarded up. Only on his third and final visit did he climb through the window to find something waiting for him.

As he was climbing down on the other side, the then 13-year-old child turned to face a panting K9 who was as hot as he was. His tongue was hanging out and his focus was on the child burglar. Immediately the two became friends. "Hey, boy. Whatcha' doin'?" Drew said as he pet the large German Shepard. The dog seemed to be immediately in love and Drew loved the dog back. He nearly couldn't stand to leave the dog behind as he liked it so much.

Drew wondered if he'd remembered the past because he wanted to make amends to the people he'd wronged in his earlier years. He knew it would be impossible to make everyone happy and that he could never fix his past because, after all, it was the past. Drew had never assaulted anyone that hadn't first assaulted him. He did, however, have his issues with stealing things that didn't belong to him. He'd broken into a house next door to his parents at the age of 10. He'd stolen some jewelry and sold it to one of his older kid friends. He often stole because the other kids dared him, especially from stores. But now he'd come to realize what a complete jerk he'd been all those years ago. He wished he could just tell the world he was sorry and forget about his past but he knew while he himself was perfectly capable of forgiving those who had done him wrong, others might not see it the same way. It had been years since his first act as an inconsiderate jerk. People grew old and with age many became bitter. Many were just looking for someone else to blame their unhappy lives on. He could approach the wrong person to make amends and just become another statistic or the topic of an unwanted conversation. It could cause serious problems for what little family he had.

Drew decided that one day when and if he could afford it, he would try and make amends to some of the people he'd wronged. For now, the thoughts of his past behavior lingered more as reminders than guilt.

Drew left his thoughts for a moment to chop some onion into his spinach. He added a little Irish butter and garlic to taste. As he cut the onion, he remembered struggling to cut a piece of government-issued cheese from a huge block while his friend wasn't looking. Again, he had been stealing. When he was 14 years old, he'd run away from home so much that they finally just left him alone. Stealing a piece of cheese at his friend's house was a stressful task. His friend Tojo had gone outside to check the mail when Drew went for the cheese at lightning speed. He grabbed the knife that Tojo's papa used to constantly sharpen and raced to cut a piece because he was starving and they wouldn't give him anything to eat. He pushed down hard on the super sharp knife. Halfway through he sliced half of his finger off. Blood gushed and showered the cheese. He panicked and wrapped his finger with paper towels before rinsing the cheese off and quickly putting it back. He would never again steal cheese, to say the least. He remembered feeling like a guilty idiot.

No matter how many times he tried to analyze himself and his mischievous activities, Drew couldn't figure out why he had behaved the way he had. His behavior could be compared to Tom Sawyer.

Drew dumped the onions in the spinach. Then he pulled the ribs from the oven and smeared BBQ sauce all over them. He'd mixed Jack Daniel's BBQ sauce with a little brown sugar to make it scrumptious. As he put it back into the oven, he remembered having stolen some ribs to trade for crack at a Kroger grocery store in Memphis years ago. And before that he'd stolen a carton of Marlboros with his buddies Paul, Daniel, Kelly, Scott, Jamie, and Jason. It nearly made him feel guilty for cooking the ribs he had now. He thought that no one really deserved anything anyway. He remembered having seen someone post an article on social media that protested that looters and rioters should lose their food stamp benefits and or any government assistance. When he heard this, the first thing came to mind was how this would affect the children or family members of those convicted. He couldn't believe he was living in such a harsh world especially having grown up in the land of the free and home of the brave. Of course, his family insisted he focus more on flowers and puppy dogs than what was wrong with the world. He knew they were older than him and that he should respect their point of view whether they respected his or not. However, he was becoming more and more sure that they had experienced far fewer violence than he. They stood up for the justice system and policing despite the violent videos because they were, in fact, never on the other side of the law. They hadn't experienced and or witnessed the severity of the life he'd lived and had seen only what was presented to them. They'd surely never witnessed the discrimination and violence he'd witnessed firsthand when it came to justice and the impoverished. They wouldn't even compromise and meet him halfway on his views so he decided to spend less time on social media. Sure there were other people he didn't know out there who shared his views but he wasn't interested in meeting them. Meeting new people was nearly the last thing he wanted to do right now considering his current situation with unknown assailants.

Whoever had played games with him for years gone by had added to his life's trauma in such a way that really set Drew off. Yet on the other hand, he strongly believed that what didn't kill him would most definitely make him stronger. He never pitied himself or blamed his past for anything and he wasn't going to start now. He couldn't understand the nature of those who did feel sorry for themselves. And although he knew that those type of people were sick and struggling within themselves he still felt disgusted when a grown adult cried over something that couldn't be changed. In Drew's world, he demanded that we all be optimistic with an overall positive outlook on life. If he'd had it his way, we would all love our neighbors as ourselves. A hello and a smile. Consideration. Qualities that would make the world a much better place to live.

He stirred his spinach before preparing some corn muffins as he enjoyed the little yellow buttery guys especially with a crock pot full of beans and some hot sauce. He often prepared this dish for he and Missy. Drew's thoughts shifted and he again began trying to piece the puzzle together that lay scattered in his head, despite the fact that he'd tried to put it away in a file in the back of his mind.

Drew poured himself some milk to drink. He loved it and could drink it throughout the day with no problem. It never bothered his stomach and he assumed it kept him extra healthy. He'd once been in a $33-a-night motel in Everett, Washington where he'd tried watching a dirty movie. He remembered finding it strange that after one particular sex scene, the two girls held up a gallon of milk and said something to the effect of, "He drinks a lot of milk. He must be healthy." He had hardly expected to be taunted again in a cheap motel watching a dirty movie. He knew that he drank a considerable amount of milk and had done so for most of his life. He also knew if someone had been watching him and playing games with him, that individual or individuals would know he enjoyed more milk than most people. But to get that idea into a movie he was watching late at night in a cheap motel would have taken some doing. In the back of his mind, he had expected something strange to happen while he was there. It had already been happening in excess prior to visiting the motel. Odd wasn't the word for what he'd experienced in Everett, Washington. It deserved a word far more extreme than odd, strange or weird. It felt to him as if he were on one giant movie set and that everyone he met was part of a game directed precisely toward Drew. He never felt famous for one moment. He did, however, feel infamous like a villain who had secretly been introduced as a game piece on a board unbeknownst to him.

The truth was that pornography served more as a distraction than a turn on. The entire time believed someone was watching him watching the video. He hated the feeling of playing this game but was able to get the person or persons to once more respond in doing so whether it be by making noises around his door or TV interference. A response could leave a clue in some way whether it be purposely or unintentional. And he wanted a clue so badly that he was willing to pretend he didn't know that someone was playing games with him in order to catch them. He had humbled himself enough to pretend that he didn't know someone was watching him constantly. It took every ounce of courage he could muster to play the game over and over and over again. But he wanted to know he wasn't losing his mind. He was sure he was more in his right mind now than the person who'd spent so much time and money playing games with him. Drew was sure of himself.

The actions he took to draw out a response were usually out of his character. Buying drugs just to get an anticipated reaction seemed to serve no purpose. He truly believed he was being watched and that someone was trying to distract him but he couldn't catch them. There were noises here and there. People looked strangely at him. Passers buy pointed at him ... something was indeed happening.

He'd grown out of the need to gratify himself physically. That sickness in his life that had nearly haunted him for years was now dormant. Although it was a natural thing he'd clung to from a very early age, masturbation wasn't meant to be part of an excessive routine. It began sometime as a young child no doubt because he'd been molested. By the age of 12, he was ejaculating sometimes up to 10 times a day. Today he felt no want or need for it. He was over it.

One day years ago in Everett, Washington, Drew was marching down the road probably headed nowhere important and listening to his headphones when he realized his feet were hurting considerably. Drew had always walked on his toes but today was a little harder on his feet than usual. But because of the games played on him in the past and present, Drew felt suspicious. He was dressed in a white button down and tie with dress shoes to match that he'd long since purchased at Ross clothing store. He stopped where he was standing on the sidewalk and pulled off one shoe to inspect it closely. He noticed immediately that there was a very slight, thin layer of glue at the sole. He pulled the shoe apart to find a hole cut into the base where a thin and narrow, very rusty piece of iron lay hidden. A flat rusty bar of iron was hindering his walk. He found the same thing in his other shoe and threw them both to the sidewalk in hopes that the culprit was watching.

Another time, he'd put on his suit quickly because he was late for work. On his way out the door, he realized the suit smelled like feces. Possibly some sort of sulfuric liquid had been splashed throughout his wardrobe like the stink bombs you could once buy as a practical joke at any Spencer's in any mall. He sprayed himself down with cheap cologne and took his chances as he headed out the door. The first thing he heard when he walked into the call center was a co-worker named Jessica lifting her voice a little as he walked by to say, "Okay, who smells like ass?" Embarrassed, he left the office immediately and went back to his apartment. Jessica helped him to understand that not only had the smell not gone anywhere but that being late would be the least of his worries if he didn't fix the problem quickly. The joke was only on him for a minute. He went home to find all of his clothes stunk the same. To solve the problem, he washed his pants and his shirt in the bathtub thoroughly. They now smelled downy fresh. He rung them and shook them with stronger than average human strength before shaking them senseless. They were slightly damp but they would be dry in no time. When he walked back into the call center, he greeted Jessica with a smile as if to say, "It's all good now." Jessica seemed to appreciate he was now smelling nice, almost as if she had been in on it. He saw the admiration in her smile. His esteem was high. He was sure his lousy excuse for a roommate had something to do with it; he and his associates. The whole scene of people there seemed motley. Odd, if you will.

The women in Everett had peer-pressured him into using the amphetamine on a regular basis. He indulged, of course, of his own free will and enjoyed their company somewhat. He enjoyed the mystery about them and wouldn't dare make a pass at any of them, not only because he was a gentleman but he didn't want to destroy their mysterious relationships. Something about their demeanor intrigued him. It had always felt as if they were there at his disposal for sex and also as if they were placed there for him but sleeping with them may have open unwanted doors. He chose to keep enough distance from them to allow for observation. But every now and then the women would take him and for that he was weak. The only time he slept with any of the women of Everett was when they forced themselves onto him or made themselves fully available to him. They had to be extremely suggestive in order for Drew to have coitus with them. One of them had once gotten drunk and pulled him out of his chair and into her bedroom after bluntly telling him, "You are going to do it to me and you're not gonna tell anyone." Once she was on the bed, she passed out. Drew merely did his best to cover her up with blankets before going to sleep on the floor. The next morning as soon as she woke up she said, "OMG, what did we do last night? Oh, no, what happened?" She didn't remember if they'd done it or not so Drew took advantage with a joke. "You mean you don't remember what we had together last night? No, I'm just kidding." They laughed it off and she was relieved.

He was with Missy now and none of those chicks mattered anymore. Missy wasn't all about sex and neither was Drew. They shared many qualities that allowed them to live together without strife. They got along like champions. He made her laugh and gave her hugs and kisses. She confided in him and loved him back. She listened to his point of view on life and stories of what had happened to him in his bumpy and odd past. And she assured him he wasn't crazy. She had seen a lot of it for herself. When he first met Missy she had her own problems and, believing he had no problems of his own, he felt the selfless need to help Missy with hers. For years they both endured a journey that eventually resulted in bouncing up onto the right track. But that is another entirely different story.

LOVE OF MUSIC

DREW LEFT THE KITCHEN and headed to the room with the television. He turned the TV on. There was a movie starring a famous rapper. Drew loved music. The rapper seemed to feel the same way that Drew did concerning the government and abuse of authority. He loved the statements he had made in some of the rap he'd created and he respected his point of view. Drew respected men for who they were and not what they looked like. He looked up to the rapper and his views and loved the adrenaline rush he experienced from listening to the music. This adrenaline rush was conjured up through hard beats and or guitar riffs. He loved a wide variety of music and hundreds of artists. He could listen to rap one minute and country the next minute. It didn't stop there either. He liked all music and could switch at any given moment.

Drew decided to turn off the movie and go for a walk in the fresh air. He put his headphones into his ears and marched out without fear. He thought he had just charged his small iPod shuffle just the other day but as life would have it the dang thing was dead. On his way back home, someone hollered from their car window "yayee yayee!" It sounded like a trademark phrase that his favorite rapper used. He walked on home and tried not to make much of the coincidence as to remain humble. But how could he forget about what had happened while it was still happening? Was it coincidence after coincidence or something more? This was yet to be discovered.

He walked in the door and for some reason remembered a jerk in Tacoma whom he'd bought pot from all the time. The guy was, or at least pretended to be, a Nazi skinhead whose hair had grown out. The guy always told Drew stories about how dirty he had done other people. He boasted about how he and a friend knocked another fella out just to defecate on his head. This guy was sick and Drew could hardly stand his company so he basically got his pot and usually left as quickly as possible. The weed dealer seemed to sometimes make a funny sound with his throat. Drew presumed it must have something to do with the guy's heroin habit. Drew was talking about him to a girl who did not know the weed dealer. Drew had made fun of the guy's funny, throaty gasp of breath by mocking the sound from his own throat. He felt somewhat guilty immediately afterward because what if it happened to him? Unfortunately for Drew, the following day he himself began ever so slightly to make the same funny noise. It felt like some sort of weird bronchial issue and he wondered now if it had been some kind of contagious virus and not actually from the guy's heroin abuse. Whatever it was stayed with him for months. It got worse before it got better and then finally vanished. Drew took it as a lesson not to make fun of people whether they knew about it or not. However, he often did so in hopes of getting a response. As crazy as he knew it looked, the clown incident left him thinking that possibly people were listening to him and or watching him through his own television set. For a while, he talked bad aloud about everything from celebrities to newscasters so that maybe he could get an answer to what was going on with his life. No one ever came forward. There were no signs on social media of angry celebrities of angry family members whom he'd talked bad about in the apartment with the TV on. He didn't get it. He didn't enjoy having to think through the mind of paranoia because he wasn't a paranoid person. He was very on guard but not afraid.

Drew pulled the ribs out of the oven and put in the corn muffins before sitting down and turning the television back on. On the TV, people on motorcycles were going super-duper fast while jamming music played. Drew cranked up the volume and stole adrenaline from the hard sound of the song. He turned it back down and wondered if maybe he was a bit manic in nature. He didn't want to be manic but the music really excited him. He thought maybe he should quit the music and write to all his favorite hard music artists and tell 'em, "It's been a ball but that's all y'all. Thanks for years of physically motivating music but I have to calm down now." Drew had always felt that if he were put in a ring to fight someone and was able to wear headphones that he could beat dang near any man. Karate or not. Didn't matter. It was what was in the heart that won fights. He had started thinkin' it was time to start thinkin' about getting himself a gun. He was getting older and didn't have quite the wind that he used to. He knew all too well what it was like to be bullied around by someone with more power. The power to defend oneself was important to Drew.

The movie ended and Drew took the muffins out of the oven and sat them next to the ribs. He went to pick Missy up from work. He couldn't wait for her to try his BBQ ribs when she got home. He hoped she would like them. She was very picky when it came to meat. She was more into vegetables but still ate meat when there wasn't too much fat and it was cooked just right.

He blew into his new DUI interlock ignition device before he was able to crank his van. He drove down the road wanting to do 60 miles per hour but abiding by the law that said no more than 40. Even though it seemed the police avoided pulling him over he didn't want to entice them. He still didn't know for sure what had been going on or who it had been with enough money and power to play games with him. He didn't particularly want to anger the police for obvious reasons. Someone with enough time and money to play these games was most likely going to be tied in with them somewhere. He drove down the road a little way before noticing a woman driving with keys still stuck into her car door. He pulled up next to her and honked but she seemed to be ignoring him. She waved him away and sped off. He didn't know what to make of it. He assumed that she must have known the keys were in her car door and wanted to be left alone. He thought maybe she had endured some kind of argument or fight with her other half who had possibly stuck their own keys in to unlock the door. Apparently, the other person hadn't been quick enough and she'd driven off. He felt it was irrelevant and made himself stop thinking about it. He pulled into Missy's place of employment and scooped her up.

That night they both enjoyed the beautiful baby back ribs, spinach, French fries, and corn muffins. They then retired to bed for nine hours. They liked to play and giggle before falling asleep. The following morning, they woke up to hear policemen shouting through a loudspeaker for apartment number seven to come out with their hands up. Drew was in apartment number 11 and couldn't picture where number seven might be. Drew and Missy both watched from the window as men dressed in tactical clothes walked rapidly to and from the SWAT team armored vehicle. What Drew found odd was that he saw no one being arrested. Hours went by before the SWAT team finally left the apartment complex. When they left, Drew went out to see what all the hoo-ha was about and to maybe catch a glimpse of the apartment in question. When he got outside he realized there was no apartment seven. He chalked it up to just another weird thing that he couldn't explain by just observing.

He went back inside and began to make pancakes. He hadn't made any in quite some time. Some butter and syrup could make most pancakes a tasty delight. When he was done he brought Malory a plate and returned to the kitchen to make his own. He wondered to himself how healthy the sweet syrup actually was. He wasn't a health nut but he understood he needed to watch what he ate. He had to compensate with his diet somewhat to counteract the negative effects of smoking marijuana and tobacco. There had to be a discipline. Moderation with smoking and eating his vegetables seemed to balance him out physically. Veggies and milk seemed to add to his quality of life. He knew others who might disagree with him.

When Drew sat down with Missy he turned on the television. It seemed coincidence would visit him bright and early before even leaving the house. The story after the local weather boasted of maple syrup's healthy qualities. This was no big deal to Drew but Missy chuckled. She hadn't observed all the coincidence Drew had. In a sense, Drew had grown numb to the coincidental and ironic course of the life that he'd become accustomed to. While it didn't bother him as much anymore, it still lingered a bit uncomfortably in his mind. Pushing it aside never really made it go away. It merely sat in his mind's periphery, always on the shelf to his right.

After they ate, Drew took Missy to work. He rolled his eyes as he turned the key and the landline dial tone sounded from his speakers. He ignored it again as he cranked the van. Missy chuckled once again. He dropped her at the front door of the hotel she worked at. He gave her kisses and went on his way. On his way back, he noticed that, as usual, he was the only vehicle in his lane. He couldn't make sense of it. Often he was the only driver in his lane along a stretch of road called Mill Plain; the very same stretch of road that the policeman turned his headlights off then on while he and Missy discussed whether or not it was against the law to not be using headlights while the windshield wipers were on. The very same stretch of road that the brakes gave out on his vehicle when he was charged with the DUI. The same road that Drew found himself guilty of putting the lives of other people at risk. Don't drink and drive!

He also noticed no one was looking in his direction at all. He knew all too well that when people were trying too hard not to see you that they looked everywhere but at the subject such as in the case of the Mega Market grocery store that he'd one stolen cigarettes from. Before his arrest, he'd noticed none of the sack boys who'd gathered around the exit would look in his direction. No matter how hard he stared at them he couldn't get any of them to acknowledge him. Only then did he realize he was the target. While putting the cigarettes back on the shelf seemed like the smart and morally right thing to do, it still got him arrested. Little did he know that a security guard upstairs had been watching him the entire time via 12 different camera positions including his hands up close. Once he returned the cigs to the shelf, the security guard came down the steps from in front of the registers to make the arrest. She informed Drew as she cuffed him that concealing an item was against the law whether you put it back or not.

He thought perhaps he was reading too much into what he saw but his esteem assured him that it was okay. It was okay because having too much information was greater than nothing to sort through. And overall it was okay because deep down inside he kept the most positive attitude in the world. Not being afraid and not being concerned with what tomorrow would bring proved useful in humbling himself. He'd once read that tomorrow wasn't promised today and that tomorrow brought with it its own challenges and that we should focus solely on today. Drew believed it to be true and tried as best he could to live by it at as much as he could. Being human assured that there would still be times that he would be concerned about tomorrow anyway at some point in his life. Only now, he was learning better how to deal with his worries as opposed to letting them run away with him into some kind of drug and alcohol-induced oblivion. He'd learned to accept death and tragedy were inevitable parts of life here on the beautiful planet Earth. Manning up and swinging back at life's low blows now seemed far more reasonable than drinking or taking drugs.

Looking back upon his own character, he could see how much of a jerk he'd been for years. He could fully understand the problem he'd once posed his parents and couldn't imagine what it must have felt like to be responsible for him. He guessed that back then he didn't fully understand he was harming anyone. In his youth, he had thought it innocent and fun to play with fire. He didn't realize the reality of what might happen. At that age what "might" or "could" happen didn't frighten him enough to shew him from entertaining his own natural curiosity. He was simply a mischievous child who was too smart for his own good and bored with sitting still and being good. A therapist might tell him that what he'd done at five with fire may have stemmed from the fact that he'd been molested, psychologically abused and punished to extremes. Life had proved brutal and scary for him as a child. It was almost as if he'd been frightened so much that nothing could scare him anymore as an adult.

Looking back he still couldn't believe someone had gone completely out of the way to play with him by moving a train in front of him so many times in Tacoma when he needed to simply walk over the tracks. He couldn't believe that so many different episodes could be a coincidence. Not with a giant train. He still couldn't believe someone had gone so far out of the way to send hobos into the woods after him so many times. He could not believe any of this had happened. He couldn't believe the police did U-turns behind him so many times after appearing to run his tags. He couldn't believe there had been surveillance cameras in his home. Today he entertained nothing less than patience with regards to answers. When he got home, he sat in his van long enough to roll and smoke about four puffs of a marijuana cigarette to calm his anxieties. He put the rest out for later and went in to sit down in his room. He had to come up with his own way of making money. Again he entertained writing a book. This time he decided he would do it. He would write a book with the hopes of becoming a published author. It was true that he only had a sixth-grade education as far as the record went but he'd managed to pick up on reading and spelling rather well throughout the years especially during his incarceration. He couldn't stand seeing the justice system walk all over the people and spent many of his years in the law library writing about the law. He sued for himself and others who were treated unjustly. He never got any financial reward or otherwise credited to him directly but did manage to help others. He was able to educate some of the uneducated people in their own street with language enough to help them get started fighting for their own rights. He filed papers for another inmate once and had gotten him released. He'd always been willing to help other people to defend themselves. In his eyes, he saw the judicial system as bullying those uneducated about the law. Namely the poor.

Once he had decided to write his book, he wrote down his first words on a Google Docs account. He got bored rather quickly when it came to writing his first page. He began to reconsider writing a book because his first thought was that it wouldn't get him anywhere and that he would be a failure as an author. Besides, what did he know enough about to actually write a novel about? He wasn't an expert about anything.

Knowing full well that he was allowing negativity to invade his positive decision to write a book, he forced himself to move on and continue to write. He wrote until he'd completed the first three pages and felt inspired by what he'd written. After about 20 pages or so, Drew stopped writing. He had so many things weighing on his thought processes that he allowed himself to quit. He wasn't so sure anyone would buy his novel anyway. About three days after Drew quit writing, he began to notice that most movies he found on his free channel television set were about authors and their lives. Some were funny, some sad, and some dramatic. He wondered if this unknown "thing" that had been part of his life was trying to encourage him to write his story. Encouraging him to write about the many experiences in his life that the unknowns had caused through their manipulation. Although it had been very strange in Washington with people playing games, it had been much stranger with something else that they hadn't seen. It wasn't nearly as strange to him that he could say, write or look something up in his home and later hear or see something totally relevant in the outside world as it was that he thought of things and saw something about them after only thinking it in his mind. It happened quite often with him but seemed to serve no purpose. For example, he would sometimes have a song in his head. That very song would be on the radio when he turned it on. No one could have put the song on to play games with him because he hadn't so much as hummed it aloud. It was only in his mind and then on the radio at the same time. Sometimes it was a song rarely heard on the radio yet he'd turn on the radio and there it was. When lightning followed him down the street in Memphis, it hadn't been people playing games with him. When his frog gigging friends were run over where he also should have been, it wasn't a coincidence or a trick. When he'd climbed out of the van in Memphis that he'd wrapped around a telephone pole, it hadn't been someone playing games with him. He knew there was something more serious out there than all of the people in the world. An entity far more powerful than humans. One that laid down a path for each individual. A path that no one could escape because it was inevitable that people did what they did.

Drew felt that each step we took in life was a predestined one. It was what it was and if a change was destined to come, then it would come. The truth was that the past could not be changed. And the past wouldn't be so if it weren't meant to be.

He had a different outlook on life than most of the people he knew. And although he could get along great with nearly anyone, very few could carry on interesting enough conversation to keep him interested in talking. It seemed most people refused to take a look at the other side in Drew's eyes. It was lonely.

One day, on his way to pick up Missy, he noticed a lit sign in front of a Vancouver high school just down the road from his home. The sign read: "The Power of Story. Don't let someone else write your story." This hit a nerve within him that said maybe other people had been playing games with him and writing stories about it; the same people that had watched him use the bathroom and the same ones that watched him scratch his butt in what should have been the privacy of his own home. Was he in a reality TV show or was someone playing games to try and convince him that he was on a TV show in order to try and scare him straight into getting a job? Or were they just trying to get him never to use drugs again? Were they getting even with him for something he'd once stolen? And who were they? His suspects included but weren't limited to his family from down south, his ex-bosses, a film director or producer, police, and his biological father. Which one it was he couldn't point to for sure. For all he knew, it could be all of the above.

He'd grown weary from thinking about what had happened to him in Washington and reminded himself that he didn't want to think about it. So he pushed his thoughts in yet another direction of memory. He remembered back to the week he'd first lost his virginity to a woman. At 19 years old, he would hardly consider himself to have been an adult. Mating like a wild animal seemed to be a new world completely. Looking back he couldn't believe he was able to lie so well as to juggle women the way he did. Hiding relationships from other women really pulled him down and often into the drink. But he chose to live that way and faulted no one. The first girl asked him to walk her to her car. The next day, another girl's mother asked him out for her daughter who had a secret crush on him. The day after that, another girl invited him to Red Lobster for dinner and then back to her place. Two days later, another girl asked him to a party and another just started making out with him at the grocery store. He was overwhelmed and absolutely stupid with sex – drunk from it if you will. Thankfully, now, that flame was under control. He saw many a beautiful woman but didn't look at them in the same frame of mind that he used to. Filth was filth no matter how ya' looked at it. Sex was often not worth what he'd felt afterward. Guilty and dirty were not feelings he wanted to live with and sex with women just to be having sex felt guilty and dirty to him especially when it was pure lust. He still remembered that feeling: the desire for a shower and the need to forget.

Drew got his lady home and continued struggling to write his book, stopping at times for days to deal with what seemed to be a long-term trauma that had built up over the years. There was simply just too much on his mind. The strange things seemed to have mostly occurred in the state of Washington when he was using or pretending to use drugs. It seemed his aggressor watched him constantly but would only make stupid mistakes when they thought he was high or drunk. He had to figure out how to draw them out while he was sober. That old drug game had played out for him. Until he could figure out how to do what was necessary, he would merely live his life and try and write a book. At least he could get the honor of being a published author. For now, he felt watched by a quiet eye. And despite the fact that he was sure there was surveillance equipment somewhere in his apartment, he refused to tear his apartment up looking for it like some kind of "tweaker". He refused to use drugs anymore even though that was the only time he could get them to react anymore. There must be another way.

Interrogating people wasn't his style either. At least not yet. He could hire a private detective but was afraid that whoever it was would just buy out the detective. To his knowledge, everything he had access to was controlled: his phone, his computer, and even his television. After all, why would anyone go to the trouble of installing hidden camera sprinkler heads only to stop now? It was going to take something drastic to make them stop watching him. He could count on the F.B.I. but wasn't willing to go so far as to have them look into it. He wasn't fond of the government and his pride wouldn't allow him to request their help. He felt that if he did that then he would be no better than they were. He wanted to put it together on his own. He wanted to know who was so interested in him that they would violate his rights as a human being.

He squirted just more than a pea size amount of enamel protecting toothpaste onto his smashed toothbrush. When he began to brush he noticed an oddly shaped indention in his bathroom carpet. He bent closer for a better look. There he could see that it was a large dog's footprint. "Why me?" he thought to himself. To his knowledge, there had never been a dog in his apartment. He didn't smell a dog or see any dog hair, just a dog's footprint. The only dog in the area that could fit the print belonged to a woman downstairs. Amber had a large black dog that howled when she was gone. She seemed to be the sociable partying type, not the nosy type. He dismissed the dog paw print for now and finished brushing his teeth.

There was only one person that he knew for sure that would certainly know what had happened with the sprinkler heads – his landlord Mishelle. He knew without a doubt that she had at least something to do with it. He'd seen her face on the internet as having been busted by the F.B.I. for selling fake designer purses but wasn't sure how true it was. That underhanded type of crime told him she was capable of being sneaky and deceitful once again if there was an opportunity to capitalize. She seemed to be a nice person yet hungry for control. She wasn't the owner but the manager of the complex. While he couldn't see anyone getting a job like hers who had a prior felony, he always felt that anything was possible. When the time was right, he would find out exactly how she was involved. For now, she got by. But she didn't get away. He got back to writing his book, remembering having seen look-a-likes of his grandfather's wife, his uncle, and his brothers. He wrote about it but then closed the document because it was starting to bother him. He tried to fight it but the trauma seemed to have got the best of him.

He changed the channel just after the news began discussing how President Donald Trump had given the order to fire 59 Tomahawk missiles on a Syrian airbase. Instead, he landed on a program about a man named Luis Diaz who had been falsely accused by the police and several women of rape. The man had been sentenced to umpteen life sentences in prison because police had manipulated the women into thinking he was the culprit. Twenty-six years later, they discovered that the detective had blatantly lied just to be hateful. The man was released but so many years of his life had been stolen from him by the very state government he paid taxes to and trusted. It sickened Drew. How America could be the head stone throwers was completely beyond him.

His heart ached for the millions of people who had been falsely convicted in the world since the beginning of time. His heart also tried to hate those who had inspired the government to do as it pleased. He wanted to hate people in authority because they'd been responsible for taking so many innocent lives that they didn't deserve to judge. He fought the hate from entering his heart with all his might even though he'd watched repeatedly throughout the years as innocent people were set free without sometimes so much as an apology. Watching it on television helped him to understand why people shouldn't be so quick to pass judgment on one another. To Drew, it was far more serious a subject than the media gave credit. It was like an epidemic yet it was ignored. Brushed to the side, it wasn't important to anyone until it happened to them as an individual. It amazed him how little people cared about each other. And how quick they were to point a finger. It appalled him.

Drew deemed it impossible to change monsters into furry little bunnies so he lived with the idea that most of the world would only get worse. Governments would continue to have their way with anyone they chose and it was just part of life. The downside was inevitable. Throughout Drew's younger years he'd been beaten and falsely arrested by the police of Memphis, Tennessee. Most of the arrests were his own fault. The violent beatings were not. To this very day, the perma knot on his forehead reminded him of an altercation when he was 11 when an officer at the Memphis Juvenile Court hit Drew in the back of his head and slammed him headfirst into the metal stairwell. The officer had been angry with him because he'd been rocking in his chair too much.

To stay positive, Drew remembered the harsh situations he'd been in and as always it helped him to be thankful. He thought about the times he was homeless with no way to take a shower. His feet would begin to burn from the sweat and filth that lurked within every crevice of his toes. Sometimes it was so bad that it felt like acid mud squishing between his toes. It had stunk of urine, rendering it impossible to be around other people for fear of grossing them out with the smell. Being homeless was horrid at times. At other times, it was the freest feeling on Earth. He didn't have to answer to anyone or pay money to people that he didn't want to. He had been free. The price for freedom didn't include showers or baths though. And he didn't appreciate being nasty. The government and rich people these days owned most everything, including the water that people had a human right to. Because of that, people weren't allowed to bathe themselves without the money to own or rent their own property. The government didn't supply anyone with showers either. The only hope for those who chose to live outside the machine was to ask church missions to help them.

One thing he could never forget no matter how hard he tried, was the many times he'd tried for hours to sleep in the freezing or near freezing cold without layers or cover. It had been horrible. Shaking and shivering while too tired to do anything about it had made a lasting impression on him. He would be more careful if he were ever to live outside again. He had no intention of doing so but as a friend once said, "Never say never."

The thoughts that often crowded his mind made it harder for him to pay attention to the present. He'd once spoken with a therapist who told him that ultimately he was, in fact, suffering from trauma. The therapist, known only as Ms. Mang, had only one session with him before pissing him off enough to not come back. She'd first accused him of faking he thought people were watching him before she realized that he wasn't. She apologized before he left and told him she believed he was suffering from a lot of trauma stemming from his past. It made more sense to Drew than being diagnosed as having psychotic episodes with hallucinations. This was the diagnosis a psych doctor in Tacoma had presented him with. He fully understood how his story may have sounded to her but hallucinating? He didn't think so.

Drew went back to concentrating on his half attempt to write a book. After looking over the small portion that he'd already written, he could see how it could become a best seller yet he still allowed thoughts of editing and publishing to get in his way. He anticipated that it would take forever to get it written and then another forever to edit it himself before sending it to an actual editor. Editing was going to be a huge job. But if he could get his foot in the door of a publishing company with a nice advance, he would continue to write and be happy doing it. He could become, at last, a success.

Contributing to the rest of the world by doing something all on his own sounded appealing. Being his own boss was absolutely what he needed. He longed for it. He wrote short stories while he thought about his life and how he could relieve himself of something but wasn't sure what.

Drew grew tired and fell asleep writing his novel. A soft song somehow sneaked into his head and it soothed him. "I loved you. You didn't feel the same. Though we're apart, you're in my heart..." He glided into another dream. He dreamed vaguely about a woman he'd lived with as a child who he addressed as Big Mama. Her image was barely available in his dream, he only dreamed of the time he'd been introduced to her. He could see bushy sort of grey hair and glasses. He'd been so small that she had seemed like a giant to him. But then the music changed and went to another song. "She ran calling wildfire..." The venue changed as well as he dreamed now of lying in bed, waiting for his mother to get up and make him go to school. Softer more pleasant songs often followed him to sleep. It didn't matter how wild or mild the dreams were or if he remembered them, he always woke up with the remainder of a soft song in his head that counteracted any disturbing dreams.

His dreamed moved to a time he was riding bitch on the back seat of his buddy's souped-up R1 motorcycle. His friend Jason had popped a wheelie and was passing traffic on the interstate for a good few minutes at 100 mph. It was a good time when it happened and still a good time today in his dreams. He'd had a lot of good times with Jason and wished he were still alive despite their fallout.

He woke from the cluster of memories turned dreams and went to bed. Missy lay waiting for him. She didn't like going to bed without him. She felt secure with him. He was her other half. And she was his. He had someone to share his mysteries with that would at least try and see them from his point of view. She supported him in so many ways that she helped him to be secure with himself and the person that he was.

The following day after he took her to work, Drew had a talk with himself about thinking too much. He tried to convince himself it was best to leave everything involving his past alone.

And that included not only Washington but Tennessee as well. He really needed to move forward with his life. However, as usual, the thoughts would eventually come busting back into his mind. He thought it might drive him crazy to try not to think about any of it. What was he going to do? He felt too strong and too stubborn to allow it to ever get the best of him. But what if he became too old and didn't have the answers? It might be harder for him. He didn't want this thing lingering around his mind for the rest of his life. So he had no choice but to solve it. He chuckled to himself and thought, "Just not right now." It bothered him but he would maintain his sanity at least long enough to cross the finish line of mystery.

He walked into their apartment and made coffee right before plopping down on the bed to watch more news. He was a little warm so he turned on his box fan. When he did so the picture and signal clicked on his television. He couldn't understand how a fan plugged into an outlet opposite his television could affect his TV that sat clean across the room.

He also noticed that sometimes when he spoke out loud either to himself or to Missy that his digital analog TV signal would break up. He began speaking out loud on issues such as the news shortly after his arrival in Washington state. He wondered if any of it had to do with listening devices or cameras hidden in his apartment. He truly loathed the thought of having to stoop to think this way. He wished he could believe that since the sprinkler heads were gone that the unknown pest was gone too. The smarter part of his brain assured him that they were still there somewhere watching, listening and waiting. Waiting for what he didn't know but he could sense that there was some sort of secret wait. Maybe a wait for an ex-burglar to strike again. That most definitely wasn't going to happen. Perhaps what the people of Washington didn't understand was that despite his record of crime he'd outgrown the aspect of theft.

He'd matured enough to realize how wrong he'd been and the seriousness of the stealing he'd once done. Since he'd moved to Washington he'd learned a lot from looking back on his old self that he'd long since left in Tennessee. He'd become a different person. There had been far less pressure on him here than when he'd lived in Tennessee despite the sneaky, slithering watchers that made every attempt to drive him nuts. Hot Tennessee sun, extreme poverty, humidity, homelessness, and violence had all contributed to his past criminal behavior. In Washington, it was much cooler outside and far less stressful for Drew both physically and emotionally. Washington State had helped him get to his feet.

The south expected him to do it on his own. Understandable, he thought. After all, he wasn't entitled to assistance of any kind in this harsh world and he knew it but he was grateful to Washington. The police were far more humane here than they were in Memphis and people didn't assault one another around every corner. Washington had proved to be far less harsh than what Drew had experienced in the southern states. He'd gained a respect for Washington's local government. The only part he wasn't fond of was the congregations of gossipers and underhanded people, which, of course, included the privacy-invading spies.

He flipped through the television stations until he found something he liked. The problem this morning, as with many other mornings here in Washington, was that every time he tried to listen to what was being said either by actors or journalists on the news, the signal would break up long enough to cut out important words. The newsman might say something along the lines of, "Today's highs will be in the upper..." Where the heck did the important part go? He just knew it couldn't possibly be coincidence on one hand and yet, on the other, he simply could not be sure.

He was now enjoying a Kung Fu series on television. Everything seemed fine right up until Master was trying to explain something to Grasshopper in a parable. Then he heard, "Grasshopper, you must … before you can …" It had really gotten old and Drew had mostly humbled himself but it still ruined the moment. Drew tried adjusting the antenna but to absolutely no avail. If someone actually were responsible for this, then they deserved anything bad they had coming. He wondered to himself if they would ever be able to redeem themselves…

MORE HORRIBLE TV

WHEN THE TELEVISION BEGAN to act up again, Drew decided to connect to the internet and find out if the market sold devices that could purposely cause TV signals to break up. He found that indeed there were devices like this for sale. They even sold devices that could drop your cell phone calls for you which could possibly explain why his cell phone worked horribly at home and dropped many a call. He couldn't believe that people could be so evil as to even try and invent things like this. "Bastards," he thought.

He turned off his television so as to win the battle. They wouldn't make him angry this morning. By cutting himself off from his anger, he felt that he'd won. The only thing they'd accomplished was him turning off the television. They'd accomplished nothing more than that. In Drew's eyes, they were losing at their own game of manipulation. "Why would they even waste their time?" he mumbled to himself.

He looked back and could remember that every time he settled into a new area, his television and telephone worked just fine. It was usually a couple of days, give or take, before the signals began to disrupt on his phone or television. To him, this was just one more red flag that someone was intentionally trying to disrupt his personal life. Or was it just plain bad service all around? What if the national weather service had a warning? Would he be left uninformed because he couldn't afford cable or satellite TV? He considered dropping television altogether but he knew Missy enjoyed it. "What is wrong with people?" he asked aloud. "Why can't people just mind their own business?" He listened but there was no answer. He wasn't mad but disgusted and saddened by the idea that anyone would lower themselves to such a standard just to get a rise out of another human being. He was still no closer to knowing for sure who had been responsible for derailing him from his track of life. As much as he hated to admit it, the mysterious someone had helped him to become a stronger person than he'd been prior to his arrival in Washington State. What didn't kill Drew made him just that much stronger. Washington offered him a completely different kind of stress. It was by far more psychological than the physical stress he'd subjected himself to in Memphis. He'd become more responsible than he'd ever thought about becoming in Tennessee. In Memphis, Tennessee every dollar he made went on alcohol that made him forget how horrible he'd felt about being homeless and completely uncomfortable with heat and mosquitos. The drink helped him forget why he couldn't understand all of the violence he'd seen and endured throughout the year.

Now in his 40s and sober, he wasn't blinded anymore about who he was and what he had been. He still had a love of the south and he reckoned he always would. But the change in atmosphere and culture seemed to have done him some good. He'd somehow managed to restart his brain like you would any smartphone. Out of its normal element, his mind seemed to relax and open up allowing him to repair himself. Had he not learned how to control his anger Washington it may well have driven him mad. Drew had become much more of a humble person than he once was. For that he was thankful. However, he'd learned not to trust anyone. He realized that not trusting people was a good exercise when you were just getting by. So many times in his past he'd trusted his "friends" who often sent him out for their own entertainment. He'd been a follower of the wrong kind of people when he should have been leading. He'd fallen for the "okey-dokey" too many times in his life to allow it anymore. He despised people who talked him into helping them do stupid things such as stealing or invited him along as a scapegoat. People who wanted someone to take the fall with irked him. He'd dealt with it for so long that he recognized them very quickly and avoided them at all costs. "Where were the good people?" he thought.

He'd had to cut off his neighbors who once bothered him to no end about a ride. Frequent interruptions eventually grew tiresome though and Drew dropped the neighbor "friends" like a hot potato. He knew they were in on what he'd learned to endure and it had once raised his blood pressure. The people who once pretended that Drew was their personal taxi had all day to call Drew but chose only to do so when he was busy concentrating or entertaining himself. They never called when he was merely watching a television show or browsing the internet but only when he needed personal time for himself, which wasn't all that often. When he used drugs he noticed it set the watcher off. Yes. Strange things happened when he used drugs and alcohol but it wasn't a result of the actual drug use.

Strange things happened because some nosy ass son of a biscuit eater was all up in what was supposed to be Drew's private life.

He chose to stick to his guns when it came to handling his own business. Yelling "help" wasn't Drew Shaw's style and he wasn't about to start now. He was a true believer in things done in the dark being eventually and inevitably brought to the light. The phrase "in due time" crossed his mind.

Drew surfed the internet again while searching his own crowded brain for something to search for. Sometimes his mind was just a giant question mark because so many issues crowded his thoughts. He could only imagine how brilliant and productive he might be were he free of anxiety and puzzling thoughts. It disturbed him somewhat to think about what great things he was capable of if he could just put his mind to it.

As he surfed the web, he looked for more information on any newer info about his name. He searched for signs that someone somewhere, even if it weren't him, were being filmed without knowledge for the sake of a show. He found things, yet again, that pointed towards himself as being the character of a secret show. If there was indeed a modern-day secret show then certainly his life was fitting the criteria. Had he fallen victim to a kind of secret entertainment? Or had he angered the police somehow with his social media postings? Or maybe he'd angered someone whose beliefs in the system superseded morality?

Drew ran across partial blogs about a character who was, in fact, being filmed for an up and coming movie and possible series. The guy being secretly filmed had no idea about it. He also read that there had been others too who were caught up in this attempt to produce something of the same nature. He read that one of them figured it out because of the bad acting and had gone to the feds to have it stopped. He was also in the process of suing them. And while he could find this information he couldn't seem to find any names or pictures. When he connected this scenario to the film producer who seemed to have broken into his email account, he couldn't help but entertain the idea that it was, after all, what he thought. A movie or at least a filming of a portion of his life here in Washington. If it wasn't, then it was an attempt to make him think so at the very least.

Drew felt that this show was an attempt to slander him. He wondered what could be so interesting about him other than his slight dry sense of humor and his open-voiced outlook on life in general. Maybe someone liked his sarcasm. Or maybe they hated him so bad that they wanted him to feel stupid or humiliated. Somehow, he'd humiliated himself enough along with their help that humiliation no longer existed for him. It was an armor he wore proudly. He'd learned to shut off fear in Tennessee. And in Washington, he'd learned to shut off humiliation and embarrassment.

Nothing he did made the invisible bug reveal itself for who or what it was. He always got the answer that he was looking for in the form of loud and sometimes strange noises. He wanted to know sometimes more than anything if it was just a rich nobody playing with his life for their own sick satisfaction. Or even sicker would be his own family pretending that they had been doing it for his own good. He simply wanted to know who it was. He wanted it all to make sense to him so that his mind could rest. And no matter what happened, he always gave his family the benefit of the doubt.

Continuing to browse the internet made Drew feel tired. Not finding any answers didn't help. He pretty well knew that someone was controlling what he could see on his computer. But he still took to the challenge of attempting to get around them. He tried different search engines and sometimes got better results before his internet connection was interrupted.

It seemed to be a common thing to happen when he felt he was getting closer to answers. His computer never failed to fail him at this point. He decided to stop browsing and start writing. He opened his up and coming novel and tried to write again when he decided to nap. Colors began to fill his mind and once again his mind escaped into the past.

His mind was back in "Mempho" and his dream was in midtown. He'd called to meet up with Pooky the six-foot-nine-inch tall crack dealer. When Pooky asked him if he even remembered the night before, Drew honestly didn't because he'd been whiskey drunk and Superman.

Pooky and Cory "Black" who rode with Pooky, began to inform Drew that in his drunken state he had told them he wanted $20 worth of crack. When Pooky handed Drew the crack, he'd started to walk off without paying because he didn't have any money, to begin with. Pooky told him to give him his money or the crack back when Drew threw it on the concrete and stomped on it. Cory "Black" told Drew he needed to slow his role. Drew knew that meant if he tried something like that again he might get hurt. Drew couldn't believe he'd done what they were telling him as it was completely out of character. It was humiliating. They could have killed him but the humiliation was all he felt. He was thankful to have visited the crack scene while escaping with his life. He wanted nothing more than to never have anything else to do with it. Lesson learned.

His dream changed to another scene of humiliation where he'd been smoking pot in the bathroom and his mother dang near kicked in the door to bust him. He'd lied and said he hadn't been smoking but he had. Standing on the toilet while blowing the smoke into the vent had evidently done nothing to help conceal what he'd been doing. From there, his thoughts jumped to times when his mother defended him against his stepfather for having stolen his pot. He often heard her telling his stepdad that he was just being paranoid. However, Drew had stolen his pot. This was the same guy who had forced Drew to smoke against his will as a child but Drew still didn't feel justified to steal from the man. He stole marijuana from his stepfather for years before finally being caught crawling on his belly like a snake in his parents' dark bedroom. He didn't feel fear for what his stepdad might do but he felt extreme humiliation and embarrassment in front of his mother who had once defended him. Even in his dream state he felt the humiliation and thought to himself, "Why, why, why am I doing this?" When he woke up he felt uncomfortable. He felt the mixed emotions of humiliation, anger, and disappointment. He felt the strain of having let his mother down all those years ago. He still loved her and could not explain to her why he'd been the bad child he'd been because he truly didn't know. He could only conclude that he was sick and had gotten better.

He climbed out of bed to go pee and to get a glass of milk. He was parched and of course, he loved milk. He lit a joint and took a few puffs before retiring a bit longer. It was only 4:20 am in the morning and time to go back to sleep. The thc would help. He fell asleep, this time without a single dream. Dead to the world, he got the rest his mind and body needed before waking up refreshed later in the morning.

Drew remembered his friend Jimmy who had also often needed rides to the methadone clinic in Vancouver years ago. Drew hadn't minded giving Jimmy rides so much because he liked him and Jimmy paid him properly. Jimmy did, however, call at the most inconvenient times like all the others after him. When he woke he wondered if Jimmy had been some sort of actor as well. He also questioned whether or not Jimmy had actually died on that April fool's day years ago in Washington.

Drew had taken Jimmy to the methadone clinic and McDonald's earlier that day before the police knocked on

Drew's door to inform him of Jimmy's death. It had been one hell of an interruption. And while he wasn't sure Jimmy really was dead, he had to believe he was in order to preserve his memory of Jimmy's respectfully.

The morning following Jimmy's untimely demise, Drew saw that police were loading what appeared to have been a body with a sheet over it into an ambulance. It didn't make sense because there seemed to be no police car in attendance. And why would they load a dead body into an ambulance and not a coroner's vehicle? And why he had to think about this years later while brushing his teeth was beyond him. He wished the thoughts would just go away.

When he was done brushing his teeth he had some very strong coffee. These days he preferred coffee over meth or crack. But, of course, it would always be someone's opinion that coffee too was bad for him. As he drank his coffee, he thought about how American media deemed almost everything was bad for you. Breathing the air itself could give you cancer. Fruit was bad for your teeth. Milk could give you kidney stones and boiled vegetables had no nutritional value. It seemed there was a bad side to everything in life. The news media said fish were dangerous because of the mercury levels they contained. Butter was bad and then called a great part of a nutritional breakfast. People were putting butter in their coffee. Marijuana damaged your lungs 20 times worse than a pack of cigarettes. Everything was made to look dangerous as if to scare people into thinking they needed to be told these things. As to manipulate the people of America into thinking they needed protection from themselves. It did not seem to matter to Drew. In his opinion, no one could cheat death.

He drank his coffee and watched the morning news. Bored with the news on Donald Trump's taxes, he changed the channel to PBS where an unknown show discussed humiliation. These sort of consistent coincidences confused Drew to no end. He couldn't figure out how they could possibly be important. Dreaming about past feelings of humiliation and waking up to see a segment on the very topics he'd dreamed seemed to be important to him but made no sense. He'd somehow managed not to make too much of an issue of it within himself even though there were times it astounded him. He thought it must serve a purpose but for now, it was only confusing. How could he find a motive for this when the man wasn't really even involved? No one knew what he'd dreamed the night before and there was no way the TV show could have been intentionally aired for him. How could this be happening on a regular basis and how could it be tied into the other odd things he'd been experiencing? Maybe these were two separate issues that he was trying to connect that actually were not connected. It was all too much for him to start thinking about again this early in the morning. He listened to some music. It soothed him as he enjoyed his coffee.

The man on the radio sang "Nothing Else Compares." He flipped through his newsfeeds before seeing an old story from a show concerning a man who felt people had been playing serious games with him on his computer and in his home. The man didn't seem to be crazy but the host insisted that the man needed help. Drew entertained the thought that maybe the drugs and alcohol had driven him crazy, but only for a moment before he laughed it off. He was not crazy by far. Only slightly disturbed.

He flipped the channel on his television back to the news although he didn't know why. Surely he wasn't interested in bad news. Perhaps this was Drew's way of chasing an expectation of excitement. Could he have replaced his drug and alcohol use with watching the news and social media? When he thought about this he felt slightly pathetic. He decided to write more of his book in the hope of redeeming himself.

Drew understood that life was full of mystery and intrigue and that experimenting with drugs and alcohol was weakening and overrated. He would put this in his book and leave it at that. Just like the turn of a page in a book, so too would be that dark episode in a life that he'd once lived. He would move on but he would not forget. He would not forget where he came from and he would not forget what had happened to him in the great state of Washington. He would simply remember it in a sober state of mind.

For months Drew wrote in his book. The coincidences remained but the oddball occurrences stopped. People stopped pointing and staring. He stopped meeting weird people and life seemed to relax for him just a little more. He still daydreamed and night dreamed about his past and coincidental occurrences still occurred but nothing out of the ordinary like people coming into his home. His vehicles were no longer being played with as they had before. Sometimes, on the mornings after he'd used drugs, his car drove as if it had no shocks or suddenly overheated. He no longer felt the aura of aggression and hostility that seemed to leak from the minds of the culprits. It seemed they had run away. He figured that by now if he hadn't gotten them to reveal themselves they weren't going to. He was going to have to go in after them. Just not today. He enjoyed procrastination.

GOD

DREW HAD ALWAYS KNOWN and was fully aware that the man upstairs had been watching out for him. He'd often been celled with a violent inmate. And right when he knew there was about to be another violent confrontation, he'd prayed. Whenever he'd prayed, they were somehow mysteriously rehoused or shipped elsewhere. After years of fighting off violent criminals, he began to pray to the only Father he knew. The Father he'd used to replace the biological father who was not there. The Father who had saved his life so many times before despite his rebellious acts of thievery and disconcern. The One who allowed him to be drunk on the night of the frog gigging incident. The One that allowed him to get out of the van that was wrapped around a telephone pole. The Father who allowed the knife that had been jabbed into his chest to narrowly miss a vital organ. The Father who gave a clumsy goof the reflex and strength to fight off a Pitbull that had only killing on its mind as it lurched for his throat. And the very same Father who spoke to him about his anger through lightning and again with mosquitos. Drew knew he'd not been living right when the mosquitos attacked him in Arkansas and that they wouldn't allow him to sleep. He knew he hadn't been living right when lightning smashed down next to him in Memphis.

Drew looked back on his encounter with a drone when he'd left Everett and walked into another city. A drone had been following him high up in the sky through the city. Drew knew and had been through so much by then that it didn't upset him too much. He had to accept that there wasn't a thing he could do about it so before he laid down to try and get some sleep in a somewhat remote field he spoke out loud to the drone. He asked the drone questions without expecting any answers because obviously drones don't talk and, besides that, the drone was a good couple hundred feet above him. "Why are you following me? What kind of game are you playing with me?" he asked as he lay on a concrete slab in the middle of a field. It was late at night and the drone shone like a star above him. He'd watched as the drone seemed to shimmer through the sky behind him earlier. Because of everything he'd experienced in Everett, he had a pretty good idea that not only was the drone watching him but listening to him somehow as well. He'd come up with the bright idea to tell the drone to move a little from side to side for no and up and down for yes. He asked the drone if it would answer yes and no questions in this manner. Oddly enough the drone agreed with him by moving in an up and down motion. He could hardly believe he was right. It was both watching and listening to him.

He'd asked the drone if they were male or female watching him. But he forgot only for an instant that he could only get answers to yes or no questions. So he rephrased the question by asking if they were female. The drone bobbed up and down to say yes. It was a female. If it hadn't been a female watching him then they wanted him to think it was. He asked if he was on video and got yet another yes.

He got up and went into the busier area of town solely to hunt down what homeless people referred to as "snipes". "Snipes" was slang used for half-smoked cigarettes. Drew really needed a smoke and had none left. He gathered some snipes from around town and was heading back to the concrete slab when he nearly got lost. He asked the drone that still followed him if he was going the right way when it went into a side to side motion. So he turned back around only to realize the drone was correct.

He'd just missed the entrance to the field and found it moments after the drone acknowledged that he was going the wrong way. He'd grown very tired as he had walked for miles earlier that day to get to the city he was now nearly in. He lay on the outskirts of some town looking at a nosy person's drone that hovered far above him in the night sky. He asked it a few more stupid questions before pulling himself out of his pants to offend the spy in the sky. He got a reaction when an automobile pulled up and sat with its lights off near the field entrance obscured from view. He gathered that whoever had the drone was driving the car. He wished someone would get out and come to him running their mouth off but no one did. Eventually, the vehicle backed right back out and never made it within a naked eye view of Drew. By that point in his life, he was so disgusted with feeling spied on that he wanted ever so badly just to know of one person involved in watching him. He thought that if he could just find one of them, then the rest would come out to protect the one he caught. He didn't care by what means which at the time included the most vulgar and offensive things he could think of to anger the nosy bastards.

It truly disgusted him and he would never forget having sunk to this level as long as he lived. He could have been arrested and called a sex offender for exposing himself in the field despite the fact that no one but a drone was within viewing distance of him. Or in the woods in Tacoma when the hobos seemed to invade him of privacy. Because nowadays getting caught peeing could be construed as a sexual offense in the eyes of judicial hypocrisy. He didn't enjoy being forced to mix something so normal and natural with defending himself of an actual offense. Everything was a problem when he was homeless. Someone had to have been paying the other homeless to aggravate him. Someone didn't want him to have so much as a moment alone. At one point, he even asked the drone if other people were watching in Washington and it motioned a yes. He asked it if people from Tennessee were watching him and the drone responded no. Eventually, the drone vanished amongst the stars in the clear night sky.

Drew thought deeply about another way to get a reaction from his hidden aggressors without exposing himself or using drugs but could think of no other way than to continue to write his book in hopes of discovering something he hadn't seen before. He thought if nothing else, perhaps he could piece something together in writing as opposed to sorting things out in his head. There was more to write because, after all, this book was not solely for profit but also for him to better understand who and what he was. And who had been so interested in his life?

Drew booted up his computer and turned off his radio. He'd seen an RV online that he and Missy could afford to make payments on and decided to drive his van down and check it out. As usual, when he turned the key to start it, the van speakers blared with what sounded like a landline dial tone. Drew laughed a crazy quick laugh before rolling his eyes and moving on. He wished he knew who had been responsible for all of this. He thought it might be nice to hit them so hard that it knocked their jaw loose. Or box their ears as his gramma always said. But he knew he would never physically harm anyone unless he was defending himself. He wasn't so arrogant as to believe that he himself could get the justice he needed. Drew had a Maker. He refused to believe that humans had once crawled from the sea before turning into monkeys and then humans. He knew better than this.

During his drive toward destination RV, he saw an old black man in a field holding a lawnmower blade. From what he could see the man was merely doing some kind of work. It reminded Drew of when he'd been in the chow hall in a Tennessee prison. He sat with an inmate who had told him to watch the chow line because something was about to happen. He could feel someone was about to attack someone else but couldn't tell where or who.

"Watch that guy in the coat over there," the inmate told Drew. Drew watched and said, "Yea, that's just one of the crazies isn't it?" It was in the middle of June and the guy was wearing a coat, as some of them did all-year around. Drew took a bite of his vegetable stew and cornbread as he waited in anticipation for what could be a hardcore fist fight. He took another bite of the bland carrots, water, and potatoes. Just then he saw what was really on the sweaty man's agenda.

The coat-wearing convict suddenly began to shake his right arm. From his coat sleeve, he shook out an object that seemed to come out forever. When the convict's arm was done shaking, the object could clearly be identified as an overly sharpened lawnmower blade with a cloth wrapped around one end to serve as a handle. The coated convict quickly made known his intentions. He walked straight up behind an inmate who'd been accused of snitching. As the snitch leaned forward to take a bite of his watery prison cuisine, the coated bandit took a swift swing that landed the blade dead in the middle of his neck. He dropped the blade and walked off quickly. Drew could hardly believe what he was seeing. The man's head now lay in vegetable stew and cornbread still attached to his body by only a thin layer of bloody skin. He'd heard snitches get stitches but this really took the cake. Only one thing was for sure: this man would never snitch again.

ANTONIO AND LINO A AND L AUTO SALES

HE ARRIVED AT HIS destination. A and L Auto Sales. And there was the RV. A very polite and well-mannered gentleman who introduced himself as Antonio greeted him with a genuine smile. He smelled of a mild yet expensive cologne and was pleasant with an assuring handshake. Antonio introduced him to his partner Lino. Lino was also a gentleman of dominate hygiene and he smelled great. Both were of Hispanic descent. Drew understood why men bought expensive colognes now. It was very welcoming. After meeting these guys, he decided never again to wear cheap cologne. They looked and smelled great. They were two of Americas few honest auto salesmen.

They sold Drew a 1996 Holiday Rambler 34-foot Endeavor for $4000 down and one year of payments. Everything worked including the shower, toilet, and stove. It came complete with a giant gasoline-powered generator and was self-contained. It even came with a portable black water tote to empty waste into for easy disposal. They could survive anywhere and they wouldn't have to deal with skyrocketing rental prices on apartments. In two years, they would outright own their own home. And if perhaps they didn't like where they were at, they could simply drive away.

Neither Drew nor Missy needed much space as they weren't entirely fond of buying "stuff". They always sat close by one another anyway. The RV was large enough that it could be compared to a studio apartment. Now they had to find somewhere to park it until they were ready to move into it. Finding a lot with a space available would prove nearly impossible.

Drew searched high and low for a space in town and came up with absolutely nothing. He had to settle for a spot in the mountains of Washougal where a nice lady who was nursing her uncle because of a stroke allowed them to park and live for a while. They paid her $300 and parked the RV on gravel next to her home. Drew informed her that they wouldn't be moving in immediately and that they still had a few weeks left in their apartment. One Friday morning, he woke up because the moon was so bright it was like a flashlight in his eyes. He lay awake staring at it. He was grateful it wasn't a drone.

Drew lay thinking in his bed as he stared into the brighter than usual moon, dreaming to himself soft memories like that time when he was maybe seven years old and anticipating his mother getting him ready for school. He could remember thinking that he would be glad not to go to school, while at the same time enjoying listening to his mother's alarm clock play AM radio. It was a pleasant feeling from the past that soothed any current mental anguish for Drew at least at that moment.

He seemed to be able to smell the past while his mind was there. The smell of the past felt very comforting. It seemed to contain within it something he'd lost along the way so many years ago. Sometimes when he remembered the smell of a certain time, he first experienced a strange ammonia type aftertaste in his throat. He couldn't understand why and never would, but he enjoyed the smells of his childhood – at least some of them.

Drew never could figure out what exactly the smells were and couldn't compare them to anything at all. They could only be described as a strong déjà vu. It was sometimes such an incredible trip into the past that he truly enjoyed. However, it sometimes left him puzzled and in a trance-like state. Often, it was very relaxing. Whatever bad situations he'd ever been in also contained a bright side somewhere in his perception and that is where they remained. He looked at only the bright side of most everything, even in his dreams.

The moon began to vanish behind the seemingly alive trees. They looked nearly animated in the mist of sweet Washington rain. He always slept with his window open because he was a warmer than normal person who was at his best in the cool weather. He smelled the breeze and it warranted a smile. As he lay and watched the early morning moon, he remembered the werewolf movies he'd enjoyed growing up. He wondered where all the really scary movies had gone until he realized that in maturing he had lost the thrill of the genre. It must happen to most people. They must outgrow their fears. It couldn't be the movie industry.

He snapped back to reality and back into the now as the moon was no more. He thought, "Why does someone want me to go back home?" He felt that the whole neighborhood, who he did not know, wanted him to leave. Yet no one knew him or even seemed to look at him most of the time. It seemed that sometimes people crowded him when he was getting ready to do something important. That's why he didn't much know many people. Falling prey to peer pressure had been one of his earlier problems. Trying to be nice to people who took advantage of him had long since taken its toll. Meeting people who only wanted him to do something for them all the time had introduced skepticism into his personality. He didn't like meeting new people mainly because he perceived them as a threat to his freedom. When he was a child, other kids encouraged him to steal. They then lead him into vandalism, which in turn lead to juvenile court. When he was a young adult, they got him to help them steal cars or three-wheelers and moved from there to hard drugs and alcohol. The adults also lead an adult Drew to jail.

Perhaps he had decided that because he couldn't find good friends that he was supposed to remain without friends. It wasn't that he didn't like people in general but that he had to look out for his own rump. Life had taught him this much if nothing else.

He remembered the woman telling him, in a way that seemed to be genuine bad acting, about her lost cat named Slander in Everett. And how cats needed help getting home once they were out of their domain. She told him that the only reason that they generally left their area was because something had spooked them really bad. He laughed to himself as he thought about how she might have been trying to plant a subliminal message somewhere in the back of his mind. It was as if she were telling him to go back to Tennessee. It had angered him when people in Everett, Washington spoke to him in a manner seemingly rehearsed yet casual. It was as if people were watching him and trying to manipulate him in some way by using someone else to make their statements. Almost like someone was telling them what to say in a concealed earpiece. He could always tell when they were being deceitful. It wasn't something he enjoyed. He felt like a schizophrenic person might feel if they thought everyone they knew was being nice to their face but a jerk behind their back. Because he lacked the fear, it was a little different. He need only to humble himself. He'd had no physical proof at the time and was left with only one option to merely observe. But he could hardly go around town shaking everyone by the shoulders asking them what was going on as then they would have accomplished what he thought they had set out to accomplish – to have him gone or going crazy.

Looking back on his endeavors in Everett, he could only figure at one point that neighborhood groups must have gotten together to fight the drug epidemic and were running users one by one out of town and possibly out of the state. He realized now it had been deeper than he'd thought. In the last year, he'd discovered more than he wanted to know about a possible reality series involving a man who didn't know about it. The fact that someone using a producer's name had hacked his email account months ago, hadn't helped him to look in another direction. When he looked the hacker up it showed him a man who worked for a movie company. Were all these instances connected or were they all fabricated in his mind somehow? Then there was the Drew Truman account who had hacked into his social media. When he looked the guy up, he discovered that the supposed hacker was an app designer for the web. However, there was also the other possibilities. Maybe some oddball people were playing games with him to get him to think that someone had been making a show out of his life. All of this information went through his mind instantly and soon he was back to sleep.

Later in the morning when the sun finally dawned, he woke to a cup of coffee that his love and comrade Missy had brought him. She was happy as long as he was happy and vice versa. She was meant for him it seemed. They both enjoyed cuddling every night and expressing their opinions about current news topics. She usually saw things his way so they got along well. He liked her coffee. She was his little "squishy". At least, when they could pretend that's whom she was when they were in a private setting hugging.

He sipped his coffee as Missy turned on the news. It was nearly May Day and the media warned of possible riots due to political protests. The people often protested here in the northwest. It was something he hadn't seen much of in the south. The southern United States appeared a bit too divided for protesting. They were mostly Republicans whether they knew what it meant or not. Racism added to the statewide division as well. If the blacks and whites could all come together in the south, he thought for sure they would be a power to be reckoned with. Drew held hope for this in his heart.

Police in the southern and east coast states had slacked off quite a bit on shooting unarmed black men to death. The only time he'd seen protesting and riots down there was when police shot and killed people without good cause. Other than that, they strongly believed in nothing more than voting your opinion when it came to politics, or so it seemed to Drew.

Police were now being focused on for beating people and manhandling them. The news aired a story with video of an officer beating a jaywalker in the middle of the street and a girl being slammed to the ground for not producing identification while jogging. He began to see these guys as a circus or clowns, like the ones on tricycles, in barrels, or coming from a small Volkswagen. They were most likely doing as their departments told them. A paycheck was their motive to clown on people. He tried to imagine being in their shoes and what it must be like to work with immoral directives in order to feed their families. What it must be like to have to fill a quota of citations, tickets, and arrests by the end of each month so that you could pay the mortgage. It was sad but it was life in the U.S.

He laughed at himself and reminded himself not to point too many fingers at anyone else. He knew it was God Almighty who had looked out for him and God who had allowed him to once get a Bronchial infection for making fun of someone who had the same infection. The guy had been a jerk but Drew realized it was not nice to belittle other people, even to yourself in what should be the privacy of your own home. Judging whether someone was okay to be around was one thing but judging them for who and what you thought they should be was quite another. Drew believed that if you liked someone that you should accept them for who they were and not try and twist them into your perfect friend. If you really liked Joe Shmoe down the road, then you should allow him or her to keep being himself as long as there was no imminent danger. You shouldn't try and tell Joe Shmoe that he fishes too much when he could be doing something more productive. You should only congratulate him and ask him how many fish he caught and what kind, not criticize. Don't ask him why he does what he does and then disagree with him because then he's not gonna like you anymore and in turn you'll stop liking him. Surely we were meant to live in harmony, he thought.

And although the police were responsible for giving Drew a perma knot on his forehead and had once paralyzed the left side of his face, he knew all cops truly weren't the same. He did not hold a psychotic grudge against police in general but a grudge against the departments who seemed to have a God complex. Other departments were humble. It seemed to depend on what city you were in and what precinct. Drew thought most people were okay until they proved him wrong.

The news wasn't really news. It was full of rubbish to him. Nothing good ever came of it. The occasional saving of an animal caught on tape or a child recorded nearly missing death as cars run over him without harming him. Little caught on tape today was promising. He was tired of the news and wanted something more in life. He considered listening to music in the mornings rather than watching the news but he was aware that sometimes music had triggered his drinking. Music had its own way of making him slip away. The wrong song could send his adrenaline shooting straight through the roof for hours. And when the adrenaline rush did finally go away, his nerves were shot. Alcohol had sometimes helped for a moment but eventually only made things worse. Music was good if it were the right kind. Listening to hard rock or rap riled Drew up. He didn't want to be prepared to fight every time he walked into a room with people anymore. He didn't enjoy always being on the defensive. However, the violence he'd long since lived with in Memphis had molded his demeanor into a gentlemanly but expectant warrior. He expected an attack and still carried it with him in his walk.

In truth, he had never been physically attacked in the state of Washington but he wasn't living in racially divided neighborhoods anymore and he wasn't going to prison anymore. His commute into Washington State had done him good. It allowed him to see another form of an aggressor. A silent aggressor. One who tried and would have succeeded in running him back to where he came from had he been your average guy. An aggressor who pushed and pushed without laying a hand on him. Drew had, by design, become a leader without followers. A leader in the sense that he would do things his way because he felt in his bones that he was right. It really did not matter to him if the whole world jumped off of the cliff because he wasn't going to. It was as simple as that. He would at least try and stand for what he believed in as long as it didn't land him in a cage where a married homosexual man had the right to order you to lift your penis off of your testicles for a thorough search. Today it seemed that if you spoke out too much against the government, you could end up in that cage. Protestors always ended up locked up for protesting. Often those who hadn't done anything but hold up a sign were slammed and arrested just because police couldn't grab the one they wanted.

Police stopped shooting unarmed black men so much after the people rioted violently and tore up their cities. It was funny how violence seemed to get more done than Wile E. Coyote with a "help" sign. Still, people everywhere shouted that violence wasn't the answer. Unfortunately, these were mostly the same people who defended police violence. The world had too many people in it and it was crazy. Standing up for himself, his friends, and his family would be as far as he would go. Standing up against immoral policies was a waste of his time and he knew it. The government was set in its ways and would do as it pleased because it had too much momentum.

Drew got back into his book writing project. He typed until doubt seeped into his brain that writing his book would be worthwhile. The doubt that he would be successful at it and the doubt that he could afford a good editor. He didn't know anything about the writing world that he assumed also had its own politics to deal with. He stopped for a while and decided to button it up again until he felt ready. He walked outside for a smoke and a little sunshine.

Reaching into his pocket for his lighter, he let loose a small giggle. He recalled the officer that had slammed him into the wall once in Portland, Oregon for offensive littering. He'd reached into his pocket and pulled out his lighter when the officer had seen a receipt accidentally fall from his pocket. He looked down this time to make sure no paper fell from his pocket as he pulled out the lighter. He lit his smoke and blew the first puff out through his nose. He wondered where this trail called life was going to lead him to next.

They moved into the mountains of Washougal, Washington where Drew continued to write his book. The drive into Vancouver now took 45 minutes when once it had taken 10 minutes to get anywhere they needed to be. Drew had faith that everything would work out the way that it needed to. One day while Drew and Missy watched television in their Holiday Rambler, Drew heard helicopters. He casually walked outside to see what they were doing. Although he knew they were flying like most helicopters do, he wanted to see if they were covering news that he might not yet be aware of. When he got outside he noticed that for a moment they hovered a few hundred feet above their motorhome. It was about the same distance that the drone had hovered years ago. They flew off as he remembered the night he'd stayed up late in Vancouver listening to Dee Snider host a radio show called "House of Hair". He remembered that Dee said, "Here come the choppers," just as he started an Aldo Nova song called "Life is Just a Fantasy". At the very same moment, a helicopter flew straight over the apartment at a very close range. That night he'd been using amphetamine. And that night, the unknown entity was hard at work playing some serious games. Although he had no proof that it wasn't just coincidence, he felt it was not. Nor had the giant train in Tacoma, Washington been coincidence.

Drew Shaw was battling something he'd never battled before. Drew was battling himself. He was fighting against himself and his own perception. Fighting against the thoughts that sometimes spelled regret. He had to force himself to be okay with everything he endured, whether mentally or physically. Drew was far too hard-headed and would never allow himself to be angered or upset for very long. He was determined to live as happily as possible regardless of the circumstances. "Kill 'em with kindness," someone had once said to Drew. Drew had met many a hater in his years on Earth. Matter of fact, he'd met more hateful people in his lifetime than caring people. To Drew, that was just the way the ball bounced. Encountering hateful people was part of the humbling process. He would not hate on the haters because he simply wasn't hateful.

The truth was that Drew had suffered so much trauma in his lifetime and had abused so many drugs and alcohol that it was possible his mind was fabricating bits and pieces of his life by linking everything bad together. For instance, Joe Shmoe down the road may have played games with him that in turn lead him to believe that Negative Nancy who ripped him off for a few bucks in a bad dope deal had both conspired against him when actually the two didn't even know each other. Drew felt this aspect was possible in his now-sober mind.

Maybe the landlady had spied on him with cameras in the sprinkler heads but maybe she hadn't known of the other things he'd been through. Perhaps it had been a series of unfortunate events mixed with different people and cultures. Maybe no one knew the other was playing games. Maybe he was just crazy. Whatever the case, he had to let it go. No matter how often the thoughts haunted him, he did his very best to remain mentally positive. Sometimes this meant forgetting it for a while or pushing it to the side. Bottling it up helped him to continue on with life. He was a humble elephant. What more could he really do? He could either move on or wallow in the mystery of what had actually occurred. The fact was that people had done him wrong and played games. But there was no sense in him holding onto any of it. It was life and life was bound to happen. Because he was now sober, Drew could now deal with almost anything. He felt he was now, after all these years, finally ready to take on life.

Today he was stronger. Today, Drew thanked Almighty God and Jesus Christ for allowing him to get through all the suffering. For walking him not into but through the proverbial flames of death. For sparing his life so many times and humbling him enough as not to jump to conclusions that might have changed his character. Today, it didn't bother him at all that he was behind another vehicle at a red light on the street that displayed the words, "We know" written by a finger into the dust and grime of the rear window. It didn't bother him that just before seeing the words, he was singing along with the song on the radio, "Nobody Knows It". He seemed to have grown numb to these elements of surprise. Simply put, nothing surprised him anymore.

Drew Shaw continued on with life. He continued to watch the news and continued to move on. He couldn't believe the complaints he'd seen on social media regarding people taking offense to the beliefs of others. People protested that others didn't have the right to say what they felt. He'd always been taught growing up that "sticks and stones could break my bones but words would never hurt me". And that America was the land of the free with free speech. In recent years, he'd begun to realize that the rules had changed. He wondered if maybe the government ought to subject everyone in the United States to an hour class in high school on learning to accept the opinions of others.

Along with that, they could maybe teach the importance of freedom of speech. Drew felt personally that he would rather see the warning signs of possibly dangerous people than shut them up and have no warning at all. He felt maybe it best they reserve the right to type or say whatever they felt was necessary. Perhaps this way someone could try and talk some sense into them lest they attack in surprise. He would rather know his prejudiced or psychotic neighbor for what they were than to assume they had the best of intentions.

On the other hand, Drew understood how it felt to be humiliated or made fun of. He'd felt it himself when schoolgirls had called him ugly in the seventh grade. He understood that sometimes human beings had deep emotional issues and that words could be damaging to self-esteem. Bad mouthing people for being homosexual or fat or black or even for just being police officers was plain ignorant but not illegal. Nevertheless, he believed people should have a right to move their mouths in any manner they chose short of biting someone.

Drew and Missy enjoyed their short time living in the mountains of Washougal for nearly two months before moving on as they said they would. They moved closer to the town where they parked on the street in Vancouver. While they lay in wait for someone (anyone) to respond to their ads on the internet, the street was all they had. It was fine up until the generator quit working during a rare 100-degree day. Then things went from bad to worse as an overly intoxicated punk kid came through in the middle of the night ripping off the driver's side RV mirror as well as their car mirror. The guy was screaming as if he were the female version of the incredible hulk. It was just as well Drew couldn't get dressed and get to him in time or he might have killed the guy out of sheer anger. He felt that somehow God had stopped him from getting a hold of the guy. If he'd chased someone down the road and choked them to death, he may well have wound up in prison for the rest of his life here on Earth. God had saved him once again. And also might well have saved the life of the vandal. Drew always felt bad after defending himself against the attacker. He felt their newfound fear of him and guilt for hurting them.

Drew and his love eventually got a response from a man willing to rent to them. He was a well-to-do Cuban man named Jose. He collected MR2s and rented rooms to those in need. Having a sewage hook up for their Rambler along with electricity was quite the relief. Drew questioned why it had been so difficult to find a place to park. He sat writing in his RV parked flat up against a legal marijuana shop, writing more short stories that related to the current times.

CHAPTER

MOVING ON

DREW GAVE RACISM DEEP thought on many an occasion. He put himself in the shoes of the black men and women of the United States. He pictured himself as having his entire family tree raped, beaten, and murdered. And then later hearing his government telling him to forget about it and move on. He understood where African Americans could, would, and possibly should have an attitude. It seemed to Drew, that the Southern US government had, because they lost the civil war, revised the laws in such a way as effected solely the poor, which at that time was predominately African Americans. That way they could call it "community service" or "sentenced to hard labor" as opposed to slavery.

Other issues bothered him as well, such as people mocking the Bible. Drew assumed that surely no matter what religion one followed, they all must teach respect for a person's religion short of it being violent or hateful. But ever since he'd arrived in the state of Washington, he'd heard people making fun of the Bible. Their arrogance and ignorance both angered and saddened him.

Police officers beating and killing people on video and then blatantly being let off the hook hurt his feelings as well. He'd been victim to them and understood that these people were going through an awful lot. Policemen were caught in the mix of having to defend the bad ones, which in his eyes took at least some of their good away. Good officers seemed to be made less than because of the bad ones.

And then there was his family. His grandmother never seemed satisfied with him and he couldn't blame her. She insisted on him working a hard labor job all the time. It often haunted him when he wasn't working full time, like now. He understood her concern for him but the simple fact was that Drew was clumsy, for lack of a better word. He'd nearly been killed on many a job because he was always willing to work harder than anyone else. He'd suffered many a concussion and been ripped off by enough so-called employers that he no longer trusted them. Most people got paid by their employers. Drew had a way of working for the wrong ones. His own grandmother commented to him once that he didn't need much money because he'd just be ripped off. Why someone would work him without pay was beyond him. He didn't care anymore. He concluded that he just wanted to live his life.

He had experienced enough of life that he had many a tale to tell. When he wrote stories, he put his heart into it and found he thoroughly enjoyed it. Drew Shaw left the drugs and alcohol alone, along with the once-intriguing mystery, and began writing short and mind-opening stories. Despite his decades of alcohol and drug abuse, he was able to quit without attending AA or any of the drug rehabilitation centers that were forced down your throat on daytime television. The lifetime of beating himself up was enough rehabilitation for Drew. He wrote in the peace and privacy of their RV. He began with short stories that helped him to get things off his chest and move on with life. He no longer posted to social media to hear the opinions of what he considered the opposition. Because, after all, he was an empath and he did not want to hurt the feelings of others lest he felt it himself. It hurt him to hurt someone else's feelings because in a sense he felt what they were feeling. That's why people often appeared to be acting because most people don't show their true selves. They often masked what they truly felt but Drew could feel it. Often he felt the emotions of many people at once, which could sometimes be overwhelming. This was why he was sometimes mistaken for being snobby. Socializing hurt his feelings. He would release all of what he'd absorbed while writing his stories. He wrote many stories and eventually got published. His life began to change for the better as he wrote. The following were two short stories Drew wrote while in his Holiday Rambler behind a pot shop. They take a somewhat alternative view of the world as we know it. Brace for something a little different.

THE PETERSONS

CHAPTER

BILL PETERSON

Bill Peterson was one ignorant redneck. Conceived in Kentucky and raised in the backwoods of Tennessee, Bill had a mind full of closed doors. At six feet six and 240lbs, Bill was a beanpole of a sorry excuse for a human being. Brown eyes and salt and pepper hair, he had the mediocre look of a farmer and a farmer he was. He often wore a straw hat and dangled a single straw of hay from his self- satisfied black-toothed grin. He beat his wife and hated black folks. His favorite pass time was watchin' wrestling and drinkin' brown whiskey. He loved his truck too. At 66 years, Bill was a retired farmer but still claimed his title when asked.

Today was eclipse day and frankly, Bill was tired of the dang sun anyway. He wished it away as he chugged straight whiskey and scarfed down a greasy BBQ sandwich. This morning on the day of the 2017 total solar eclipse, Bill had gotten plenty enough of everything. He was plenty disgusted by pretty much anything and everything. He was sick of his wife naggin' about this and naggin' about that. Sick of the dad-blasted weather and sick of life in general. It was the same ole same ole and the whiskey didn't seem to be workin' its magic anymore. Cruising the town in his F-150 had grown old and so had "people watching".

This early morning as Bill wiped more grease and BBQ sauce from his face, his wife was ranting and raving about his nasty socks in the floor. She was sick of it. They both basked in bitterness. His was fueled with alcohol and her with hurt. She loved him but he only seemed to love brown whiskey. The only affection he'd shown her as recently was the sour slap of his backhand across her face. Sadly, it was a behavior that she'd long since accepted. Although it was hurtful, she took the only form of affection that she could get from him. Their once beautiful and loving relationship had diminished and become something to be reckoned with. He was everything to her and the bottle was taking him away slowly and violently.

On this particular morning, as his wife nagged him, his mind began to click. He'd had enough of everything and the sound of her angry, love-starved voice aggravated him intensely. His long, narrow, greasy fingers gripped the whiskey bottle as he chugged down the brown evil spirit while attempting to drown out her whining voice. But his anger level grew faster than the whiskey could enter his old system. His blood boiling, he slammed down the bottle. Then he stood up and marched towards his target. Her mouth seemed bigger than life and he had to put a stop to it. With every bit of his rage, he pulled back his right arm towards the left side of his chest before releasing an almost spring released backhand to her mouth.

CHAPTER

THE JOURNEY OUT

HE'D SLAPPED HER ONCE again and felt none too good about it once again. Deep inside he felt it hurt him to slap her, but he also excused himself with the solipsistic feeling that she'd made him do it. If she hadn't complained about him being the pig he was, none of this would have happened. Disgusted with himself, his wife, and the entire situation, he grabbed his truck keys and quickly walked past her. As she lay sobbing and holding her face, he took off in his truck in haste. He drove out of the county and into the city of Memphis.

Another of his retirement pastimes consisted of cruising the Memphis ghetto neighborhoods just to feel the disgust that he longed for. It made him somehow feel better about himself. He drove by and gocked in disgust as the crack dealers blatantly served crack on the corners to their victims. The police didn't have enough room in their jails for all of them, so they sold it until they were busted. The key to selling was to always put away bail money. The bust was inevitable and one had to be prepared.

He couldn't stand the fact that he saw white people buying the junk and it especially angered him to see white women at the mercy of black men. Today he thought to himself, "They have another thing comin'." As he drove through a red light, he stuck his hand under his armpit and quickly smelled his hand. To him, it smelled like nothing. To anyone else, it was a lot like nasty feet. He didn't even know why he did it. It was just another of his bad habits. It seemed as normal to him as it would to blow his nose at the dinner table while eating with company. Other people's thoughts and feelings didn't matter to him. It was his world and they were just in it.

Bill drove into the drive-thru at a McDonalds to get himself one of them "Mac Rib sammiches", as he called them. He used the same hand he'd stuck under his armpit to pay for and take his food. He even licked those same fingers after inhaling the "sammich". Hell, he'd done it a million times before and nothin' bad came of it. Why not continue? Although he'd just had BBQ for breakfast, he felt like he was still hungry, partially because of the giant, drunk tapeworm hosting his body. Bill knew nothing about his host. But his host knew everything about him. Bill had been and would always be the tapeworm's entire world.

CHAPTER

CORY PETERSON

Cory Peterson was a middle-aged black man with two children and a crackhead for a wife. He lived in the housing projects of south Memphis where he took care of his two children. Cory was also a crack dealer. He sold crack to feed his children and to keep clothes on their backs and a roof over their heads. He'd stopped trying to work for "the man" years ago when he realized he was getting nowhere in doing so. He could make no more money than $6.15 an hour because he had no education and most businesses in the area were owned and operated by whites who felt blacks weren't worth the trouble. That's how it felt to Cory. When he had worked, he gave them his all with his physical labor as they weren't willing to accept any less. He shaved off years of his life in one year and for what? So that they could talk bad to him and disrespect him every chance they got? So that they could congregate at lunch without him and talk racist jokes? $6.15 wasn't nearly enough money to live on in the southern economy of Memphis, Tennessee. With crack, however, he was able to make ends meet. The cost of going to jail and losing his children to a corrupt government who would at least feed them was cheaper than standing by and watching them starve and go into depression. He truly cared for his children and his wife although, she no longer lived with them because of her own crack problem.

Cory got up early because he badly needed to sell his product to come up with the rest of the rent money. It was summer vacation for the children and "eclipse day" to boot. His children Tony and Tisha were fast asleep as they'd had themselves a long night of X box 360. They had practically celebrated all week about the coming solar eclipse and they could not wait to see it. Cory had only hours to get out of the house and make some money before his little monsters woke up. He jumped in and out of the shower before drying off and applying Jergens lotion to his legs and feet.

Dressing in his finest Adidas outfit, he sat down to smoke a marijuana cigarette that looked like a brown blimp. He felt he had to first take care of his head before hitting the streets, lest the streets played on his anxiety. He put his blunt out half way and "hit the door". Once he was outside, his tennis shoes took him to the sidewalk where he began to "beat feet". Stepping down the road in his fancy Adidas tennis shoes, he always felt half on top of the world with the other half teetering on paranoia. Selling crack was considered a serious crime and would mean years in jail.

As he hit the corner, he looked down a straight and narrow street that went on for blocks. Nothing looked any different about it today than any other, with one exception: two blocks down he could see police raiding an empty house. This was a practice of the Memphis police department that Cory had seen before and he wasn't surprised. Cory was obviously smart enough to walk in the opposite direction of the exercise all the way down a long road to a hotspot for crackheads. There he could hide in the cut behind the little Asian store and serve his crack without being seen. Occasionally, he would switch up and occupy different areas. He knew staying in one spot was how to get busted and he wanted no part of a cage.

This was the only life he knew. He also knew that if he were caught selling in territory that any gangs claimed, they might shoot at him first and still not ask any questions later. The dope game was a tricky one. Dodging law enforcement and gangs were the only setbacks. The money was usually pretty good because not only were the homeless smoking it but the rich as well. Of course, the rich always sent the poor to get their drugs in case of a bust. It wasn't hard to tell what was going on when a neighborhood crackhead pulled up in a new Lexus to buy dope. And it happened quite often. Often, the police would take the dope track themselves and sell the crack on before arresting the buyers. This was another practice of the Memphis police departments and the Shelby County Sheriff's department. Cory knew the area all too well and could practically sense when something wasn't right. The police had caught him once before, but since then he had gone out of the way to be cautious.

CHAPTER

THE SYSTEM

Cory was smart and could have lived a different life. However, he didn't know how. Most of his brain cells were always too busy thinking about how not to get caught. He was very good at what he did. He was very good with facial recognition and body language. As the old saying goes, he could smell a cop from a mile away. Cory made sure his product was safe. He stuck most of it into the crotch of his pants while keeping a few pieces in his mouth for immediate sale. He did not sell to fishy "newbies" until he'd seen them served by other dealers in the hood. He wasn't about to sell dope to someone he didn't know who might just be buying specifically for the cops. That was the key to obtaining a warrant for the Shelby County Sheriff's Department. They couldn't very well get a warrant without first saying exactly how much crack they were going in to get, so they had to get a warrant for the actual money they used to purchase the crack cocaine. This involved recording the serial numbers and requesting a warrant for those serial numbers. He knew to launder his money as quickly as possible. He was happy with making an average few hundred in a day but a couple of times a month he would hit a mean lick and gross upwards of a grand in as little as one night. The hitch was that he couldn't do it every day no matter how good the money might be. He didn't want to be predictable or even known for that matter. One prior bust wasn't enough to be "known" yet.

CHAPTER

BILL'S VIGILANT PLANS

Bill decided to head towards Summer Avenue where he would cruise around for a while and enjoy watching the hookers work the streets. He knew the regular faces but new faces always turned up. Bill liked to wonder what their stories were and how they ended up this way. He often entertained his own scenarios within his thoughts. He had never stopped to talk with any of them but he knew why they were runnin' these streets at all hours of the day and night. It was all because of them dang crack dealers. "Them dad-blasted dealers was turnin' these folks into real life zombies. Zombies who dealt only in sex and thievery. They hadn't to be trusted. None of 'em," Bill would tell you in a heartbeat.

Bill backtracked down Summer Avenue and drove not too far from Memphis into Arkansas to his favorite drive-thru liquor store. Once his flat bottom was parked in that seat, he usually liked to keep it that way, at least until he got back home to abuse his wife. At the drive-thru window, he ordered his favorite whiskey and he ordered it cold. He was a regular and they always made sure Bill had a cold pint on standby. Before he drove out back onto the highway, he pulled over to take a giant filthy swig of his pint that nearly knocked out half the bottle.

Bill got his plan together in his head as he drove back into Memphis. He drove all the way back to Summer Avenue where he rented a motel room by the hour. This hotel sat off the main road a good piece and had virtually no customers. It would be just fine for what Bill had in mind. He paid for five hours and jumped right back in his truck. Today he was going to do his part to make a difference in the world. Bill Peterson was going to hurt someone today in a very peculiar way. He was angry at the world and someone else was about to pay the price. Before he went home that evening, Bill would make a stand that he felt totally justified about. A stand that was unheard of. A stand that people everywhere would praise him for and a stand everyone would condemn him for. Bill had finally found an outlet for the burning anger he'd felt within himself for so long. Now, all he needed was that sacrificial lamb to be on the receiving end of what he had planned during the eclipse.

He drove into south Memphis where he knew the ghetto would be mostly black and with no shortage of crack dealers. He thought of how he despised the trash the city streets had turned to in the last 30 or 40 years. He drove down one street that was literally infested with crack dealers and prostitutes. He felt it best to use a little gas in passing through here. The criminal activity was far too thick for what he had in mind.

He continued to drive through one of the most dangerous neighborhoods in the United States until he couldn't see it anymore. He came to a stop sign at one point when his truck was "rushed" by 15 or more competitive dealers who were eager to show a large number of crack rocks that rolled around in their palms like dice. Each yelled over the other, "I gotcha! Watcha' need? I gotcha'." Thankfully, his windows had been rolled up and he was able to simply drive away from the mob of aggressive criminal salesmen. Through the entire drive, he was in awe and disgust. The neighborhood wasn't even policed it was so dangerous. He drove on as this was not the venue he had in mind. This place was off the hook. He slammed back another drink of evil and got completely wrong in the head. For a moment, he cocked his head to the side like an inquisitive dog. And then he was back on alert.

Bill backtracked into midtown Memphis where the dope track seemed a little less wild and the dealers were slightly harder to find. It was easier here to find prostitutes than drugs unless you put a little work into it. He decided to park his truck in an area he knew he'd seen dope deals in. It was near an alley and a ma and pa Chinese grocery store. He sat calmly in his truck as he looked around to observe anything criminal that might be taking place. Bill slid his hand down in his pants and scratched the itch between his uppermost thigh and his right testicle. He scratched for a good five seconds before sighing in relief. It was a very sweaty itch and he must have known it would stink but he still brought his fingers to his nose for a deep wafting of pure stank. His pupils dilated at the smell but his expression didn't change a bit. Since he'd retired he didn't much see any need to wash his own ass on a regular basis. His excuse was that he hadn't done no work and why would he need a shower? He didn't have any friends and saw no reason to smell good. What it did for his health didn't matter either. He'd already beat his wife on several occasions for complaining about it. He was a free white American and he could do as he dang well pleased.

He wiped his fingers off on his shirt before digging in his nose to remove a chunk of golden relief. Any average American watching him would draw the conclusion that Bill was a disgusting man. Bill didn't feel this way because first off, Bill wasn't focusing at all on himself. Bill was focusing more on what was wrong with everyone else. On what was wrong with the city streets. Angry, he asked himself, "What is wrong with these street people? Why are they so disgusting?"

Bill sipped what was left of his whiskey while he waited for that one fly to hit his web. He didn't know who his subject was but he knew someone would be. He watched as a couple of older heroin addict hookers walked up the street. He could tell they were heroin addicts because their eyes were almost closed. One of them stopped in her tracks for a moment and appeared to take a nap standing up. Out here there were fewer of these than crack addicts. He sat and waited and just when his patience wore thin and his drink was gone, he saw him. The target had just come from behind the grocery store in what Bill thought was a tacky looking jogging suit with stripes on it. He exchanged something with one of the girls who walked around the streets quickly like a chicken. In his mind, he referred to these kinds of prostitutes as "Chicken heads". They were the ones who smoked crack.

He started his truck and moved in for a better view. Like a hunter, he had to remain unseen by the target. He moved up closer to the Asian ma and pa grocery store and turned his truck off again. He sat and watched and conspired. His first move was going to be the most difficult. As he lay in wait, he saw another "Chicken head" coming up the road – a black girl with corn rolls and headphones in her ears walking along the side of the street on what looked like a mission

Bill stepped from his truck and shut the door but not before grabbing his empty pint bottle and cupping it under his larger than life hands. He wanted to throw it away but first, he wanted to make sure he was seen by the Chicken head throwing it into the street corner garbage can. He wanted her to know that he drank so that she wouldn't mistake him for a cop. He wanted to gain her trust just long enough to get what he was after. He walked down the road towards her and hesitated so that he wouldn't get to the garbage can before she did. He timed it just right as he approached the garbage can and openly threw the bottle into its wide mouth. Just as the bottle lay still and quiet in the container, Bill approached her with a, "Howdy ... I'm Bill mmmmm. I was just gonna ask ya if I can buy your pipe off of ya? I'll give ya 20 bucks for it."

"Honey for a 'Twinkie' you can get damn near anything I got," she said with a delightful smile. And in broad daylight, she began digging in her bra like she was tryin' to get a crumb out. She dug around with a blank expression on her face that looked as if she were staring into another realm for what seemed to Bill as an eternity. When she finally pulled the pipe from her bra, she first had to examine it right there on the street.

Bill began to get irritated and she eventually handed it to him in exchange for his money. Bill shoved it angrily into his pocket and seemed to almost charge back up the sidewalk towards his truck. In an instant, he was back in the truck and slamming the door while he cussed under his breath about how difficult people had to be. There was almost nothing he would have liked more than to have slapped the stupid Chicken head's pathetic face. But he had to focus on the target lest his plan be thwarted.

CHAPTER

THE CAPTURE

BILL GREW RESTLESS IN waiting again for the drug dealer to
rear himself once more. To Bill, drug dealers and addicts were
the scum of the Earth. They were the lowest of the low and
nothing would ever change his view. They were animals. He
couldn't understand why they couldn't be more like him. He
viewed himself as an upstanding citizen who'd done his duty
as a countryman and didn't rely on anyone else. And he knew
drugs were evil because he'd been told so. It was the marijuana
that caused a stir when he was growing up. The marijuana
junkies were the worst for a time. He'd watched Refer Madness
and knew marijuana made people into psychotic killers and
such. But then crack came into play in the 80s and marijuana
somehow stopped driving people crazy. Now crack was the
problem. He didn't question how marijuana had stopped being
the problem. He only knew that it was cocaine now. And

that he, for one, was gonna do something about it. During his wait, he pulled the long narrow glass pipe from his pocket and analyzed it. It was black and greasy, just the way he saw black people in general. He couldn't help the fact that he was a racist pig. He'd been brought up this way. Looking at it from a different view was out of the question. "Black was black, and white was white. If you were friends with one of them spear chunkers then you may as well be one of them," he thought. Bill Peterson wasn't gonna have any mess out of any "Wiggers" either. And no room for the weaker species. Bill felt good about himself today. Bill was prejudiced but to others, he was simply considered one of the family.

Cory stood in the cut between a rock wall divider and the back of the food market waiting on the next 15 or 20 dollars to walk by in search of his dope. He'd made $20 already and had a long way to go. He kept an eye out for cops as he leaned against the rock wall pretending to be hanging out. If the cops did see him they would certainly shake him down and find the bag in his pants. There was a 50 percent chance that they would only search his pockets and his mouth, but he accepted the fact that there was a chance he may get caught. The police in this neighborhood were particularly aggressive when it came to crack dealers. The police would go so far as to break the law themselves to convict any one of them.

They were known for civil law violations and felt completely justified within their corruption. It was worth it to them to put these monsters behind bars. The police didn't treat them as human. They were paid to think people who used drugs were violent, stole from other people, and had to be caged like animals. Never mind the fact that hundreds of thousands of people stole for money and not drugs. The crack dealers felt the same way about the cops. To them, the police stole their product and caged them up with psychotic killers for a paycheck. To the ghetto, the police didn't seem human. The feeling was mutual. The treatment wasn't.

As Cory cupped three $20 rocks in his palm, he saw in the distance what looked like a homeless alcoholic hobo heading in his direction up the alleyway next to the store. The man was looking at the ground and past Cory as if he weren't really paying attention. He was an old white man who wore dirty long johns and a gigantic dirty cowboy hat. Cory dismissed him as a threat but wished he would hurry up and get past him. As the white man began to pass by, he made a sort of sideways eye contact with Cory. It was an almost insane look. The old white man with what appeared to be food painted around his mouth twisted with a sudden move that caught Cory off-guard. In the blink of an eye, the old bandit brandished a big black pistol that boasted six shiny bullets in its round chamber. Bill jabbed his fat firearm into Cory's side to the point of pain. He first took the three pieces of crack from Cory's hand before forcing him to walk in front of him towards the truck. When he got to the passenger's side, he forced Cory in at gunpoint without explanation. Cory found it difficult to protest as he wasn't sure exactly what was happening. The size of the barrel on the gun alone was enough for Cory to keep his mouth shut. He'd seen a lot on these streets but now he seemed to be in a state of shock, at least for a moment.

"What's goin' on, man? Why are you pointin' that big ugly pistol at me? You the police?" Cory asked with true concern.

In response, and with a twisted and nervous face, Bill replied, "Hell that's a surprise. Do I look like a cop? No. I don't. But don't sweat it too much. I think you'll survive if you do what you're told. If you give me any problems though, I will not hesitate to pull the trigger. Understand me, boy?"

Cory understood enough not to try anything for now. He rode along easily, for now.

Bill held the steering wheel with his right hand as his left hand rested on his chest, aiming the fat black barrel at his subject. He drove straight to the motel where he'd earlier purchased a room. Bill wasted no time in getting out of the truck and hurrying his prisoner into the room.

The room smelled of light mildewing, badly covered smoking, and years of unmentionable DNA spatters. The walls were painted a near puke color. In the light, they were even worse. Bill promptly turned on all the lights and ordered Cory Peterson to have a seat in the corner chair. It boasted yellow and white flowers that had now faded into a light brown nicotine film. It was gross. And it felt cold and waxy. Still, Cory sat down in it disgusted and more confused than frightened.

THE FIRST JUDGMENT

ONCE CORY WAS SEATED in the chair of many tales, Bill had a seat at the corner foot of the bed and sat for a moment. He looked at Cory straight in the eye. However, for Cory, it was like Bill were staring straight through him. It was almost as if Bill seemed to know him. The truth was that Bill truly believed that he did know Cory because he thought that he surely knew his type. Bill saw Cory as the scum of the Earth. A poisoner of white women and a food stamp sucker. Bill put aside his anger and hate for a moment to have a conversation with the animal he'd just caught. He wanted to entertain himself with some questions and answers that would most likely confirm that his redneck views were completely justified.

Bill sat there looking at Cory for a moment before breaking the ice with his first question. "What's ya name boy?"

With the sucking of a gold tooth and a little arrogance, Cory said in a calm voice, "What's it to ya man? And why am I being kidnapped? You plan on shootin' me or somethin'? I mean damn it, whatever your name is, I ain't did nothin' to nobody, especially you. Man, I don't even know you. So whatever it is you got up your sleeve go on and spit it out. I got kids at home. I ain't got time for none of this man." By now Cory's anger had overridden his fear and he was beginning not to like the situation more and more.

With yet another black-toothed grin, Bill said calmly while cocking his pistol, "I said what is your name? Full name."

"My name is Cory Peterson," Cory responded with a tone of voice that crackled and secretly begged for mercy.

Bill could hardly believe his ears. This piece of hoo-ha had his precious and proud last name. "Spell it. Your last name. Spell it," Bill insisted, lifting the gun an inch above his own knee. Cory spelled it out for him and it was the same as his own. As sure as spit, this cockroach had his last name and Bill liked it none too much. "How in the hell could this happen?" Bill wallowed in disgust within his own mind but wasn't about to show it to this scum he'd just picked up off the street.

Cory began to rock back and forth in the chair in worry.

"Why do you sell this crack garbage? Don't you know this crap is destroying America? Or do you even care? Bet you sell to kids too huh?"

Cory looked now as if he were ready to cry but didn't. He responded to Bill in just such a way as to try and justify what he did. "Man, it is hard out there. I got two kids and can't get no job. I done tried. Every time I try, I get shot down because of my education level or because some self-righteous white man like you don't like my gold tooth. I can't afford to feed my kids and go to no school. I can't afford no babysitter neither. I live in the ghetto, man. That's where I came up and that's where my folks came up. Ain't nobody comin' through the ghetto offerin' nothin' good but maybe a free sack lunch. What am I supposed to do? I mean, c'mon, man."

Bill took a silent moment to try and take in what Cory told him. Still, Bill imagined in his head how people were stealing from hard workers who didn't deserve to suffer not only some of their own problems in life much less some unsub crackhead's problems. "The people you sell to do immoral things for that garbage. You do know that right?" Bill proclaimed leaving it open for an answer.

Cory shook his head and rubbed his eyes with irritation before responding. "Look man. I ain't told none of them people how to get their money. That's their business and I ain't got nothin' to do with that. How you gonna sit there and blame me for other folks who steal? I ain't told 'em to steal nothin'. That's on them. That would be like you blaming another person's place of employment for funding terrorism because the person sent money to ISIS. It ain't the company's fault they spent the money on terrorism, is it? I don't think so. Whatchoo gonna do if they send the crack I sold them to ISIS? Charge me with terrorism? I'm just sayin', man, you can't put that on me. That's those people's personal behavior. I shouldn't be punished 'cause they can't act right. I'm doing what makes the world go around. I sell a product that is in demand. I make a business transaction. That's it, man. The rest ain't me. I don't steal. And for your information, little kids don't buy crack. If they do, I aint seen, em. Just sayin'."

Bill was entertained with the fact that this guy had all the answers and felt completely justified in what he did. "But what about the fact that it's against the law? Don't you consider that immoral? Or do you somehow think it's okay to break certain laws but not others?" Bill asked in a somewhat civilized manner. He wanted this chump to admit and agree that he was twisted and immoral. Bill wanted a confession. Bill was starting to think that this idiot was crazy and just didn't get it. The truth was that Bill was stuck in what he believed. Bill had been taught that it was bad and that was it. Taking into consideration that the man had kids to feed wasn't part of Bill's concern. Nor was it part of Bill's concern that they might be looking for their father to come home soon.

While Bill sat deep in thought, Cory impatiently decided to point something out. "You are talkin' all this mess about morality and about obeying the law, yet here you are in a motel with another human being that you kidnapped and held at gunpoint. Ain't you breakin' the law too? Man, you really got life twisted. Y'all white folks are somethin' else. But let's get down to business, man. For real. I got two kids at home waitin' on me and you got me here … What are we doin', man?"

Bill replied with a slightly self-gratified snarl, "The police wouldn't arrest me. They share the same views. Hell, I'd be a dang hero if I shot and killed ya right now, son. Don't you get it? You are the bad guy. You are the reason these streets ain't safe to walk down. Now, I got a little idea that you ain't really gonna like. But it's for a good reason. Just trust me on this.

"If you value any portion of your worthless life you will do exactly as I tell you when I tell you. Because I will not hesitate to shoot you and make it look like you kidnapped me as opposed to vice versa. Besides that, I personally don't consider you as being kidnapped. I merely made a citizen's arrest and brought you here in the name of justice. So what we gonna do here today is see if, in fact, we can change your perspective a little. You don't mind sellin' this abomination to people who have families that care about their wellbeing. Families who are tired of their relatives stealing from them and begging for crack money. You say the other side of the picture ain't your business just as long as you can raise two more crack dealers. Because that's what

I see. You don't wanna open your eyes and look at what your kind has done. What they continue to do." Bill had waited long enough he felt. It was time to get on with the punishment. Bill flicked one of the three rocks he'd taken from Cory right into Cory's face. It bounced onto the green, once blue carpet just at Cory's feet. "Pick it up," Bill said with authority.

Cory reached down and picked up the small stone. It seemed to almost glow in the dimly lit room.

"Now look at it. This is going to be a bit of a counseling session. I want you to observe that one rock. Just look at it. Doesn't look like much to you, does it? Sure, it don't because you don't smoke it. I know because you couldn't afford that space outfit that you are wearing right now if you was a smoker. Now, what do you see when you look at it?"

Cory held it near his eye as if to examine it carefully. Then he said almost sarcastically, "I see 20 dollars. That's all I see."

Bill responded with a disgusted, "Mmmm."

Immediately, Cory Peterson's demeanor changed. He uncrossed his arms and began to press on the arms of the filthy chair nervously.

Bill pushed a plastic silencer onto the big black barrel and they both heard it pop in place. At that moment, their eyes met more deeply than they had before. They sat staring at each other silently for what seemed to Cory to be a lifetime but was mere seconds. Bill aimed the silencer that appeared to be mostly electrical tape, down towards Cory's right knee.

With a quick flinch, Cory quickly said, "Hey wait, man. Hold up a minute. We ain't got to do this, man. You can let me go and I ain't gonna say anything at all to nobody! You have my word, man. Matter of fact I won't even sell dope no more, man. You'll see. I will show you, man. Check me out. But just let me go, man, so I can get back to my family, man."

Disgusted by Cory's response, Bill told him in a fed up voice, "You either smoke or Imma shoot your knee out. After that, if I'm still having problems with you, Imma shoot out the other knee. And if that don't soften your hard head, then I will move to your elbows. And you will be even worse off than if you had just done what I told ya in the first place. If you try to run, Imma shoot you in the chest and you will most likely die. The choice is yours, boy. Now. Smoke or I'm gonna be poppin' the knee you got in about three more seconds. I suggest you get smokin'."

Angrily, Cory shoved the crack cocaine into the straight and narrow glass conduit. The piece was a little wider than the hole in the pipe and caused a layer to shave off to the side and fall into Cory's lap. Once the pipe was caked full, Cory reached in his pocket for his lighter. The lighter he used only for weed would serve another purpose today. He had no choice but to accept what he had to do to go free. He'd never smoked crack or any hard drugs before. His mind raced as he tried to weigh out his options as quickly as possible and came to the only conclusion available. He knew he must submit. Jumping into the unknown sounded more pleasant than a bullet in the knee or chest. Cory flicked his Bic lighter and pulled on the glass pole as if it were weed. He entertained the chance that it may not affect him at all. As he pulled in the smoke he boasted a look in his eyes that tried to convince Bill that it wasn't nothin' but a thang. Cory looked at Bill as if to say, "I can take anything you got, you prejudice old white fool." But as Cory began to blow out the smoke, he thought he heard a train or a tornado when it first formed nearby. It felt as though wings flew by his ears and were forcing air into them just for a moment. Colors flashed before his eyes that he'd never seen. And it was mixed with a most orgasmic feeling that one couldn't deny being human. Cory's tongue lay hanging on his lip as he caught his breath from what may have been the most intense 20 seconds of his entire life. For those few seconds, everything was like a fantasy. It was a complete escape from everything and everyone. It was a release of all anger and sadness all at once and was absolutely astounding. It was like having sex with the woman of his dreams. It was like nothing else he'd ever experienced in life. For those 20 seconds, he had totally forgotten where he was and what was happening. He focused solely on that which had control of him. That feeling.

As soon as that 20 seconds passed by, Cory felt like his hearing had intensified. He thought he could hear people talking in the next room. Paranoia also immediately set into his mind simultaneously. He thought he heard them maybe say his name but wasn't sure. He sat completely still for a moment so that he might hear more clearly. But Bill, who had been basking in entertainment for the last few minutes, broke up Cory's intense concentration with a giggle. Cory turned his head quickly like a chicken and looked at Bill with a dumb yet aggravated gaze.

Bill laughed a light, "Yeehaw. How's that grab ya?" Bill threw the other two rocks in Cory's lap. Bill was amused and wondered if Cory would become a crackhead now instead of a crack dealer. "Hit it again, boy! Do it now! Do it or lose that knee. We ain't done yet."

Cory looked past Bill bugged eyed and took himself another full pull. This time it felt nearly as good as the first one but not quite. Cory must have wanted to hit the shameful tube of white smoke again because Bill didn't have to tell him to do it. He did it on his own. Cory seemed to be now glued to the nasty chair and his old personality was somewhere in outer space. He stared directly into the wall behind Bill as he rubbed the pipe between his hands to cool it off. Cory continued to smoke for a couple more hours on his own and without direction from master Bill. Bill smiled as he watched his prisoner chase another hit after his first hit. Cory felt he wasn't getting enough of the feeling he'd first felt so he kept trying, hoping he could smoke enough to feel the way he did after that very first puff. Cory had forgotten about everything else in life. Because of the circumstances, all his mind would let him do was smoke. He would have to smoke until it was gone.

Cory thought about telling Bill that it wasn't so bad but he stuttered and couldn't get a full word out of his mouth. His voice seemed to be gone. Communication was going to be impossible right now and Cory knew it. It was a side effect of the drug. But that didn't stop Bill from rattling on and talking smack.

"Boy, you ain't fartin' around with that dad-blasted crack, huh? I guess you done uncovered one of your true talents. You is now a bonafide crackhead, son. That's hella funny if you ask me. See, life has a way of shiftin' things around. I might have just helped you to be your true self. A real live crackhead."

"Who'd have ever thunk it?" Cory thought about his wife who he was estranged from and began to realize now what she was doing. She'd been caught in the same trap but under less forceful circumstances. He knew now why she'd chosen it over her stressful relationship with him and the children. The first puff was all it had taken to start her on a chase that would take all her attention and her old pain. He understood now that she'd been caught in a trap that had taken something away from her. At once, Cory forgave his wife and longed to see her.

After a good deal more smoking, the room was nearly filled with white smoke. It had a sweet stink to it. And the pipe seemed to be caking up more noticeably with the oily substance. It was nearly the color of motor oil. At least it appeared that way to Bill. It reminded him that he needed to change out the oil in his truck later. Yes, sir, Bill was getting a gigantic kick out of watching this guy take a dose of his own medicine. One moment Bill was laughing at his victim and the next he looked on in disgust. He didn't know how the drug was treating Cory's mind but he could see it must have done something to his nerves. Cory was now leaning over the floor and looking at the carpet to pick up white balls of lint. He told Cory to sit back up in the chair and cocked his pistol again. Cory quickly sat back up and seemed to stare at the ceiling as he rubbed the lint between his fingers. He was beginning to get confused with Cory's behavior and it intrigued him. Cory took another puff as he had begun to long for it. As he blew it out, his eyes grew huge. They were at least the size of a silver dollar. They seemed whiter than ever now. It reminded Bill of a cartoon that had gone wrong. Bill had had himself one hell of a day. The entertainment wasn't going to stop until he was ready. Bill was interested in what Cory might say or do next. Because Cory seemed to be in outer space somewhere, Bill decided to provoke a reaction by asking Cory how he was feeling. Cory looked over at him for an instant and then passed Bill at the stained wall.

In the lowest tone, Cory responded, "Not too good."

Bill could see in Cory's eyes that "not good" was a certainty. Cory appeared to be looking at invisible monsters or ghosts. He couldn't seem to stay still in his chair while he looked around wildly at times at invisible threats. Bill was beginning to get a little agitated himself. He hadn't had a drink in hours. He sat in thought with his gun resting on his knee. Looking at the wall next to Cory, Bill pondered what to do next. He wanted to leave there feeling justified in his actions. Bill looked away from the wall and back at his prisoner.

Just as he did, Cory cocked his neck to the side like a curious dog and asked Bill in a concerned voice, "Did you hear that?"

Irritated, Bill said, "No. What did you hear? No better yet I got a question for ya'. How much of your product did I just make you smoke?"

"Forty dollars," Cory mumbled. Slobber seemed to have dried up around Cory's mouth. When he spoke, the crust crumbled from his dry lips and fell into his lap. Cory must have seen the flakes fall because he looked down and began to pick up the crust while tasting it to make sure it wasn't the precious crack. It dissolved in his mouth and then on his finger as he touched any white spot he saw. Cory was traumatized.

Bill stood up and pulled his fat wallet from his long back pocket. He flipped through a bunch of old, balled up bills and unfolded two 20-dollar bills. He threw them on the table before telling Cory, "That was on me. Next one's one you. You might wanna consider getting yourself right. Maybe find a real job. Hell, ya' might even go to church. I'm considering it myself. Have a wonderful day."

CHAPTER

THE RELEASE

Bill backed out of the hotel door and shut it behind him. He was done punishing and judging Cory Peterson. He cupped his gun up under his arm before getting back in his truck. No one was around but he knew full well to be cautious. Once in his truck, he placed the gigantic 357 Python revolver back into the glove box. As he drove away, he took note that Cory hadn't opened the door yet. He wondered if Cory was enjoying his own product. He let out a small chuckle. He felt good about what he'd done today. Before heading home, he would have to hit the liquor store up for an emergency drink. He bought a gallon of rotgut nasty before heading towards the homestead. He felt like a new man.

Meanwhile, Cory remained seated in that creepy crawly chair licking his finger and touching his lap as if he were fishing for Crack crumbs. His behavior did not, however, line up with the mass of thought circulating his brain. To add to his anxiety, he thought he could hear police outside talking about busting him. He sat perfectly still for maybe 20 minutes so that he could focus on what he was hearing. It took him that long to realize he was hearing nothing but what lurked within his mind. Once he dismissed those thoughts, his mind went back to his wife who was out there somewhere on the streets because he hadn't understood her problem. Now, he felt that he truly did understand. He couldn't wait to see her, on one hand, but on the other hand, he seemed to be stuck where he was for the time being. He took another hit of the smoke that had become an instant habit. He wasn't getting any higher. Just feeding the want.

Cory sat around tweaking on Crack cocaine for about another hour after Bill had left him there. He knew that he could leave now but was mentally stuck for a time. He finally reached a point in his high where he felt sober. At that moment, so as not to lose it, Cory ran into the bathroom and began washing his face with cold water. It helped cool him down and it helped to revive him. He straightened up his demeanor and put on his best confident look before marching out the door and back towards home. He still had a bunch of crack in a bag in his underwear but had by now smoked the three loose rocks – an entire $60 worth of the garbage. It was all paid for except for the $20 he'd smoked once Bill was gone. He didn't think he would become addicted because he couldn't wait to come down from outer space. He really wasn't much enjoying the paranoia that he so bravely fought off. This stuff was truly trash and he could now fully understand why people chose to use it. Nothing else seemed as important as that next blast. Addicts would nearly defecate on themselves in anticipation of a fresh hit first thing in the morning, which was referred to as "a wake up".

Cory exited the hotel parking lot and walked straight up to Summer Avenue where he hoped to catch a bus from here as quickly as possible. But just as he arrived at the main street he saw people everywhere with faces turned in his direction. Many of them held cameras and most were wearing sunglasses. What was happening? Was this some sort of show or was he about to be under arrest? He knew without a doubt that the entire world knew he was high. His heart raced with fear of what might happen next.

Cory stood very still at the bus stop. He prayed in his head that everything would be alright and that he could merely get home to his kids without being arrested. He felt like something wasn't right and he didn't want to draw any more attention to himself than he may already have. He made sure not to make eye contact with anyone around him. He was a considerable distance from all the agent-looking people that he saw. He looked down the road. A straight flat stretch of road for a near half mile was visible to him yet no bus was. His wait was beginning to feel like an eternity when suddenly it began to grow dark and birds began to make weird noises. Guilt smashed him in the face as he realized how stupid he'd been.

The people hadn't been looking at him after all. The people were waiting on the solar eclipse. The sunglasses had all seemed uniform to him at first and now he knew why. They were all wearing solar eclipse glasses. The cameras were for pictures and videos of the natural wonder. Cory was relieved to understand now that he hadn't been the center of attention. His heart sunk a little when he realized his kids were at home watching it without him.

Once Cory caught a bus and returned home, he hung out with his kids until he found a babysitter. He needed time to himself. His nerves were on fire. He knew what he must do in order to get relief. He had to smoke more. With his children in good hands, Cory sat down on his comfortable, clean couch before reaching in his pocket and pulling out the crack pipe Bill had forced on him. He observed it closely for a moment before putting it into his mouth. He then lit it as if he were lighting a cigarette for an extensive period.

But instead of holding the flame to it he tapped the flame to it several times while taking in the smoke very slowly and fully. Many people had died this way. When he blew it out it was as if all his problems had disappeared. In short, he was comfortably dumb, complete with his tongue hanging from his mouth. His nerves dead. He was relaxed in his own world for another 20 seconds before chaos broke out in his mind. The sounds of police radios outside and the thought that they may be coming to get him riddled him with fright and paranoia. He took another hit of the mystery smoke. Although it wasn't as good as the last one, it took all the crowded emotions away instantly for another 20 seconds before it all crashed down on him again. Cory continued this for some time before resorting to his marijuana. He lit his half blunt and was able to make himself discontinue smoking the cocaine. Now that he felt his head was okay for travel, he headed out into the hood in search of his wife whom he'd pushed away to save the children. Now he felt the need to try and save her.

Cory walked through the ghetto in search of his wife whom he'd always vowed never to sell crack to. He found her relatively quickly and told her that he'd missed her and was sorry for pushing her away. He explained to her in full detail that he wanted her back and that they could both fight this thing together. She'd been asleep after a long smoke out and was still waking up when he began talking to her. She welcomed what she was hearing and shed a single tear as he told her he understood. He made a deal with her and she was more than happy to oblige. He told her that he would smoke the crack he had left with her if she promised that they would both seek to become better people at the end of the party. She agreed she wanted to live differently and promised him that she would back him if he backed her. Together they'd made an unexpected pact to move on to a better life and without the cocaine.

Cory pulled out his pipe and together they both smoked so much crack that it was gross. They got drunk together to come down before they both returned home to try again to live life without fear of police, cages, and financial ruin. They both laid down in the bed and went to sleep. By nightfall, the two kids were home and Cory and his wife reunited with them in a way that they never had. Tonight they realized what was really important.

Bill Peterson drove home on his high horse knowing he'd done a great deed for his nation. He was prouder than ever and couldn't wait to brag to his wife about what he'd done. He headed north in his pickup truck on Highway 51 out of city limits and into the county. There was less traffic up here and Bill could tip up his gallon of whiskey without being seen and drive at the same time. The truth was that Bill drove better drunk. He'd been drinking whiskey since childhood and it was now a part of him.

Only other lifetime drinkers could ever understand. Heaven forbid one of those women from M.A.D.D. see him. They'd hurry up and call the police on him. Safety was their middle name. They'd probably call the police if they saw someone riding in the back of a pickup truck, he thought to himself. That's how concerned about folk's business he thought they were. He grumbled to himself a bit as he drank and drove. Bill was far from being drunk or out of control of his vehicle. He felt fine until he noticed it suddenly had become darker. He'd forgotten all about the solar eclipse but there it was. He looked up at it in amazement. He didn't think he really cared about it when he'd woken up that morning but now he was in awe. He looked back down at the road and back up at the eclipse while juggling a drink of brown hell in between. Bill looked up one last time before a dog ran out in front of his speeding truck. It was unavoidable. He swerved to avoid it but inevitably ran over it. At the same time, his truck lost control.

As his truck slid out of control, he saw the telephone pole getting closer and closer. Before he was done sliding, his truck had slammed into the pole but fortunately on the passenger's side. Bill's head smashed against his driver's side window knocking him completely out. When he came to moments later, he remembered what had just happened. But somehow, he felt better now than he had before. He couldn't believe he'd just survived this wreck. He turned the key and the truck started right up. He was able to drive away with a dented side. His body felt fine and he felt thankful. He was thankful to be alive and thankful he had a beautiful wife to go home to. It's possible that the bump on the head may have changed Bill's perspective for the better. Whatever the case, he felt the now urgent need to get home to his wife. He threw out the gallon of whiskey. He didn't even know why. An emotion came over him that he'd never felt before and he felt guilty about slapping his wife that morning. Bill had no idea why he felt that way, but it felt good. He had to get home to tell her that he loved her and that he was sorry for the unnecessary punishment he'd put her through for years. Bill roared through town in his truck until he pulled into his own driveway. He didn't even crave another drink of alcohol right now. His only concern was his wife.

CHAPTER

THE SECOND JUDGMENT

BILL RAN UP TO his screen door on the front porch. He slung it open with an almost uncontrollable joy. Before he could get completely in the house, he saw his wife standing maybe six feet away from him against the refrigerator door. A drying stream of earlier tears glistened on her cheeks as she held a small, nickel-plated 9mm Beretta out in front of her, pointed directly at Bill's chest with both hands. Bill's face changed from a smile to one of confusion and hurt.

With a calm voice, his wife began to explain to him what the rest of today held in store. She said, "You sorry no good excuse for a human being. I've had all I can stand of your abuse. You come in here smiling and looking all high and mighty in my face and then you turn around and put your hands on me like I'm a punching bag."

Before she could finish, Bill tried to interrupt but she wasn't having it.

"I'm talking right now!" she screamed in anger and protest. "It's my turn you bastard. Now I've taken the liberty of going to the liquor store for you today. I spent money we didn't have to make sure I got your favorite whiskey. So, pick up that bottle right there and get to drinkin'! Go on pick it up! Now!" She let off a shot from her Beretta that struck the door next to him.

His reaction was to do as he was told. He wanted so badly to tell her that he'd seen himself today for what he was but she wouldn't allow him a word in edgewise. With no choice, Bill accepted his wife's orders and he grabbed the bottle. He tipped it up like it was nothing and took a long, ugly drink that ran down his mouth like a thirsty pig. And although it was a big drink, it didn't even begin to make the fat bottle look less full. "You happy?" he said to her behind a tear.

"Nope. Take another one," she said with anticipation.

So he drank. He took another and another and another. He had to stop for a moment to avoid vomiting but she never let up.

"Drink some more you lousy piece of garbage. Drink!"

He drank. And he drank. He knew she wasn't playing and if he didn't do as he was told she may well kill him. His mamma taught him long ago that if a woman holds a gun on you she is 10 times more likely to use it than a man. Halfway through the bottle, Bill was drunker than he'd ever been. He didn't by any means enjoy it, yet part of him was now beginning to respect her. He was realizing now more than ever that he loved and respected his wife. He began to apologize to her with clear words even as drunk as he was. "Baby, I am so sorry. A lot has happened today and the way I feel about what I've been doing is horrible. I never wanted to hurt you. I was angry and losing it. I realized today just before I got home how much I was in love with you. And the guilt was so overwhelming that I wanted to hurry home to you and tell you that I am sorry."

"Liar!" she proclaimed. "Now drink up!"

Bill felt saddened and he felt that it was unfair that just as he'd come to his senses, life had slapped him in the face. Bill continued to drink down the rest of the corn water nightmare until it was almost gone. Within an hour, Bill had consumed over a gallon of whiskey and he was starting to feel very sick.

Meanwhile, his wife was slowly digesting what he'd said to her earlier about being sorry. He sounded convincing and she'd never heard anything like this from him before. She was about ready to give in and tell him she was sorry when Bill began to heave. He was gagging as if he were trying to throw up something more solid than whiskey. She dropped her gun on the counter and ran to nurse him. She held him as he started falling sloppily into the floor. Soon his head was in her lap and she caressed him. They lay on the kitchen floor. He continued to gag in her lap without producing any liquid. She started to think that she may have killed him. She sobbed in a rocking motion with his head. She wasn't sure now what to do. She couldn't just let him die. This was her husband of many years and she loved him very much. She concluded that she had to get up and call him an ambulance. She got up from the floor careful to lay his head back down without bumping it. Before she could reach for the phone, Bill started to throw up. Something was gagging him as his body was trying to force out the alcohol. Something else seemed to be in the way of the booze. Something huge and nasty.

Bill got to his knees and on all fours and he began to hurl. Something that looked like a giant pot sticker began to protrude from his mouth. He pushed to gag through his mouth. He pushed from deep within his stomach as the long, noodle-like thing fell from his mouth followed by brown liquid that gushed out like a cracked fire hydrant. He sat for a moment as he caught his breath. His wife looking down at him and the slimy intestine-like blob in the middle of the floor. She was starting to gather that perhaps now he would be okay. He looked up at her and sat back against the dishwasher with a laugh. He was laughing uncontrollably. She could understand why. By the same token, she was concerned with what it was he'd just spit out into the floor. It was a giant tapeworm. Bill now felt like a new man. A drunk happy one. She laughed back and the two of them laughed together although they weren't entirely sure what they were laughing at. She got down on the floor with him and cradled him.

"What in the good Lord's name was that?" she asked mid-laugh.

He said to her with relief, "That, my dear, is a tapeworm that I didn't know I had. I feel so much better now that that thing is out that I don't know what to do first. But I do know one thing. I'm done drinkin' after today and I love you more than ever. I promise never to be mean to you again, sweetheart. Other than that tapeworm and the whiskey, I don't know what got into me. You're my wife and I'm gonna' start behaving like a husband."

They both lay on the floor laughing when the worm twitched. For a second they grew quiet. Then their laughter resumed when it stopped moving.

Bill and his wife soon renewed their vows. Bill quit drinking and hadn't drunk since the last one his wife forced on him. Bill never laid his hands on his wife again unless it was a hug. He loved her so much that he took up going to church with her and taking walks through the park like they had once upon a time in their younger years. The two of them began to watch what they ate. And they got more exercise. Their skin cleared up and they began to look younger. They even went to homeless missions and volunteered their services every other weekend. They were finally back on the track of loving one another and other people as well. They began caring more and more about life. And although they had forgiven each other for their shortcomings and anyone else in life that had crossed them, Bill couldn't forget what he'd done to Cory Peterson. Now 10 years later, he often wondered to himself if Cory was even still alive. Bill had surrendered his prejudice since that day of the solar eclipse. That day, on his way home from terrorizing Cory Peterson, he had somehow let go of hate. Bill became a loving and caring man. He was now truly sorry for what he'd done. Every now and then, Bill would ride through Memphis hoping to catch a glimpse of Cory either selling or buying crack cocaine. But he never saw him there again. He had long since outgrown the hatred that drove him to ride through the ghetto and judge people. He only drove through these days in search of his once prisoner.

Bill had long since gotten rid of his big man truck. He and his wife now had one vehicle, which was a convertible Chrysler Lebaron. What they had now was a family car for the two of them. When he had his truck, it was considered his. Drinking and basking in hate had made him selfish and violent once. Now, he involved his wife in almost everything he did. The exception was driving through Memphis from time to time. He never got around to telling her what he'd done that day and saw no reason to tell her now. She had never asked him what he'd done that day and it remained his secret. He thought perhaps he would tell her one day. Just not today.

Today he and his wife were going to the zoo in Memphis and then later in the evening they were visiting a church to help serve food to the homeless people. The zoo was beautiful. It was nice walking outside in the beautiful weather while observing so many different wild animals. In a sense, Bill felt sorry for them. He couldn't imagine being forced to live in a cage under someone else's rule. Ten years ago, he couldn't remember having cared less about an animal. Now he seemed to have a compassion for all living things. Bill had done a complete 360 with his and his wife's life. He'd become a different person and he himself could see it clearly. He'd dropped the ball and chain of hatred. He saw black people as human beings now. He saw himself as having once been a hypocrite. He even changed from Republican to Democrat. Everything had changed.

Cory Peterson was showering and getting ready to start his new job. For the last 10 years, he'd been working part-time at the regional medical center while his wife worked full-time at the Pink Palace Museum. Cory did all of the cooking and kid watching to take up her slack. Nine years ago they both decided to move into the country and away from the influence of anyone or anything negative. Cory and his wife had decided to turn their lives around together. Their commute was long but it had been worth it to move away from all of the people who were once bad influences. Their two children were now nearly grown up. They were good kids and turned out fine.

Today was Sunday. Normally, Cory would have been at the hospital working janitorial but today he was starting a full-time job. It was a job he'd un-officially studied for during the last 10 years. In his heart, he knew he was ready for it. He turned off the shower before stepping out where his wife handed him a towel. He'd forgotten to grab a towel and she'd realized it. When he came out, she cracked the door and handed him one. He smiled as he took it from her hand. He was thankful to and for her. They didn't argue anymore like they once had years and years ago. Today they loved each other. Today crack and alcohol were out of their lives and love was in.

Cory's wife was off work today. She cooked breakfast in the kitchen while Cory dressed and groomed himself. She whisked the eggs with milk, chopped onions, shallots, and fresh jalapeno peppers. Long ago they'd decided together to start eating right. They rarely ever got sick now. Depression had long since gone. They were living their lives the best way they knew how. A good, clean life. Cory had stopped selling crack years ago after having an altercation with a corrupt old man. He didn't stop necessarily because of the old man though. He stopped because he was tired of being a victim and he wanted to be happy with his wife. He stopped selling not because most people were against it and not because it was against the law but for his family. His wife stopped smoking because she wanted the same thing and to live a normal life free of humiliation and free of cages. She didn't particularly enjoy men with badges touching her all over her body from time to time in search of drugs either. She didn't enjoy having police dogs ordered on her because she was homeless and looking for privacy. The street life had taken its toll on her but she wouldn't allow it any victory. She too had refused to be beaten just as her man had. They finally faced their guilt together and were able to deal with it. And guilt was strong for parents who couldn't live up to the rest of society's expectations. Using a substance to ease the burden of parenting wasn't acceptable to society. Alcohol was. They wanted no part of either.

Cory sat down in the kitchen ready for breakfast in a fancy suit. Tie and all. He looked sharp as sharp could be. His wife told him how nice he looked in the suit. If his skin had been a little lighter, you might have seen him blush. He felt good. He was hungry too. Breakfast was served. Cory cleaned his plate like he was raised to do. He didn't believe in wasting food. When his wife took a shower, Cory sat and pondered. He thought back to the dirty old man that'd kidnapped him all those years ago. He wondered if the man had finally drunk himself to death or if he'd ever changed and lost his bitterness.

Back then, Cory hadn't known what to think of the old man and he'd never much focused on it until this moment eating breakfast. Cory thought if he ever saw that man again he might forgive him for what he'd done. The old man hadn't really done him any harm and Cory didn't want to hold contempt in his heart for anyone. He wanted to be free of that. He was now all about letting go. He dismissed the thought and moved into the other room. He picked up his marijuana pipe and took three puffs. Cory had slowed down on the marijuana over the years and now used it very lightly. He used just enough every morning to keep his nerves calm. It did not leave him feeling out of control nor did it seem to have an intoxicating effect. For Cory, it was a natural medicine. His use was completely harmless and marijuana had been decriminalized.

After Cory's wife was dressed and ready, she came into the living room where she relaxed for a moment on the couch. She could see Cory in the mirror from the hallway. He wanted to make a good impression this morning at his new job. Once he was done making sure everything was in place, he walked into the living room and asked his wife, "Are you ready?" With a nod of her head, they set out towards his new place of employment. Along the way, they picked up their two teenagers from their friend's house where they'd spent the night. They too were dressed to a "T". The kids knew today was important for their dad and they knew to be dressed properly for the occasion. They traveled for a few more minutes in silence before pulling in to a parking lot where a few homeless people were hanging out as if they were waiting on something. In fact, they were waiting for food.

Cory parked the car. He and his family walked around to the front of the building where a giant cross built of dogwood seemed to stand guard. They were at a church that had no name. The church had been standing for many years and its people decided not to give it a name because they preached only from the Bible and to them that was all that mattered. It was an old building. Many people had passed through it over the years. It also had its fair share of regulars who came every Sunday.

Cory's new job was at a church with no name. A church he and his family had frequented for the last seven years. On this day, Cory was being accepted as the new assistant pastor. He would work full-time for the church. His new duties were now to assist people who needed help in any way. This included listening to people who wanted to get something off their chests and people who just needed someone to pray with. Cory would also do sermons and assist in taking care of the church's bills. He'd long since volunteered to help time and time again and now it had turned into a job. Today, they would have a sermon and introduce Cory as the new assistant pastor. Afterward, they would feed the homeless people who came to eat.

He and his family entered the front door where they were greeted by everyone. They all seemed to love Cory and were happy he was there. There were also many volunteers there for the sermon and feeding. The church was predominately black but always had new volunteers come in for a visit. Today was just as any other. A mixture of blacks and whites attended and all seemed happy to do so. People felt comfortable here and with each other. In fact, it almost seemed as though an unseen force held hatred at bay and away from the building entirely.

Cory shook a few hands and gave everyone a genuine smile. He attempted a zigzag through the people who talked amongst themselves and to each other. Along the way, he was stopped by the pastor who gave him a hug and congratulations. The pastor asked him how he was doing as he lay hands on Cory's shoulders.

Cory said, "Pastor, I'm doing just fine this mornin', sir. Aside from getting a little aggravated with traffic, I'm great."

The pastor quoted one simple verse from the Bible to him in response. "Forgive them. For they know not what they do."

Cory laughed lightly as he knew it to be true. The pastor broke eye contact to greet another person and Cory moved on through. When he turned, he bumped into one of the older white gentlemen who was attending and volunteering to help feed. As Cory's Bible fell to the floor, the man instantly bent down to pick it up for him. He handed it back to Cory and said, "I'm sorry. Please forgive me." Cory looked into the man's face. Before he realized who he was talking to he replied, "I forgive you." with a smile. Bill Peterson and Cory Peterson were face to face again.

Inside of a church with no name the two may have thought for an instant that they recognized one another. They shook hands and both moved on. Neither was sure who the other was but they were sure they had met once upon a time.

When the service was over, the head pastor announced Cory Peterson as the new assistant pastor. Bill Peterson could hardly believe what he was hearing. He was seeing Cory Peterson for the first time since the day of the solar eclipse and he didn't know what to do. He was so incredibly overwhelmed that shivers ran down his spine and his grey neck hair stood up. Bill was torn between being extremely happy for Cory and thoughts of how to break it to him that he'd been that angry, drunk, old man who had held him at gunpoint and forced him to use drugs. Bill was himself now in shock. He excused himself to the bathroom where he washed his face and even smacked himself a little to make sure that this was real. Questions flooded his mind as he splashed more water on his face. "Would this guy forgive him? Would he try and get even? Would his family be affected? Might Cory try to even kill him?" Bill lost his faith for a moment and decided he should get his wife and leave. He pulled a brown paper towel from the receptor and began to dry his face, lost in thought and concern. He threw the paper towel into the garbage and reached for another to finish the job. Just as he placed the new paper towel to his face, something poked against the bottom of his lower back. At the same time, a familiar voice said to him with confidence, "Don't move." Bill was frozen in place. He knew he'd done that man wrong years ago and now he was going to have to own it.

REDEMPTION

BILL KNEW CORY'S VOICE well and he now felt vulnerable and under Cory's power. Cory's weapon pressed ever so lightly into Bill's lower back. Bill stood still and waited for death or kidnapping. As Bill stood in silence, he accepted the inevitable. He knew full well that he deserved whatever he was about to receive at this moment.

Cory said to him firmly, "I don't yet know what your name is, but you kidnapped me years ago and forced me at gunpoint to smoke crack cocaine in that nasty hotel room. Are you still that person?"

Bill said sharply, "No."

Cory smiled and shook his head. "Turn around then and feel what I feel."

Bill turned around ready for his punishment and Cory lifted his Bible from the small of Bill's back.

"Forgiveness. That's what I feel from God today. I forgive you for what you did to me all of those years ago. I forgive you."

When Bill realized it hadn't been a weapon he was tickled. A weight so great was lifted from Bill's heart as Cory forgave him for what he'd done to him. When Cory hugged him, Bill not only hugged him back but began to cry uncontrollably. He was so happy he nearly couldn't quit crying. When he finally did stop he felt much lighter.

Cory and Bill Peterson became good friends after that. Bill attended Cory's church on a regular basis and the two of them helped each other whenever necessary. They went on to live their lives and came to love one another as brothers. Brothers who no longer saw color.

THE END

ENTRAPMENT

AND

DECEIT

CHAPTER

KENNETH JAMES

BULLETS RIPPED THROUGH THE wall next to Kenneth James. He ducked and dodged with stealth. He had no body armor on today and it entered his mind that one bullet from his assailant could end his life. He stood and faced the two bandits for just long enough to fire off five rounds from his police-issue 38 Special. He hit one in the leg and the other ducked behind a concrete pillar. By now, Kenneth was nearly out of bullets and hoping backup would arrive soon.

Kenneth was an honest police officer. He'd been on the force for nearly a decade. Before that he'd been an attorney. Now at 61 years old, Kenneth had white hair. He had blue eyes of old knowledge as he'd kept his face buried in the books for many a year. Being a police officer didn't leave him much reading time but retirement was near. He would have plenty of time to read later. For now, he had to work the beat. For now, he had to figure out what to do about these guys robbing the grocery store. He'd walked in just in time to see it happening. It wasn't what he was looking forward to when he came in to by milk and chicken batter.

Kenneth wasn't a tall man. He stood somewhere between five feet seven inches and five feet 10 inches. He weighed 170 lbs. He wasn't a big man by any means. But he was big at heart and full of courage. He'd been in the Army when he was a younger man, which had taught him discipline. Ten years of police work had taught him street smarts. Kenneth had it together. He was an experienced man who was proud to be an American. His parents were German but he was full blooded American. A man who believed in freedom. A man who believed that the people of the United States should be protected.

Kenneth fired back a few more shots at the monster behind the pillar. This time when the crook shot back, the bullet went through the wall and whizzed right next to Kenneth's ear. It was too close for comfort and he only had one shot left. Today, all of the experience in the world wouldn't matter if, in fact, he were shot dead. Even more than surviving, he wanted to catch this guy before he could hurt anyone else. His own life didn't even matter to him right now. It was all about the objective.

The subject must've known that he was about out of time because he ran for it. His buddy had long since hopped out the door after being shot in the leg. Kenneth instantly knew that his time was about to run out as well if the crook made it out that door. The thief ran down the aisle and just as he made it to the door jamb, his ankle cracked violently and poured blood. In that instant he fell, dropping his gun.

Almost immediately, he was in cuffs and being carried to an ambulance. Kenneth was a very good shot. He had hit the runaway criminal right where he'd wanted to in the ankle. Kenneth had never killed anyone aside from a car accident in his younger years and it hadn't been his fault. The car was noted to have issues with tipping over at sharp turns.

Killing when it wasn't necessary was a basic standard Kenneth held. He'd faced a number of situations throughout his police career that would have warranted his killing someone but he never did. He always found a way to wound them as opposed to killing them. Although an officer of the law, he still didn't believe in taking the life of another human being if not absolutely necessary. There was something wrong with taking human life.

Kenneth had heard stories over the years of fellow officers shooting people to death because they'd feared for their lives. And some he felt, did it twice too often. But that was none of his business. He always had faith that the department handled things in a manner in which they should. Officer Kenneth James usually worked the beat alone in uniform and without a partner. Today was supposed to have been his off day. He should have been frying chicken by now.

Both wounded robbers were apprehended and Kenneth was given a pat on the back. After a few hours of paperwork, he headed home. He picked up his milk and chicken coating from another store. Later, while Kenneth ate his chicken, he watched the news. He shook his head as he listened to a story of cops shooting a man in the back on camera. He couldn't believe that any police force could hire a guy like this and not have seen any signs. It happened so often these days that he was merely thankful not to have been working in those precincts. He quickly dismissed it as not being his problem.

CHAPTER

THE ASSIGNMENT

KENNETH HAD NEARLY FINISHED his food when the phone rang. He wondered who it could be. Was it his long-lost son who would now be 46-years-old? He'd had a wife when he was just 18-years-old. She took off with the newborn and he went on with life. They hadn't been mature enough to have a family together and were at one another's throats. She did what she wanted just as he did. He'd never paid a dime of child support and sometimes wondered if it would ever come back to bite him in the you know what. But it never had. And now at 61, he wasn't really concerned with it. He'd gone out to check on his now-adult son once but did not like what he'd seen. He spied long enough to know that his paternal son was a drug-using idiot. He wanted no part of him. Oddly enough, he had expected to see his son doing great. He'd excused his son's behavior because someone hadn't raised him right. It'd never crossed his mind that perhaps his son behaved like a party animal because his real father hadn't been there to guide him. If it had crossed his mind, then he'd missed it. Whatever the case, Kenneth wasn't happy with his son and didn't want to meet him anytime soon. Thankfully the phone call was only from his boss. The captain didn't call often. When he did, it was important. Tonight he would receive instructions to meet up with Sargent Lathrop pending an investigation.

"Detective James, I need you to hook up with Sgt. Lathrop tomorrow. They have a drug case they are working on over in the east precinct and they need a few extra hands," the voice on the other end said with authority.

"Yes, sir. I can do that," Kenneth responded before hanging up. He ate his last bite of fried chicken and retired to bed until morning.

The following morning, he got up and made himself breakfast. Bacon and eggs wouldn't hold him long but it would hold him long enough. After he was done eating, he put on his uniform and grabbed his guns. He headed out the door to go meet Sgt. Lathrop and his crew.

At first sight, Kenneth drew the impression that Lathrop was a rootin' tootin' gunslinger. He wore tactical gear in what seemed to be excess. He carried himself like a soldier in the military. Kenneth thought to himself that maybe Sgt. Lathrop should be in the Marines and not the police force. But to each his own. They were all on the same side.

"Today's objective is to make a bust on a guy we've been watching, folks. He hasn't made a move in over a month. It almost seems like he has retired yet we know dealing marijuana is how he puts bread on the table. His last move was a delivery that we weren't able to detect until after it was done. Before that, we watched what we believed to be deliveries here, here, and here," Lathrop said as he pointed to the map. He was desperate for an arrest.

There were eight of them in total. Cyclops was second in rank. They called him Cyclops because he had a scar in the middle of his forehead. At least that's what everybody assumed. The rest were just grunts – football players with guns. Lathrop was the coach and Cyclops was the quarterback. The other six were players who followed a plan well. As big as defensive ends and as fast as running backs, these guys usually apprehended the perp without issue. None of them had any reason to think that today would be any different. Kenneth made nine and today was going to be real work. He could tell by their demeanors that they were all pumped up for success. Being 61 years old wouldn't help much by way of a physical confrontation, but it would certainly come in handy where experience, knowledge, and insight came into play. Knowing the importance of being alert had paid off. Being old enough to read what the other guy was thinking had made the difference between life or death in many a past situation. Kenneth had played his cards carefully throughout his life. He hadn't gotten this far without experience and discipline. Kenneth was a straight shooter and mostly by the book. He was as good an atheist as they got.

While they loaded up the vehicles, Cyclops explained to Kenneth what position he was expected to hold. "Here's the deal. I just need you to cover the back of the line as well as the front door. Just have your gun drawn and be ready for whatever might occur. We don't expect this guy to fight. He's pretty much a pushover. Once we are there, simply come behind us and guard the front door. Got it?"

Kenneth nodded in confirmation. Everyone was on the same page. It was a go. When they arrived, everyone took up formation and kicked the door in. It was a somewhat quiet neighborhood without much traffic. As Sgt. Lathrop counted down from four, Kenneth could hear the birds singing at what seemed to him an abnormal volume. When his fingers got down to one, Cyclops mouthed the word "go." Together, they were able to smash the front door in and drag out the curly, red-headed 19-year-old man who lived there. They made sure the house was clear before they began to tear it apart. When they found nothing, their tempers began to swell and Kenneth could sense something was wrong. He saw Sgt. Lathrop whispering to Cyclops.

Cyclops walked urgently passed Kenneth and out the door. He went directly to the back door of the tactical vehicle and pulled out a large green tote bag. Kenneth took notice as Cyclops walked back into the home with the large tote. Kenneth thought for an instant that he smelled pot coming from the bag as the other officer passed by. Kenneth's gears began to turn within his head. Pieces began to click. "Please, God, don't let this be what I think it is," he thought.

Kenneth walked to the back room where he saw exactly what he never wanted to have to see. He witnessed Sgt. Lathrop pulling a large blue bag from the tote bag. It was filled with marijuana and nearly airtight. When Sgt. Lathrop turned to see Kenneth James standing behind him he snapped at him, "I gave orders for you to cover the front door. Now get the front door officer!"

Officer Kenneth James did as he was told. Chain of command was very important. Following orders from higher ranking officers was a sworn duty. Ratting on other officers was also an abomination amongst the department. Kenneth had hoped never to see anything like this but there it was. Corruption in his face. Corruption he felt sworn to overlook.

Later that evening, and after the red-headed kid was arrested for a number of drug charges, Sgt. Lathrop called Officer Kenneth James into his office. Kenneth sat in a chair opposite the higher ranking officer's desk. He shifted a bit to get comfortable. As the Sgt. finished his paperwork he started off the conversation.

"Officer James, I see you are almost at retirement age. Nice job making it so far. Never had to shoot anybody. You are a good example for everyone here." He laid his pen down and looked Kenneth straight in the eye, which wasn't easy for the sergeant. He may have outranked Officer James, but there was the elder factor. Lathrop had a respect for his elders because he knew without a doubt that they had more life experience than he had. He knew that he himself had got wiser as he aged and he was careful not to be put in his place for saying the wrong things to someone who knew better than he. He felt the desire to explain to Officer James his side of what had occurred during the drug planting bust.

Lathrop crossed his fingers and looked to his left and down at his paperwork. He said, "Officer James, these people, these drug dealers are tearing our country apart. Every day we have people stopping it at our borders and every day most still manage to get through. We can't catch them all obviously but we get 'em when and where we can. This is a war and sometimes, as we both well know, war isn't pleasant. These marijuana addicts are out there stealing for a living. They do drive-by shootings and they even rape people. I've read enough about it to know. It's threatening our way of life every day. People like that kid we arrested only add to the problem. We know for a fact that this guy was already selling prior to his arrest. We just didn't catch him this time."

Sgt. Lathrop paused for a moment and took in a deep breath while cracking his knuckles. Then he continued. "The fact is, whether this guy had it on him today or not, he would have. And who knows if we would have caught him. Every day that he is out there free on the streets is another day that he can distribute that poisonous herb. He may as well be a terrorist. So sometimes we have to be the ones to make the first move. It's prevention at its most aggressive. I know sometimes it might not look right and it ain't fair, but life ain't fair. We have to look out for our people. Our safety. Our kids. They come first. So I just wanted to make sure that we are all still on the same page. I'm sorry I snapped at ya earlier about covering the door. But, believe it or not, it was hard for me too. It's not something I enjoy doing. I look at it like this. If we want to eat we gotta skin the deer. We sometimes are forced to do things we don't wanna do for the greater good. Know what I mean? You okay?" He looked to Kenneth for a response.

Kenneth rubbed his white mustache and considered the best response. And in the least defensive and most subtle way, Kenneth said, "Don't sweat it. It's not like I'm going to IA to blackball myself. Cops don't rat on cops, remember? And besides, you are probably right. The kid will just sell again. And there will be more local pot distribution. However, being the gentleman that I am I would like to express to you a side you may well not see. If I may…"

Sgt. Lathrop responded, "I'm all ears."

CHAPTER

FEELINGS

KENNETH CONTINUED, "FIRST OFF, I have personally tried marijuana. It was an exercise we did years ago within the department in an attempt to advance our thinking. A way for us to relate to the purp's thinking. Before policies changed it was a way for us to better identify potheads as well as think like them. In order to beat them, we felt we had to become them. The thing is, something happened after we used it that we didn't expect. We were all intense and braced ourselves after having induced it. We were expecting a wave of possible hallucinations and aggressive behavior to overcome us. At least temporarily, until the THC toxicity wore off. But then, the strangest thing happened. One of the senior officers began to laugh. Ever so slightly at first but then louder. When we looked at him, he looked back at us and laughed even louder. Immediately, I knew what he was laughing at. You wanna know why he was laughing, Sgt. Lathrop?"

Lathrop nodded his head and Officer James continued.

"He was laughing because none of what he'd seen on television or read in the papers about marijuana had ever been true. All those years of watching and reading about the God-awful devil weed had implanted an impression into our brains. It was an impression broken only by experience. We saw firsthand that the marijuana crisis had been a farce the entire time. All the herb did to us was to relax our anxieties and make us hungry. I guess, in a sense, we were the zombies they made pot smokers out to be in that we were ready to eat anything we could get a hold of. We found that there was nothing to fear in the pot smoker nor within the plant itself. It wasn't a physical threat.

"We could only assume it was made illegal for some other reason; that reason most likely being money. I'm not disputing that it's against the law. Don't get me wrong. But people ain't doin' driveby shootings for it and I don't know if they ever were. What you did yourself was more immoral than smoking pot. And now that I've had my say, so I suppose I'll head home. My old back is killing me."

Kenneth left the office on good terms but not without first giving the sergeant what he assumed was a sort of fatherly advice. The sergeant didn't mind. His only concern had been a rat and now he knew he didn't have that problem. It was all good.

Later in the evening, Kenneth sat in his chair wondering why men did what men did. And why life was what it was. He soon turned off his pondering by turning on the television. He thoroughly enjoyed watching re-runs of "Archie Bunker" and "All in the Family". Those were the days. He liked a show called "Night Court" too. He was a simple man who only wanted to live a private life of TV and microwaved food. Drama was the last thing he wanted in life. He'd only become a police officer because he thought he had the morals that it took and he wanted the life experience.

The following morning, Kenneth was called into the captain's office. The captain merely wanted to see how things went. Kenneth informed him that it had all gone great and that Lathrop had his work cut out for him. It was a relatively short-lived meeting. Kenneth went back to the beat as he always had. He preferred working alone. It was enough to accept responsibility for himself. It was quite another to have to accept responsibility for a partner as well. Some of these young bucks were gun happy with a chip on their shoulders. And some preferred to stay ignorant when it came to race. Heaven forbid he get stuck with an idiot racist partner who liked to talk. On top of that, the talkers seemed never to listen thus getting no smarter than they were the day before. Kenneth had grown older and wiser than each year past. He sometimes wished he hadn't had the wisdom to see right from wrong in the depth that he did. Through the years, he'd also developed a conscience with his wisdom. He was feeling it on the beat today in his heart. He felt a guilt seeping in that he assumed he avoided. He began to think about having been part of a drug planting. Planting evidence for an arrest didn't taste good in his mouth. The thought made his mouth dry up. Nevertheless, he wouldn't ever say anything about it lest he was ousted or made an accomplice. What was done was done but the guilt lingered. He wouldn't dwell on it and would most likely forget about it, eventually. But knowing this didn't make it any more comfortable.

Kenneth was suddenly compelled to check up on the case in the marijuana arrest. He didn't know for certain exactly why. Perhaps he wanted to assure himself that the 19-year-old red-headed kid had it coming. He wanted to feel justified. Officer James paid a visit to the county jail to perform his own quick, face to face interview. He got the kid into the interview room and simply told him, "Tell me a little about yourself."

The kid looked disgusted and he had the worst attitude in the world. His facial expression said it all. His mouth hung open and he exposed his front teeth as if he were deeply analyzing something before responding, "Tell you what about myself. I haven't done anything. That pot was planted and you and your Commie buddies know it. You guys don't have anything good coming behind what you did to me. I admit I used to deal pot but I quit like six months ago. I realized not only how big of a deal it was for you Republican types but that I didn't want to live my life being controlled in a small cage with murderers and rapists.

"Marijuana shouldn't even warrant punishment but you guys pretend it's something it isn't. It's like that expression Donald Trump uses about collusion. It's a national witch hunt. Weed isn't dangerous, man. You guys are. Go figure. I still smoke it. I just don't sell it. I'm in college and trying to get a degree. You authoritarians want everything done your way. Well, what about my way? I'm not hurting anyone in any way. I'm living my life. That's it, dude. Minding my own business." The young man crossed his arms and looked away as if to say he was done talking to his enemy.

Officer James dismissed him and sent him back to his housing unit. Kenneth didn't like the inmate's attitude but couldn't use it to his advantage in feeling justified. He could see the kid didn't belong in a cage. He might have been better off not interviewing the guy in the first place. Now he felt even more guilty. Yet he was still able to justify it in one way or another. In time, he could simply forget just as he had done with any other negative aspect of his life. Carrying extra weight in the form of guilt never did anyone any good. He thought it best to move on and so he did.

Today he watched the impoverished people on the streets shuffling around to buy their drugs. He felt a sense of compassion for them because he knew they were merely in search of some relief from the hand that life had certainly dealt them. Some were destined to feel the pain and others weren't.

That was just how life was. Kenneth had begun to feel the need for relief himself as of late and fully understood where the users were coming from. And although he felt a compassion, he himself would never use anything short of a refreshing alcoholic beverage. He was a good cop. Too much alcohol was worse than too much marijuana from his standpoint but the law was the law.

Narcotics officers were working an area close to Kenneth's beat. He overheard them discussing it on the police radio. After giving it a little thought, he decided to go and check it out. He wasn't allowed in the area because he could compromise the undercover work. He pulled up at a great distance away before pulling out a large pair of extremely high-power police-issued binoculars. He viewed the operation area in clarity. There he was. In the center of his focus was Cyclops. Dressed in thuggish looking clothes, he was selling dope to the homeless. The homeless were then arrested around the corner. One after another, the buyers were put into a paddy wagon on their knees with their hands zip tied behind their backs. They would fill the wagon up with users before being mass transported to jail. This practice made the department a lot of money. More cases meant more money and that was the way it was. Kenneth stayed watching long enough to see 40 people carted off to a cage in just an hour's time. He put his binoculars away and sat for a moment shaking his head and wondering why there had to be victims. He could see that it was because people suffered. He wondered why they couldn't all just get along.

Officer Kenneth James headed back to his beat. He cruised his posts until he saw a scuffle. This was the norm on his beat. As Kenneth broke up the scuffle, he realized just then that working for a corrupt police department wasn't what he wanted for himself. Not to mention the poor bastards that couldn't afford attorneys. He was beginning to grow disgusted with the thought of working for people like this. He felt like part of the problem despite the fact that his hands were tied. He knew saying something to IA would cause nothing but more problems and in the long run, justice would not be done. The police were protected, favored, and, in some cases, nearly worshipped. There was nothing this 61-year-old man could do to better the department he worked for but he didn't have to be part of it. He'd been feeling dirty the last few nights about being part of the immoral drug bust operation and now he'd seen the setup jump and grabs being performed on the homeless. Suddenly, his job seemed dirty to him. He'd grown some sort of conscience that he could not for the life of him shake.

After splitting up the scuffle he went straight back to the department and turned in his badge, uniform, and service pistol. He left the lieutenant in charge with the excuse that his mind wasn't right and that he merely needed some time off.

THE IDEA

DURING HIS DRIVE HOME, Kenneth thought about his life and all he'd experienced. He wanted to serve his community but policing wasn't the right road. He needed another avenue. He wanted excitement and adventure in his life and he had a passion for wanting to stand for something. It didn't seem to be working out that way as a police officer. He also had his own personal problem with the department vanity. Many of the guys there were arrogant and conceited. In Kenneth's personal opinion, some of the officers didn't deserve 21 gun salutes. There were harder jobs to die working for than the job of being a police officer. He held a high respect for firemen and fishermen. Those jobs were very dangerous and very physically demanding. In Kenneth's mind, burning to death or falling into the Baron Sea were deaths that truly warranted a 21 gun salute. Being run over while stopping people on the interstate for traffic violations was horrible but it was no more respectful a way to go than falling into the sea while catering to the wants of the rich who held a high demand for crab. Or being burned to death while trying to save a life from a burning house. Even the guy that fell into the grain bin deserved a 21 gun salute. There were so many people more deserving of a salute than some of the winners he'd met on the force that it bothered him. It bothered him that he had to see what he'd seen today. He was mad at the department. And although he often turned a blind eye he felt betrayed.

Kenneth didn't need the job. He had a few hundred thousand dollars saved up in the bank and he was also about to be eligible to draw social security. He felt a change coming and it excited him. His boring life of question and guilt as a police officer was a thing of the past and new adventure lay on the horizon. Kenneth felt optimistic and positive about having the rest of his life free. He had some ideas in mind and much planning to do. Kenneth had veered off the normal path of life and into something different. Over the last few days, Kenneth either begun to lose his mind or he had unleashed something once held back. His behavior was about to take a turn for the worst and rebellion would begin to harden in his veins. Sixty-one years of his life had gone by and still, he felt a void and a need; one he'd once felt becoming a police officer would cover. And before that as an attorney. None of his past occupations had made him full. None had truly hit the spot. Working for the man had exposed him to hypocrisy and part of him was bitter about it. He'd tried to remain humble in his work but to no avail. He thought there had to be more to life than what there had been. For now, Kenneth would go home and rest for a few weeks while collecting his thoughts. He would relax and maybe watch a movie or two. He would try and forget that he'd been part of underhanded policing and move on. He didn't have a whole lot of years ahead of him and he wasn't going to spend them basking in guilt. So he hardened his conscience and swallowed it behind a drink of Brandy.

The following morning, he awoke to the beautiful chirping of birds. The sun was shining and he felt great. A small sense of sadness attempted only for a moment to seep into his happy mind regarding the job he'd just abandoned. But he quickly dismissed it. Life was too short for sadness or regrets. And it was far too early in the day to think negative thoughts. To Kenneth, life had just begun. Retirement would be fun.

Kenneth enjoyed his days alone at home watching television, eating, and enjoying the occasional drink. When he did have a drink, he wondered to himself how it was any better than what the homeless were doing. Although it wasn't against the law, it could be considered just as dangerous as any drug on the street and often worse. Ex-officer James had seen his fair share of death and other tragedies caused by alcohol. And he could see the hypocrisy in it. He enjoyed the few careless weeks before revisiting the issue that had made him quit his job. Why couldn't he stop thinking about it? He'd dismissed it weeks ago and here it was again. He would conclude that something else must be done to make his wrong right. He thought long and hard about it.

A few days later and 20 days after having left the department, he decided to venture out and have a look-see at the department he'd once dedicated himself to. He knew the areas where drug busts were conducted and steered himself in that direction. He found himself again in the same area close to his old beat with binoculars. And as sure as shells sit on the beach, there they were. Lathrop, Cyclops, and the rest of the gang were hard at work locking people up for drugs they themselves sold them. Kenneth laughed to himself and shook his head. He couldn't believe that this was what policing had come to. He truly could not understand how no one in the department had protested this sort of behavior. Was he, in fact, the immoral one to be concerned? Or weren't they immoral in selling a substance that they themselves had banned? Whatever the case, he was going to stick with what felt right to him. Honesty was right to Kenneth James. Not winning or bureaucracy. Right was right and wrong was wrong. Entrapment was immoral and deceitful as far as this ex-cop was concerned.

Kenneth had to find a way to bring attention to what he saw as an issue. He realized he had to somehow alert the public who seemed to be asleep. If he could alert enough of the right people about what was going on, then maybe the people could open their eyes and see how badly their loved ones were being victimized. Being shoved in and out of a system designed to humiliate, scare, and belittle human beings wasn't helping those people in search of relief. It only escalated their horrible situation and Kenneth couldn't help but see it in his mind's eye.

He had to find a way to throw the underdogs a helping hand or a bone before he could retire to a life of relaxation. It simply called to him. Because of his age, he excluded the idea of becoming a vigilante. And then it came to him. He could be a sort of vigilante once and just enough to get attention to what he saw as an abuse of power and greed by the department. What he was about to do had never even been attempted by another human being but was absolutely legal.

It was as if a golden key had opened a door inside of his mind. What he had to plan now would take a very small amount of research and a giant pair of kahunas. His idea was no less than brilliant. It would deliver a small blow to entrapment that might well change the department's views for the better. The action Kenneth was about to take would most likely find itself in front of a civil and or supreme court judge. It would most certainly make headlines across the world. Without physically harming anyone or even breaking the law, Kenneth would pull one small stunt that would light the very thought of entrapment on fire. And irritate law enforcement across the U.S.

Kenneth did not see the police department as an enemy. He saw enemy policies. He firmly believed in the department as being formed to protect the weak and the elderly. He was all about it. What he wasn't about was preying on the emotionally and financially weak solely for profit. These people weren't being helped in any way and only being buried deeper in depression by a system that wasn't designed to assist with personal problems. Sure, the violent riff-raff and thieves belonged in the cooler. Not people in search of relief not provided to them. Kenneth couldn't believe that this was a thing for him. He was a police officer. Officers should grow callous to concerns for the user but for some odd reason here he was being driven by a want for justice. And he was feeding the want to help the underdog. What had gotten into him? He couldn't figure it out. He just knew it called to him.

A couple of days later, he was ready to cause a stir. The department had no clue what was coming their way but they were about to be made fools of. They were about to become the bad guy if not for only one day. Kenneth dressed in all white so that there was no confusion and he couldn't be mistaken for having a gun. He wanted this to go clean and without mistakes.

Kenneth made contact with an old friend named Kelly who worked for a news station. He wanted someone to tag along as a witness to what was about to happen. He needed someone filming and someone who knew what his intentions were before he began. A witness so to speak. Another human being to verify his intentions when the mess hit the fan.

He took a few deep breaths as he focused partially on the day's agenda and partially on the news that boasted President Trump's evil hair-brained idea to execute drug dealers. He'd once heard of Donald Trump congratulating the president of the Philippines for murdering anyone using drugs. Back then he'd dismissed it. But now it seemed to be confirmed. In the eyes of rogue police officer Kenneth James, President Donald Trump was now seen as a murderer at heart and a bully. He stood up and turned off his television in disgust. Downing the rest of his coffee, it was his cue to head out.

CHAPTER

EXECUTION

It was time to get the show on the road. He drove himself to the same spot off of the beat he once worked where he met up with his old pal Kelly. Kenneth got out of his car and Kelly likewise. With an overly firm handshake, Kenneth grabbed Kelly's hand and greeted him. "How on God's green earth are ya man?"

Kelly was the happy go lucky type who seemed not to have a care in the world. He responded with a delayed squeeze to the hand and an, "I'm great. Never been better. Where are our culprits?"

"Well now, if you'll just take these binoculars and look straight down yonder ways you will see them hard at work," Kenneth said as he passed Kelly the binoculars.

"What's this thing going on in your life right now, Kenneth? Is it revenge or what? What brought you to this point? I mean weren't you a cop just like yesterday or so?" Kelly said as he took a long look through the high-powered glass.

Kenneth chuckled just before responding. "Kelly, I'll tell you. I'm just completely fed up with the world today. It's just so dang dog eat dog nowadays that it just rattles my cage, my friend. I mean, we are here to help one another right? We ain't on this Earth to hold each other down. I'm a simple man, Kelly. And I see it one way. It is right or it is wrong. Manhandling people and throwing them in cages for purchasing a product we sold them ain't right and never will be."

Kelly took the binoculars away from his eyes and laughed. "Are you seriously going to do this, Kenneth?" he asked.

Kenneth simply responded with a smile. "Absolutely. You ready?"

Kelly was and wasn't ashamed of it. This was going to make great news and that was all Kelly cared about. A hot story. "My car or yours?" Kelly asked.

"I figured we'd take yours over to the building next to where they're burning everybody. And maybe you can come back later somehow and take my car home for me. I'm probably going to jail at least for the night."

Kelly agreed and the two of them drove towards the hidden side of the department's operation. Kelly headed to his post where he began filming Cyclops selling dope to passersby. Kenneth sat for a moment around a corner and behind another side of the building. From this side, he couldn't see or be seen but he could hear the screams of the arresting officers ordering their victims to the ground. He took in a few deep breaths before his pursuit. He needed to be calm in order for this to work. Kenneth walked to the corner of the building and peeped around the corner. He could clearly see everything happening. As the next buyer walked up to make a purchase, he had no idea what was in store for him. Today he would not make a purchase. At least not here.

The man who was walking towards Cyclops looked around rapidly and stepped quickly. Kenneth looked closely. The man looked somewhat distraught. To Kenneth, he seemed more distraught than the average user but people never ceased to amaze him. Kenneth waited right until the man got within a few steps of Cyclops and then began to march forward behind the buyer to obstruct Cyclops' view of him.

He knew Sgt. Lathrop and crew were on the other side and wouldn't be able to see him until it was too late. He walked quickly behind and up to the buyer. And just as Officer Cyclops pulled out his bag of dope, so too did the buyer a gun. The man aimed the gun directly at the selling officer without saying a word. In one second's time, it was obvious that the man intended to shoot the officer selling him dope.

Cyclops' eyes grew large just before our hero Kenneth James grabbed the man's gun from behind. He slammed the culprit to the concrete and cuffed him in three seconds time. In a flash, he'd saved the officer's life. Before the grateful officer could thank him he too was slammed to the ground. "Citizen's arrest! Do not resist. You, sir, are under arrest for the unlawful sale of illegal drugs."

Cyclops laughed. "What do you think you're doing Officer James?"

The other officers rushed from their posts to assist the officer who was being placed under a citizen's arrest.

"What in the name of capital G is your major malfunction Officer James?" Sgt. Lathrop inquired with authority.

"I'm placing this man under arrest for selling drugs. That's what I'm doing." Kenneth wasn't proud. This was merely something he had to do.

Soon high-ranking officers flooded the area trying to figure out what Kenneth had started. And although they detained Kenneth for a little while they eventually let him go. They couldn't fire him because he'd quit. And there was no law stating that he couldn't make a citizen's arrest. They'd reached an odd loophole in the law and it now had to be figured out by the court system.

Days went by and Kenneth watched on the news as many copycats began imitating his actions. Civilians across the nation began busting Sheriff's departments and police departments alike for entrapment. They were actually arresting law enforcement officers who sold drugs to make arrests. The video Kelly had taken had been run so many times on news across the globe that even Kenneth didn't care to see it again.

And so began a national debate on whether or not the Justice Department should allow entrapment. Kenneth James had lived a full enough life and decided to move to Newberg, Oregon to settle down and retire. He would never make an arrest or citizen's arrest again.

The End

CHAPTER

DREW SHAW PUTTING IT ASIDE

DREW SHAW CONTINUES TO write books today under an assumed name. He still lives in the beautiful, liberal state of Washington with wife Missy. He still experiences extreme coincidence and odd instances but he chooses to perceive it in a more positive state of mind. He is humbled. Today, when he stops to read the ingredients on a loaf of bread in the grocery store and people come to stand next to him on both sides and do the same thing, it no longer bothers him. He no longer has a drug or alcohol habit. Drew was full of empathy and had been since he was a small child. He loved all people but was afraid they would break his heart. He was bullied by many people throughout his life and had no fatherly guidance because he wouldn't accept any from anyone short of his biological father. Drew brought on himself a life of hardship that he was later able to learn from. His childhood was yet another experience in this beautiful thing that we call life. When he finally sobered up, he was astonished and excited about the life he'd actually survived to talk about. And in his misguided state of mind, he left a story to be told. One he himself learned from.

Drew had a love for people and a hurt for violence. He was no longer angry with police, albeit somewhat disappointed in the justice system. He loved everyone no matter who they were as an individual. He had long since forgiven everyone who had ever have hurt him and hoped and prayed that those he lied to or stole from could, someday, forgive him too. His paranoia was gone. And he had accepted that people would always be nosy. He went on to publish his first book where he made enough money to move out of the RV and into a small home in a small town where he and Missy lived happily ever after.

The End of The Misguided Empath

ACKNOWLEDGEMENTS

I WOULD LIKE TO thank my lovely Malory for making this book possible. Without our loved ones, where would we be? I would also like to acknowledge the United States for being the free country that it is. Anything is possible if we try hard enough. And thanks is definitely in order to both the Vancouver Police Department, The Vancouver Fire Department, and The Clark County Sheriff's Department for keeping our community safe enough to enjoy writing a book. Thanks to Memphis Tennessee and everybody in beautiful downtown Frayser and South Memphis. Special thanks to the downtown Vancouver Washington Library in Clark County. Again, thanks to my Uncle Stan Lathrop for encouraging me to write. Hi Mom, Gramma and aunts. Not high to my brothers Heath and Jarrod ☺ or my cousins Barb and Tommy. Just kidding.

Printed in the United States
By Bookmasters